Behind Every Tree

Behind Every Tree

Commies, Regime Change, and the CIA

D M Flynn

ISBN: 979-8-9947118-1-1

LA REPUBLICA BOOKS

There is no order in the world around us, we must adapt our-

selves to the requirements of chaos instead.

—Kurt Vonnegut

D M FLYNN

Prologue

"Green, Max! Green!"

A skinny woman of advancing middle age rushed in to stand before the large wooden desk behind which sat Max, blinking with fear. He feared this woman with her purplish tiara, her dirty mop of stringy blue-black hair, the necklaces of gewgaws and crystals. She was shaking some papers at Max.

"*What now?*" he thought.

"We have no time to lose. Our nation is being sapped of its vitality. Green, Max. GREEN!" His wife's insistent words bounced around inside the dictator's head like one of those new Superballs from the States. Small, black, and hard they gained strength and speed with each rebound. "GREEN!" she shrieked. After a lot of words came out of her small, hard mouth and a lot of muttering on Max's part, he knew there was no shutting her up unless he signed the papers.

So it happened that red was out, green was in. Máximo Mandamás, La República's henpecked Dictator-for-Life signed the edict making all the traffic lights in La Capital green. Every intersection. All the time. His wife, satisfied, retired to her private sanctuary somewhere inside the palace, a signed copy of the edict rolled up in her tight, ropy fist.

Outside on the streets of La Capital traffic flowed smoothly, perhaps for the last time.

Chapter 1

Máximo Mandamás

Máximo Mandamás, finally rid of his wife, poured out three fingers of Ron Aniversario into a faux-crystal glass etched with the words "Hotel Cinco Estrellas," and took a long pull. He sat back in his sumptuous chair, a classic ox-blood leather wingback chair with matching ottoman (a gift from the previous American ambassador) and began taking stock of his situation. After draining the glass, Máximo came face to face with a painful conclusion — he was washed up. The iron-fisted despot feared and respected from La Capital to the province of Aguacate, was a thing of the past. Rosemary, his harridan of a spouse, now held sway over the country along with her consultant Gregorio, a sorcerer of sorts who darkened the palace with his foreign mumbling, cape, and beard. The man had appeared out of nowhere to work his way into palace politics.

Over time, her insistent hectoring forced Mandamás to issue executive orders like tsarist diktats; one more bizarre than the next. There had been, for instance, the introduction, the **mandatory** introduction, of her byzantine pseudo-religion into La República's schools with its star charts, color wheels, and gemology. She called it astrochronology or chronoastrology or some goddam thing, he could never remember exactly. What he couldn't forget, however, was the peculiar obsession Rosemary had with crystals, particularly amethyst, which she and her advisor Gregorio, he of the beard and cape, claimed were imbued with certain powers.

Máximo feared he had become a laughingstock among his peers in the ruthless dictator community who actually had *cojones* and ruled their tiny empires with brutality, goddamit. "Even that half-wit Trujillo wouldn't allow such chivying," he said to his only companion, the portrait on the wall of the French governor "Petite Freddie" who had built the Presidential Palace Máximo called home. He stared at the bottle of Ron Aniversario, picked it off the desk, and dispensed another three fingers into the hotel's filched glassware.

This most recent half-baked idea was nonsense; he felt it was Gregorio's contention that the color red was sapping La República of its strength, draining the nation's vital bodily fluids. His wife departed with the signed edict, but the conversation was still bouncing off the walls of his office. "The color green," she carped, "Gregorio has studied this. He says green will tap into our chrono-astrological rhythms. It will infuse *republicanos* with the cosmic strength of our forebearers. It is the color of our national symbol as you know. Gregorio says green vibrates at around 500 nanometers. Five hundred, Max! That's a lot of nanometers. Gregorio knows these things."

Mandamás, who had been drinking steadily to fortify himself for his meeting with Rosemary, had no reason to know the first thing about nanometers. He had stopped paying attention and slipped into say-whatever-it-takes-to-get-out-of-this-goddam-conversation mode, "*Sí, mi vida.*"

"So, you agree, Max?"

"*Sí, mi vida.*" The dictator had responded. As he began to drain his glass of another two fingers of rum, he wistfully daydreamed about a tennis court, freshly rolled red clay, blindingly white chalk lines, lissome ball girls in starched tennis skirts waiting for —

"Max!"

"*¿Sí, mi vida?*" Max flinched, spilling Ron Aniversario on his crotch.

"Are you listening? So, you DO agree to make this pronouncement?" She shook the document emblazoned with the national seal, the half avocado, on which were written many words; the most prominent being *verde*. He signed, of course.

"See that it is issued at once, Max. At once!"

Thus, Rosemary, also known as *La Bruja,* had taken complete control; the control he, the Generalíssimo, once wielded ruthlessly over the citizens of La República. Máximo Mandamás the demoralized, defeated, and deflated dictator sat at his desk mulling over the incident of the 500 green nano-fucking-meters and wallowed in a stagnant pool of self-pity. "I am weak, weak!" He pounded on his desk with both fists, crying like Johnny Fontane in his godfather's office.

Recently, to make matters worse, with only days before the grudge match versus El Corinto, La República's sworn enemy to the north and rival in all things — especially *fútbol* —there arose a great national crisis. Luis Paredes, known as "*El Muro*" for his prowess on the soccer pitch, had defected to El Corinto. The greatest goalie in the history of La República who racked up dozens of shutouts was gone. The unstoppable Luis Paredes. The man whose performance forced a nil-nil tie against Pacific powerhouse Kiribati. Yes, **that** Paredes. He turned up missing. Failing to show up at practice, leaving only a note in his locker. "I have defected to El Corinto," it said.

"El fucking Corinto," Max said. Of all places. The country demanded immediate action on the issue of *El Muro*.

Back at MidAmerica A&M where Max had been a scholar athlete (tennis), they taught critical thinking skills useful in life: operating a business, even running a corrupt dictatorship. Had the Dictator-for-Life paid attention any attention in business class, he might have worked up a SWOT analysis to assist in "taking stock," as it were. The Threats quadrant of the SWOT analysis would be filled in as follows:

Upcoming El Corinto victory in the annual match.

My eroding power base.

Losing respect.

This green garbage Gregorio was force-feeding me.

A slight stinging sensation when urinating. UTI?

But Max did not need any analysis to tell him that it was a state of affairs that called for immediate action.

"I must take action, immediately!" he declared. "I shall create a diversion! A crisis!" He slurred to his companion, the long-dead French governor who stared back from his portrait with characteristic French imperiousness.

With that, Max's head bounced on his desktop and toppled the empty bottle of Ron Aniversario.

Chapter 2

Tirofijo

Later that month ...

Tirofijo Gómez Gómez y Gómez was the notorious crime boss of La Capital who, it was said, had a heart of gold. Among the ventures of his vast diversified criminal enterprise was extortion; namely prying monthly "taxes" from the local merchant classes. He enrolled store owners and shopkeepers into his program by employing the tried-and-true sales pitch used by thugs the world over. "Be a shame if your shop burned down." So people paid. And since nothing ever really happened in La Capital nothing happened to their dry cleaners, beauty salons, coffee shops, or corner stores. They kept paying because it was the thing to do. Anyway, Tirofijo never raised the taxes, and it was rumored that sometimes he used the money to clothe and feed the capital's many grubby street urchins. Heart of gold.

Tirofijo employed the services of an ever-present horde of gamins, young miscreants who patrolled the streets causing trouble and trying to live another day. They were young, poor, filthy, and invisible as no one cared to see them. Yet there they were in their greasy uniforms of once decent clothes worn by decent children in decent homes. Such was the life of the unwanted offspring of La República. Tirofijo was once just like them. Kids whose only defense was the slingshot, the *"gomera"* in their back pockets. It seemed not so long ago he had earned his name, Tirofijo or "Sure Shot," with his own slingshot skill.

A succession of lucky breaks propelled the young Tirofijo to begin his rise in the criminal ranks of La República. It began one night after a kind person had left a small pile of worn, yet clean, clothes by his head as he slept under a bridge. When he woke, it didn't take long for him to shed his filthy rags and put on a new cotton pullover shirt and Levi's 501 jeans. He felt respectable. The jeans' cuffs even covered his age-worn tire and rope *alpargatas*.[1]

Always smart but lacking opportunity, Tirofijo made a plan and met with a man he knew dealt in stolen cars and would pay 10,000 *tucanes*,[2] more money than Tirofijo had ever seen, in cash for a red Mercedes-Benz 280SL.

That night, Tirofijo staked out a place in the parking lot by the bar entrance of the Cinco Estrellas Hotel and waited. He had almost dozed off when he heard the gravel crunching at the entrance to the lot. There it was, the cherry red lovejoy of every successful empresario and Tirofijo's exit visa from the streets. He looked carefully to ensure that it was a 280SL. It was.

He stood up confidently, made a friendly wave to the driver and walked, his heart beating fast, to the driver's side door. The electric window lowered quietly with German efficiency.

"Yes, what is it ameego?"

¡Mierda! ¡Es un hijueputa gringo![3] Tirofijo thought, at a loss how to handle this unforeseen twist until the *gringo* added, "Valet parking? Good idea. Too much car thieving in this country. Here you go, uh, —?"

"José."

"Here you go hoezay, I'll take that."

And in a series of quick motions the *gringo* handed "José" the keys and exchanged them for a ticket he plucked from the valet parking impersonator's fingers. The ticket had been pilfered the day

---

[1] Sandals.

[2] The national currency of La República.

[3] Shit! It is a *gringo* son of a whore!

before from the city's dry-cleaning establishment that promised "Same Day One-Hour Martinizing!" Tirofijo couldn't care less about one-hour Martinizing, same day or otherwise, he just wanted a numbered ticket to add to the simulacrum he was pulling off with the *gringo* in order to steal his car. The *gringo* got his ticket stub and strutted into the Cinco Estrellas bar confident his German driving machine was now in the safe hands of the parking attendant. That same attendant slipped behind the wheel of the juicy red 280SL with CD plates and drove off to collect his 10,000 *tucanes*. How the former street urchin, common criminal, and slingshot "sure shot" was able to drive the American Ambassador's car, no one knows. But he did.

The 10,000 *tucanes* was seed money. What followed was a string of well-planned cons, usury, strategic bribes, and sound investment decisions[4] that eventually enabled the man to become a respected member of the criminal community driving his own red Mercedes 280SL.

That was then. Now, however, the gangster was glum. As he played with his favorite ball point pen, watching the clothes fall off the girl floating in its stem each time he tilted it, he began to take stock. Tip it one way, the girl's clothes floated up onto her body. Tip it another, the girl's clothes fell to the bottom of the pen. It was very relaxing.

First, there was the matter of his mistress, his **former** mistress, Violeta. She said she no longer loved him. Him! Tirofijo, the man who was hung like a horse! Not only that but the warehouse, his cherished *Escondite?* The woman was charging rent for the space attached to her shop.

Secondly, Piojo, the most trusted delinquent in his employ, seemed to be around less and less. It was Piojo who commanded

---

[4] Tirofijo was an early investor in Xerox stock.

the small army of delinquents, keeping them in line to carry out Tirofijo's criminal acts. Tirofijo missed the snot-nosed terror who reminded the man of himself at that age. He struggled with a mix of paternal anger and worry.

"If he gets hurt, I'll kill him," Tirofijo mumbled.

Thirdly, the American pilot Steve Steele had become somewhat distant. Tirofijo and Steele, who flew in and out of La Chingada International with illicit goods that Tirofijo traded at criminal margins, had become chummy over the past few months. Their arrangement was simple: in came the Macanudo Cigars, dirty magazines, Zippo lighters, Scotch scotches, and American cigarettes. Out went live animals and anthropological treasures. The animals, from the pristine rainforests of Aguacate Province, were destined for rescue sanctuaries in Florida and other states. The anthropological treasures involved the business of La República's patrimony: pre-Columbian artifacts looted from many tombs and ruins found throughout the country then resold at healthy profit margins.

Trading in endangered animals and birds had always been profitable for Tirofijo; however, he tired of the scratching and biting involved with the cats and reptiles not to mention the rare birds that were shit factories. On the other hand, the trade of indigenous artifacts, though riskier, was simpler. It was merely a matter of sending small packages wrapped in newspaper via Kiwi Airways and waiting for envelopes of dollars on the return flight.

The packages contained the latest craze of "native" art installed in sitting rooms throughout the USA from The Village to The Castro. La República's centuries-old indigenous art consisted of beautifully hand-molded mud figurines. They were little mud guys with huge erections marketed as "priapic art." Tirofijo and his shipping partner, Steele, had been surprised to learn priapic art was an honest-to-god thing or genre or whatever. There was huge demand for 400-hundred-year-old naked warriors with stiffies.

But lately, Steele seemed more involved with other trivialities and didn't have time to talk shop anymore.

Fourthly, there was the matter of finances. Tirofijo was a dedicated reader of business self-help books and knew that in business there was something called "making the nut" and Tirofijo was not making his. There were just enough *tucanes* coming in to pay key expenses like phone, water, electric, Hollywood fan magazines, and a couple of weekly sessions at the Happy Fish. But Violeta's rent was the killer. He needed another stream of positive cash flow.

As Tirofijo mulled these setbacks in his mind and distracted himself with the naked girl in his ball-point pen, his stomach began to growl. He tried to ignore it, but the stomach's nagging was insistent. Finally, Tirofijo put down the ball point pen with the girl fully clothed, and said to himself, "You have to eat, *pendejo*." Normally at this time of day, Violeta would bring him an aromatic plate of her *arroz con pollo*. But not today nor any day it seemed.

Gangsters must eat, and Tirofijo's mind full of Violeta's chicken and rice decided he must have chicken. Fortunately there was an excellent fried chicken shop only a few blocks away.

Chapter 3

The Culture Commune

One week before…

Aguacate Province was in La República's eastern lowlands. Once considered a jungle and fetid backwater, it had been rebranded as pristine rain forest in order to attract tourists. The rebranding brought hordes of Nordic youth: tall, gangly people with names like Björn and Franz towing hairy-legged girlfriends with enormous backpacks and guitar cases. They happily hiked the forest singing Abba tunes, smoking ill-shaped odd-smelling cigarettes.

The local merchant class welcomed this change along with the *tucanes* that came with it as a modest mushrooming of youth hostels, yogurt stands, yoga studios, and tiny shops that sold peculiar looking glass pipes popped up. The merchants were a tight-knit group of like-minded people, an intellectual class that ran their small businesses and survived the endless tropical ennui with books. They bought books in La Capital, they read those books in Aguacate Province, and they discussed the books in their club which was facetiously called, "The Culture Commune."

Rafael Izquierdo Junior or "Yunior" was given the honor of hosting and leading the bibliophiles in their twice-monthly gatherings. Jocularly referred to as *El Supremo Comandante de la Comuna Cultural,* Yunior was known for cultivating lively discussions that oftentimes turned to politics. As the English public school-educated son of Rafael Izquierdo, Yunior's views were widely respected.

Yunior managed a handful of properties for his father and lead a humdrum existence in the outlying province. Thus, he was glad of the occasional company of the book lovers. Well-read, especially in the English classics he had gobbled up as a lad in England, he counted Dickens, Fielding, Coleridge among his best friends. By mutual arrangement, his parents had agreed that growing up in England would offer the young boy experiences out of reach of the rank-and-file *republicano* youth.

Yunior had lived with his mother in her home village of Blandings near Shropshire, England, during his formative years. His parents met at an International Communism Symposium back in the heady days of marches, strikes, love-ins, and other crippling impediments to the global status quo.

The close-minded Mrs. Izquierdo who embarrassingly referred to her husband's countrymen as "wogs," opted to take Yunior back to Merry Old so he could get a proper education. Izquierdo relented but insisted on having the boy back at 18 and then the lad could decide for himself where to live.

Yunior was in Aguacate Province, in his twenties, still deciding his future. The fact was, he didn't mind the isolation. He had only a few tenants to manage, he had his book club, and he had his library, including the entire Penguin Books collection of P.G. Wodehouse novels and stories. Wodehouse was a happy discovery while shopping with his mother in the Blandings Book Market, and the bug never left him. Sometimes he felt that he shared his quarters in Aguacate with Bertie and Jeeves.

The young Izquierdo's needs were modest — he lived at the back of one of the family's small hotels occupying just enough space to eat, sleep, read, and host his friends. It was there that the club gathered, ready to share their love of reading and expound on a Corin Tellado potboiler they had all read that month. When Yunior entered, they rose and welcomed him with their tongue-in-cheek salute: "Bienvenido Supremo Comandante to the Meeting of the Comuna Cultural of Aguacate Province!"

One of the members said, "Supreme Commander, I thought we agreed on Benevolent Dictator-for-Life?"

"No. No. It was Chief Librarian Sir Quiet!"

"Or... Earl of Overdue Books!"

"*Jajaja*," a round of good-natured laughter at the absurdity of the titles was suddenly cut off by a loud BANG! Someone had slammed the back door and was running away through the muddy alley. It was a scene right out of a spy thriller they had shared the month before and caused a bit of giggling.

Chapter 4

The Interior Minister Reports

Back at the stately Presidential Palace, Máximo Mandamás, the nation's supreme Dictator-for-Life, had come to. Still boozy from the previous evening's drinking, he was standing and looking into an elaborately gilded XVIII century French Baroque wall mirror. What he saw were the remains of what was a once a proud man, a graduate of the nation's prestigious Academia Militar Lempira Lenco. An Olympian (tennis) who had even traveled to *La Yunae*, to the United States. Once a member in good standing of the totalitarian community, feared and respected from La Capital to Aguacate province, he was but a timid milquetoast, henpecked by Rosemary, first lady and ogress.

The Minister of the Interior was standing across the wide office just inside the door ready to be invited into the *sanctum sanctorum* of the dictatorship. He was on a mission of national urgency, ready to report the findings of his extensive investigation. Max ignored him and instead continued to examine himself in the cloudy mirror. "It is her," he rasped. "Her, that witch. And her 'consultant' that sorcerer." The Minister knew the generalíssimo was referring to Gregorio, the new hire at the Presidential Palace, but said nothing.

"That beard, that cape, that throat-clearing he claims is a language, very strange do you not agree, Minister?"

The Minister had never met Gregorio yet agreed wholeheartedly. "I agree wholeheartedly," he told his boss as he entered apprehensively.

Gregorio's presence in La República was hardly a coincidence. The scion of a diamond dealing dynasty on W 47th, Gregorio was not cut out for the business and after several costly mistakes with the inventory which angered his father, he was forced to retreat somewhere safe until everything blew over. His father's much elder brother, and his uncle Milton the Mohel, took Gregorio aside and spoke to him of La República. "Go there. Make friends. Come back in a year, all will be forgiven."

Milton the Mohel slipped Gregorio a couple of hundred bucks and a plane ticket on Kiwi Airways Flight 1 leaving that very week. He warned his nephew, "It's not the Upper West Side, so be careful, they still have anti-heretic laws or something. Very Catholic." Gregorio packed some shirts, undergarments, socks and, unsure of the climate facing him in La República, a warm cape with a cowl.

The dictator back-marched four steps away from his reflection, made a military right turn, and marched to his large desk scoring the floor as he went. After maneuvering his ample presidential self around the desk, he sat and waited for the minister to cross the room. Sitting, Max took time to admire his imposing desk, the trappings of dictatorial power. He loved to caress the smooth, polished surface of finely crafted rare woods harvested from virgin trees in Aguacate Province. It pleased him to pass his hands over the satiny surface that seemed to respond to his touch. After a minute or so feeling up the furniture, he glanced up at the straight-backed gentleman standing before him.

As in other countries, the leader of the citizens of La República was concerned with great matters of state. The modern-day despot is not immune to issues regarding trade deficits, balance of payments, national strikes, diplomatic relations, or defecting netminders. It was the latter that ate at Máximo's guts like a bad *baleada*.[1] He was getting impatient with the whole business.

"Tell me, Minister, who defects to Corinto? Tell me!" Máximo demanded. Before the trembling minister could offer a response, Max continued, "Who defects to that backwater country from this paradise?" Mandamás indicated the paradise in question by making a vague gesture to the window behind him. The minister made a gesture of agreement that the La República outside the palace window was, indeed, paradise.

"Ever since we defeated them in the War of Aguacate, those *comemierda*[2] Corinthians have been conspiring against me. I suspect Paredes was kidnapped to make me look weak. Or maybe the CIA, they might have it in for me. Look what they are doing to my friend Fidel. Making his beard fall out! *¡Por dios!* Is that what is going on? Do not be afraid to report your findings to your President-for-Life. I will not kill the minister, uh, messenger. What have you discovered about our missing goalkeeper, Minister Menéndez?"

Minister Menéndez was not used to being in the presence of the Dictator-for-Life and had never had so much as a meeting with Max, much less make a report. Minister Menéndez was a simple man. One who didn't smoke or drink. Married. One child. A girl, Lydia. Very churchgoing. So much so that the minister of state was also the minister of the First Baptist Church of La Capital. The FBCLC.

The minister minister had been listening uncomfortably to Mandamás' kvetching in front of the mirror and feared the situation was extremely unsavory. Nervous and quivering in his double-breasted burnt-umber suit, Interior Minister Menéndez tried to look

---

[1] A local staple consisting of eggs, cheese, beans, avocado, etc. wrapped in a pillowy tortilla.

[2] Shit eaters.

officious by making ministerial motions, examining specific pages of his report and nodding with authority, uffishly gazing out the window. The report itself was a large volume containing vast evidence thanks to the cooperation of the armed forces of La República. Using the army's most efficient technology to extract information from the "usual suspects," the answer to Máximo's query on the desertion of the greatest goalie in the history of La República was discovered within 48 hours.

"They say it is a matter of love, Your Excellency," (the minister was uncertain as to how address the Dictator-for-Life) he declared as he thumped the top sheet — the executive summary, a single-space typed page on official letterhead with the national symbol. "It was a woman that made Paredes extricate himself across the border."

"*Puta madre*, a woman you say? How so?"

Paging through the dense report, the minister hesitantly went on, "Well, your Excellency, it seems that, uh, one of the cheerleaders, uh, a flower of La Republica, well it seems Paredes and the girl's ... they secretly carried out their passion in a way that was unseemly, Your Excellency."

Minister Menéndez was very uncomfortable when it came to discussing or participating in matters of sex. He had trouble finding the exact wording when describing it and as far as participation went, he had only had it once (Lydia) and didn't really enjoy it. Nor was he enjoying his tête-à-tête with the unhappy, impatient Máximo Mandamás.

"Excellency, Paredes was answering his desperate longing," he read from the executive summary. The Interior Minister was red in the face with sweat oozing and knees knocking.

"Desperate longing?" the dictator asked.

"Indeed. In his, uh, loins and what not."

"Explain, minister."

"Well, excellency, our goalkeeper was committing coital congress … copulating … The Flowers of La República —"

"Stop dithering, *imbecil!*" The dictator disliked dithering. "What flowers?"

"The Flowers of La Republica, that's what they are called."

"Who?" asked Mandamás.

"Whom. The cheerleaders, that's whom. That is what they are called — 'The Flowers of La Republica.'"

"So he deflowered one of the flowers?" Max was calmer, curious and intrigued about the deflowering of a cheerleader by that nitwit goalie.

"Not quite, my Liege. Paredes sowed his oats in another stable."

"What in the Virgen de Aguacate are you talking about? Stables? Oats? Flowers? Did he take the cheerleader, the flower, back to the stable to —"

"Not with the flower, but with the mare, excellency."

"Clarify, please, for the love of God."

The Minister girded his loins (figuratively, of course) and came to the point. "The goalie, well, he did not deflower the flower, he mounted the mare."

Mandamás looked up at the ceiling, which he saw needed dusting, and said, "Minister Menéndez, if you wish to live, will you please speak clearly and in one sentence tell me what happened."

"Our goalie had indecent coital relations, Your Highness-ness." The minister minister meekly blubbered, his face as red as the fake velvet walls of the Happy Fish.

"Are you telling me that Paredes was playing the beast with two backs with a mere cheerleader? This flower of La Republica? Is that all?"

"Not the cheerleader, per se, Your Grace, but her mother, Excellency. Paredes knocked up one of the parents. Of the cheerleaders. The flower's mother."

"The flower's mother?! Not the flower, but her mother? *¡Qué pendejo!* What an idiot."

Mandamás, furious and incredulous at the same time, stood up to pace some more. The Interior Minister was frightened, aware that the Dictator-for-Life could blame him for the goalie's indiscrete flower/mother fornication.

"That motherfucker," Max said as he stared menacingly at the minister, the messenger of this ludicrous news. He ignored the urge to kill the messenger but, instead said, "Thank you, Minister Menéndez, for your report. You may now leave my presence."

Minister Menéndez, visibly shaken by his boss's anger but relieved that he would not be executed, left said presence by walking backward, his head held reverently down as if examining the grooves in the wooden flooring.

I need a miracle, Max murmured.

Chapter 5

Whence Máximo Mandamás

Máximo Mandamás was a traditional Latin American strong-man who relished his totalitarian role and its attendant job benefits — the bowing, the scraping, the fawning, the toadying, medals of peace, gifts, prizes, idolatry, and comfortable furniture. What was not to like?

Short-tempered, with a commanding military mien and larger-than-life presence, Máximo was straight out of central casting. Though a coward who avoided conflict wherever possible, he managed to live up to the image of a military dictator and its demands mostly thanks to the largess of the Americans who saw in him a bulwark against creeping communism. The Americanos were always in the market for a good bulwark.

He was Máximo Mandamás. He was not a simp. He was not a play toy of Rosemary and her mystic advisor. The wagging tongues in the market, The Cinco Estrellas Bar, the love chambers of the Happy Fish be damned. A domino not yet fallen. He was bulwark against communist infestation by the *Virgen de Aguacate*!

But there were leaks in the bulwark and the *gringos* did not like leaky bulwarks.

The Dictator-for-Life needed cheering up.

So absorbed had the generalíssimo been in his despair after meeting the minister minister, he had forgotten about Güicho, his inept son-in-law. Güicho, who tended to disappear into the furniture, was standing across the room in front of a closet door. He had remained there witnessing the Interior Minister's awkward testimony.

For Güicho, who was terrified of his father-in-law, it had been an uncomfortable spectacle causing him to sweat profusely. Large dark, damp rings had formed around the armpits of his imported English navy-blue blazer. Seeing his wife's father, the supreme ruler of La República, in such a state was the catalyst to Güicho's anxiety and open pores. As the dictator's right hand, it was up to him to offer his *suegro*[1] something to lighten the mood. Something to get his mind off the heavy burdens that were the affairs of state. Perhaps some distractions, some activities to gladden the glum Máximo? Güicho came upon a solution, an old standby sure to raise spirits of any tyrant.

"*Suegro*. How about maybe some arrests? A public beating or two?" he cheerily offered.

Máximo's response was a slow panther-like growl. The younger man was secretly hoping for something, anything, to break the torpor of daily life in the palace. So he pressed on with another suggestion.

"Who shall we arrest *mi general?*"

"Whom, *idiota.*"

Güicho blinked, "What?"

"Never mind. Go back to your closet."

Rebuffed, Güicho slunk back to his office which had served as a closet during the previous regime.

The Generalíssimo stood up to stretch his dictatorial legs. He walked once again to the ornate mirror on the wall opposite his desk and renewed the self-torture. Staring back from the reflecting glass was a doughy middle-aged man with a soft, muddy soccer ball for a head. The face, once the face of a proud man respected even

---

[1] Father-in-law.

by the *gringos*, was now beginning to sag from the weight of his office. His jowls were starting to look like the bean and cheese *baleadas* he ate for lunch.

Despite the backsliding, Max still maintained the pride of a well-dressed despot. He wore a uniform from the Central American Dictator catalogue — starting with brown knee-length English riding boots superbly shined into submission. The kind with showy brass spurs. He always liked the way they ching-chingled so nicely when he walked and made grooves in the Frenchman's wooden flooring. Moving northward from the boots were the creased khaki-colored jodhpurs that gave the appearance of a man who knew his way around horses. Máximo Mandamás, however, did not know his way around horses. Máximo Mandamás was a tennis player and, thus, naturally afraid of horses. Above the pants, he wore a starched cacao-colored *guayabera*.[2] Máximo looked with pride at the national symbol atop the epaulets on each of his once square shoulders: the half-avocado.

Grabbing his excess belly fat with both of his meaty hands he mumbled, "I must get on the courts." With that, Máximo wistfully thought back to when he was a national Olympian and scholarship athlete at the prestigious MidAmerica A&M (Go Indians!).

Back then, I was a legend. On the courts and at the frat mixers with my compadre Larree Muncie. The smell of a rain-soaked clay court still makes my heart ache.

Turning, Max looked at the expensive racket propped up against a corner wall. It was no ordinary racket. It was a Wilson Pro Staff Original, and Máximo Mandamás loved it so. A gift from Larry Muncie to his old pal. He thought of those days and walked slowly back to the dictatorial desk and sat down to resume caressing the fine wood.

---

[2] A multi-pocketed dress shirt.

It was smooth. Cool and warm at the same time. He ran his right hand down the near leg, slowly enjoying the curvature of the virgin wood hauled all the way from Provincia de Aguacate, and crafted into the magnificent piece before him. Slower still, he ran his hand back up the leg, to the top and paused to feel where the tenon filled the hole of the mortise joining the leg to the tabletop.

Máximo felt a desperate longing. A romp with one of the girls at the Happy Fish brothel was in order. He would have to pay for it, of course, but he was the Dictator-for-Life and dictators-for-life always had ready cash. Money was no object for the man with many *tucanes*, all with his own face, in the shirt pocket of his dress *guayabera*. He confidently arrived at an executive decision, like any dictator worth his mettle. Máximo Mandamás, the supreme leader of all *republicanos*, stopped groping the office furnishings and yelled at the closed closet door, "Güicho, to the Happy Fish!"

"*Sí, mi generalíssimo,*" came the muffled reply.

Chapter 6

The Happy Fish

In every capital of that region of the world there were notorious and often dangerous neighborhoods with cynical nicknames; *Calle de la Navaja, Paseo de Sangre, Al Costado de Gualmar.* These were "Knife Street," "Walk of Blood," and "Next to Wal-Mart," respectively. In La Capital that neighborhood was known as the "Bitter Zone," or *Zona de Amargura.*

The Happy Fish was a fashionable bordello, an oasis ensconced in La Zona de Amargura where disreputable saloons sold liquor by the shot and cars would be stripped if allowed to linger. The Zona had its appeal for those who wished to slum it in La Capital and rub shoulders with the ruffian classes.

The brothel, however, offered a safe haven for those who sought to enjoy the pleasures therein. It had serviced generations of *republicanos* who often bragged of their exploits inside the whorehouse: incredible and unsubstantiated claims of stamina, virility, and girth were among the most common.

The Happy Fish operated on the simple business model of offering clean girls to a dirty public of politicians, businessmen, bureaucrats, and the occasional Central American strongman who was ringing the street side doorbell.

Inside, the unctuous and disreputable concierge Tomás heard the chimes playing *La donna è mobile* and minced his way to the foyer. He opened the front door just one centimeter so as to peek out onto the street. There, on the sidewalk one step below him, Tomás observed through the sliver of the opened door a long rectangle of bad skin and a cacao-brown *guayabera.*

"Generalissssimo!" Tomás hissed as he fully opened the door to welcome and admit the dictator. "You look sssplendid, Generalissssimo. Those boots, spurs, and a whip? Oh, how deliciousss."

"It is a riding crop, *pendejo*."

"Oooh, who have you been riding, Genera —"

"*Calláte, mariposa!*[1] I came to see Paola."

With that Mandamás shouldered past the sibilant concierge and into the bar lounge where he immediately sat with his back to the wall. He looked around expectantly and took in the furnishings. The Happy Fish had been a frequent haunt of a younger Max during happier days. Bathing in nostalgia, Max soaked up the atmosphere of 1850s San Francisco gold rush: a lot of shiny red velvet, an overhead swing, and several plush love seats for conversing with the ladies and sipping Ron Aniversario. He appreciated that little had changed over the years — the famous wooden bar, the hammered steel ceiling, and even the swinging saloon doors that led to the seraglio's sex chambers.

A small garish neon sign sat atop a plaster of Paris Ionian column. It was a fish with a lecherous smile smoking a large torpedo-shaped cigar. Mandamás admired the mirthfulness of the sign, stifling a chuckle (ruthless dictators do not chuckle). "Is that new, Wulther?"

Wulther, the bartender, blended honest drinks and dispensed them to a world of dishonest people. Famously, he blended daiquiris in the sleek, modern atmosphere of the bar in the Hotel Cinco Estrellas to an appreciative audience seeking respite from the heat. Now, however, Wulther was on his day off from the five-star establishment and engaged in serving up refreshments in the plush

---

[1] Shut up, you butterfly.

environs of the Happy Fish where he presented Max with his pre-ferred drink of two fingers of Ron Aniversario.

Wulther waved his bar towel at the sign, and answered, "*Sí, Generalíssimo,* it was a gift from the pilot Esteeve Steele. Do you like it?" Both men looked at the sign as if they were a pair of art critics in the Uffizi.

"Yes, it classes up the joint." Max liked to pepper his speech with Americanisms picked up at Gluteus House, his dorm at MidAmerica. "My compliments to the pilot, is he here?"

"Esteeve Steele cannot come here anymore. He is banned from the Happy Fish."

"Banned? From a whorehouse? That's incredible! Why, Wulther?"

"Paola said —"

"— Paola said, what?" On cue, in stepped Paola, the one-time budding film star known as Paola Labios,[2] now returned to her role as part-time employee of the Happy Fish and fulltime president of the PTA. She sashayed toward the lounge where she stopped and leaned her elbow on the end of the wooden bar. The Happy Fish was equally renowned for its massive bar, an intricately hand-crafted piece of furniture made of polished endangered woods from the Province of Aguacate. The magnificent item was part of the war reparations to La República under the Guacamole Act, the peace agreement which followed La Guerra de Aguacate against El Corinto.

Both men were speechless, neither offering to answer her question, both taking in the countenance of Paola. From head to toe she was as unforgettable as one of Botticelli's lusty renditions

---

[2] See "The Kidnapping of Dennis Martin," by this same author.

of Venus. A paragon of La Republican seductive beauty, Paola possessed a fine set of breasts which she aimed like tractor beams at the generalíssimo. Mesmerized, Max was motionless. He managed to look up into her eyes and lost himself in their allure.

"*Hola, mi capitán.*"[3] The fact that Paola could so insouciantly address the country's supreme leader as a mere captain was of no surprise to Wulther. He was well aware of Paola's charm and her grip on Máximo Mandamás. Only she could demote the generalíssimo and elicit a well-flossed smile from the same.

Formerly the favorite of Steve Steele, the handsome Chief Pilot of Kiwi Airways, Paola had moved on and resumed her role as a Happy Fish part-timer when not occupied with motherly responsibilities away from the bordello. The raising of her two sons, Axl and Slash, along with PTA duties at Colegio James Monroe (school motto: "Manifest Destiny!") took up most of her time. She secretly harbored political ambitions to lift her country from third world status to "developing" nation and did a lot of reading on the subject: from Marx to Montesquieu to Madison and the Federalist papers. This was unbeknownst to Mandamás who would have frowned at the prospect of having to deal with a politicized Paola away from the friendly confines of the Happy Fish.

Right then, Max was taking her in; she was exotic for a *republicana* with her black and deep-set alluring eyes like those of an ancient biblical queen in a Cecil B. De Mille classic. *Her cleavage is glorious, a national monument!* Max thought. Unfortunately, as he continued to admire the pulchritude of La República, a vision of his carping missus walked into his brain. The pressure of taking in a lovely Paola and kicking out the sight of Rosemary and her beads

---

[3] My captain.

almost caused a short circuit of Max's synapses. *That ogress is everywhere. Even in my head while I am looking at this … this glorious gift from the gods!*

"Is that a *plátano*[4] in your pocket or are you glad to see me, *capitán?*" Again, Paola addressed the generalíssimo as a mere captain — it was a running gag, Happy Fish foreplay. As the nation's supreme leader and his concubine-for-hire engaged in the timeless tradition of flirtation, he rose from the plush faux-leather chesterfield and offered his arm to the lady; together, arm-in-arm, they swung open the vintage saloon doors and proceeded to chase unchaste pleasures within.

Their ritual was vigorous and short-lasting to the great satisfaction of both; one for proving yet again his block and tackle could still perform like a horny frat boy's, and the other for it lasting only six minutes. After telling the dictator that, yes, he was hung just like a horse and, yes, she achieved orgasm twice, he arose from the bed and began the ritual of changing back into his dictator outfit. As he dressed, Mandamás started to pour out his troubles to the courtesan. Many men address their assignations with women like Paola as if they were sessions with a psychiatrist. Sharing inner thoughts and problems with a third party, a professional, has its benefits. Actually, there is little difference between a psychiatrist and a prostitute, except psychiatrists do not get naked and engage in coitus.

"Things are a mess, Paola. *Una mierda.* I just learned we have lost El Muro. He has defected to Corinto, if you can believe that, and will not be available for our big match. Everybody expects me to do something about it.

"I get no respect, no respect. I used to feel, *tú sabes*, in charge. Now that *comemierda*, that monk, is telling her the crystals

---

[4] Plantain.

say this, the stars say that. And that ridiculous costume?! He looks like Mickey Mouse in the 'Sorcerer's Apprentice,' only all in black, with a greasy beard, and with breath that could knock out Goofy. My wife is always with the beads this and the colors that, the crystals, the *amatista*,[5] plus she is making me pass these ridiculous decrees!"

"*Yo sé, capitán*. Maybe you should stand your ground like a man! Stop this religious chrono-astrologyomy *mierda* in the schools! Colors and crystals my ass. My sons Axl and Slash are falling behind in mathematics! Why in last night's PTA meeting we —"

"PTA? Do not talk to me about your PTA. Who's paying for this session? Let's stay on point, Paola! Which is me. I need a miracle."

The miracle would be if you used the head on your shoulders, jueputa.

Just then there was a commotion outside Paola's cell. A very loud, very American voice said, "My goodness, honey, I oughta take you back to Flawriduh with me. Give the girls at Velvet Plush a run for their money. Har-har." They heard a slap, probably to the derrière of Kandi, the only other girl working that afternoon.

Máximo gave Paola a quizzical look.

"*El embajador,*" she mouthed not wanting to call the boorish man's attention.

Wishing to escape the spectacle of an awkward meeting with the American ambassador in the bordello, the Dictator-for-Life tried to slip out Paola's cell door and through the saloon doors to the bar while the *gringo* finished groping Kandi. It was all for naught for immediately behind him, the swinging doors disgorged a sun-burned, ham-fisted man thoroughly pleased with himself. The ambassador recognized the Dictator-for-Life and grabbed Max's

----

[5] Amethyst

hand vigorously pumping it like they were at a $100 a plate fund-raiser back in Apalachicola, Florida.

"Max, hot damn! Good to see you, buddy!"

"I suppose." *I'm the "Generalíssimo," you syphilitic sheep schtuper!*

"Look, my wife is coming back from her shopping adventure in Miami, and we're having cocktails tonight back at the house. Would love it if you and Mrs… Mrs. uh, Mrs. Generalíssimo could join us. Only the top people, quality people, will be there. Say you'll join us, Max!"

The dictator looked distracted and offered only a sly smile and a glazed stare.

Undeterred, the ambassador pressed on for an answer. "Dammit, Max, you will join us for drinks won't you?"

"Oh, I will" said Max with honest enthusiasm as he turned to leave. "I certainly will."

Walking through the bar of the Happy Fish, Máximo Mandamás seemed pleased with himself. But it wasn't the pleasure of Paola's company, it was something else.

"I just found my miracle," he thought with a chuckle.

Chapter 7

Cocktails at the Embassy

Later that evening …

The Honorable Ambassador and Mrs. Richard Dix requested the honor of the presence of La República's hoi polloi, both foreign and domestic. It was an infrequent event, perhaps twice a year, as the ambassador's wife was usually in Miami on a shopping mission. But, according to State Department dictates, they were obliged to fulfill these social obligations.

In fact, Richard Dix was not a career diplomat. Until he became ambassador Richard Dix or "Two Dix" to close friends and fishing buddies, had never even heard of the State Department. After raising millions for The Party, he was appointed to the ambassadorship of La República and promised a more desirable posting once one less humid became available.

Dix had made his millions in the entertainment industry. The gentlemen's entertainment industry to be precise. He owned the biggest chain of gentlemen's clubs in the South and Midwest, including the iconic Velvet Plush, a jiggle joint with a cross-cultural following, catered equally to blue- and white-collar gentlemen in tier-two cities. Whether you wore a three-piece leisure suit or camouflage sweatpants mattered not so long as you could pay the $20 cover charge and two drink minimum. Velvet Plush and its famous "$4.99 All You Can Eat Strip Steak Special" were known coast-to-coast-to-coast and had been featured in "Swank," "Tang," and "Tent Pole," the trade journal of the strip club economic sector.

Another Dix holding in the lucrative "titty bar" segment was "Amish Joy," a joint that claimed the largest selection of Mennonite girls in Pennsylvania Dutch country. The club's trademarked "Barn Raising" was considered an art form among the local farming and ranching cognoscenti.

The Dix empire also infiltrated mass media with a network of AM stations under the call sign WASP, its affiliates throughout the Midwest broadcasting only wholesome American programs. The ratings leader and flagship franchise was the groundbreaking "Where the White Women At?" hosted by the former Miss Florida, Aleta Bryan.

All in all, these cash businesses brought ungodly sums into the coffers of the very godly Dix. Further, the gentlemen's entertainment trade and media holdings offered ample opportunity to make friends and influence people in high places. Not one to turn his back on spiritual investments, Dix was well-established as a contributor to the Fishing and Worship Tabernacle, Christ Up a Creek.

Though he missed his buddies and good times back home, Two Dix had settled into the life of dissipation enjoyed by the idle rich in La República: Ron Aniversario, Macanudo cigars (he preferred the "Empresario" line), coastal fishing, and rogering the local talent at the Happy Fish. He thusly realized that the life of a diplomat in the service of his president and party was not bad, not bad at all.

Ivana Dix, pronounced "Eye-vana," the ambassador's wife, was well-suited to the social responsibilities of an American embassy in the world's less developed outposts. She proved her worth by providing the best petit fours in La República at her famous afternoon teas. La República, being a coffee-producing nation did not have teas, so Mrs. Dix had to have her authentic southern sweet teas brought in through the diplomatic pouch. Wearing white gloves despite the 90% humidity, the ambassador's spouse proudly poured afternoon sweet tea as it should be served: iced. This was a novelty much discussed in the better homes of La Capital.

Coming from old money in Apalachicola, Florida, her family was originally from Canada and part of the Acadian diaspora, more fashionably referred to as Cajun. Her skin wasn't dark but wasn't white either. More like the color of garlic aioli. This had not been a deterrent to her social mobility thanks to her training at the finest finishing school on the Redneck Riviera. Thus, Ivana was used to operating at the highest levels of society. She could certainly put on the dog and lay out a spread.

Ivana met her husband when both were attending MidAmerica A&M (Go Indians!). Ivana Broque was a scholar-athlete recruited into the Silver Roundheels, the highly sought-after woman's cheer squad. There she caught the eye of Richard Dix with her sequined short skirt and tight blouse designed to accentuate her impressive southern charms. A&M football fans could not help noticing her panache when she flung the white wooden rifle high above her diamond-tiaraed head and catching it still spinning in heavy leather stagecoach drover gloves. While the girls of the Silver Roundheels might have worn the uniform, little Miss Broque owned the look.

It wasn't long before Ivana, in a breach of protocol, was made Major Majorette — the highest honor any active Roundheel could achieve, and one generally reserved for seniors. Oh, she was quite a catch; Richard Dix took note and wasted no time in inviting her to the mixer held every Wednesday and Friday at the Fiji frat house. Soon they became the biggest couple on campus where Dix himself held a lot of sway. After all, he was the son of Chet Dix. As in, "The Chet Dix Student Moral Crisis Center." Yes, that Chet Dix.

In addition to family money Dix was blessed with an enviable asset — his big Johnson, rumored to be the biggest on the MidAmerica A&M campus. It was a sweet motor, 250 throbbing horses pushing around a boss 22-foot chartreuse Bass Cat[1] with blue metal flake and a walk-thru console. No woman could resist that type of lure, certainly not Ivana, a southern gal raised on fishing largemouth bass out of her daddy's stock tank.

The wedding was held in Ivana's hometown of Apalachicola. All the local elites turned out for the event, filling the Christ Up a Creek Church from faux oak veneer panel to faux oak veneer panel to witness the blessed couple exchange vows and receive the laying of the hands from Rev. Dr. Grope himself. The assembled gasped at the dignity and majesty of the ceremony watching the happy couple march arm-in-arm out of the sanctuary to the strains of Robert Earl Keen's "Five Pound Bass."

Outside, the assembled were treated to the solemnity of the couple walking under crossed Shakespeare Ugly Stiks[2] held by the best man and his groomsmen while the members of the Apalachicola Bass Club flung Ol' Sam's All Pro Deer Corn at the newlyweds. Many felt it was a solemn celebration not seen since the War of Northern Aggression. A fact reflected in rather large headlines in the local press, specifically the Apalachicola County Tattler which proclaimed, "Broque-Dix Joined in Holy Matrimony."

Now, as ambassador and wife, the Dixes rose to the occasion to entertain La Capital's most noticeable citizens — starting with Generalíssimo Máximo Mandamás, La República's Dictator-for-Life, and his enigmatic wife. The generalíssimo, a staunch anti-communist and thus defender of American Interests and strong ally of the current American administration, was clad in his "dress blues:" a uniform of Napoleonic pastiche augmented with many as colors as possible. Mandamás sported a myriad of medals on his

---

[1] Bass Cat is a specialized high-end watercraft coveted by bass fishing enthusiasts.

[2] A brand of highly regarded fishing rods preferred by bass fishermen (and women).

manly chest and would proudly bore anyone who evinced an interest in the gaudy display of his "fruit salad."

As the dictator and his wife were announced, an embassy aide whispered to Two Dix that the generalíssimo had actually attended MidAmerica A&M (Go Indians!), his dear old alma mater. Dix was skeptical and disregarded this information as false for he believed it unlikely that someone so pockmarked and, uh, brown would be admitted into the sacred halls. Racial inclusion was not MidAmerica's strong suit. Skin the color of the Olive Garden garlic aioli sauce was about the limit for the admissions office.

Following the dictator was his wife, Rosemary Mandamás née Romero. A devout believer in her own brand of religion she called Chrono-Astrology who dabbled in mysticism and believed in the universal power of amethysts. She boasted a wardrobe of frightful creations, each accessorized with dozens of cheap beads, tarnished brass gimcracks, and colored glass strands around her chicken neck and bony wrists. The pièce de résistance, however, was the amethyst-bejeweled tiara atop her never-washed head.[3] Rather than listen to her mindless drivel, Mandamás had given in to some of his wife's questionable mandates such as the compulsory teaching of Chrono-Astroism in schools, mandatory wearing of amethyst tiaras by women, elimination of the color red in the city (it drained energy, she claimed) including traffic lights, and the official observation of solstices.

Mrs. Mandamás never left the Presidential Palace without her chief advisor Gregorio, whose behind-the-scenes manipulations of the government made him the Rasputin of La República. Claim-

---

[3] She once told her husband, "Washing dilutes the power of my hair! The Bible says Sampson never washed his hair for fear of losing his power over Delilah."

ing to be a monk from Nosuchistan, he made Mandamás so nervous the dictator felt a stabbing pain in his privates whenever the man drew near. Thus, Max did everything possible to avoid the company of the short-bearded "monk" in the cowled cape. He had smelled "phony" from the time of their first meeting and believed the monk to be from Costa Rica, thus explaining his strange accent and mutterings. Tonight, Gregorio was in full cowl and for added effect, carried a crystal orb the size of a Wilson Wimbledon series tennis ball in his left palm. It was amethyst blue. Bowing enigmatically, the mystic murmured something in his native Nosuchistani.

The fivesome exchanged chit-chat. On one side the henpecked generalíssimo and his wife with the caped counselor at her side, on the other Mr. and Mrs. ambassador. Dix had heard that the dictator was no longer master of his domain, that the day-to-day running of the business of government was in the hands of his wife, dubbed *La Bruja* by the cynical *capitalinos*. An embassy aide, the same aide who told Dix about Mandamás' academic career at MidAmerica A&M, briefed the ambassador on the first lady's craziness. He mentioned that Mrs. Dictator had gotten it into her unwashed head that the color red was bad, the color green good. This nonsense was fed to her by the Eastern European mystic who consulted with the First Lady on spiritual matters.

Dix held back from the discussion, eyeing Gregorio warily, an untrustworthy foreigner, he felt. *Where is he from?* The ambassador was thinking, *He's not one of the local crowd. I could handle him if he was a native Republican, they are sorta like Messicans, but this guy ... I don't know. With that accent he's some kind of communist I'll bet my bass boat on it.* As the ambassador was ruminating over the Rasputin of La República, Gregorio was holding forth, dominating the conversation with his familiar nonsense. "Energy values in the electromagnetic spectrum are extant in color," he proclaimed.

Rosemary interjected, "Gregorio is a genius!" Max let these outbursts on the part of his wife go without comment as the Mrs. had become rather adamant about her religiosity as curated by the robed one. As the ambassador and his wife were a new audience, Rosemary went on about the success of having the "true science" of color taught in the schools of La República. Two Dix started looking around for somebody, anybody, to talk to or get him another drink.

The first lady went on to boast about her own decree requiring women to wear tiaras with plastic amethyst-colored beads (sold by the First Lady herself through exclusive retailers) so as to channel their feminine spirituality. She was working on something for men, she added. "The head pieces really add something, don't you think Mr. Ambassador? Mrs. Ambassador?"

"They're something all right," Ivana responded while looking around for somebody, anybody to talk to or get her another drink. But the dictator's wife was on a roll. Her audience usually consisted of just the one person, her nitwit husband, who was stubbornly resisting her suggestions. She peeked over at Max and observed him looking around for somebody, anybody to talk to or get him a drink.

Outside, audible to the partygoers, was the incessant horn-blaring now common in the capital. Rosemary had her wish, all the traffic lights were now permanently green and with no reason to stop, cars and buses and trucks filled the intersections creating a chaos never before seen in La Capital. The situation was such that drivers abandoned their cars to run errands, have lunch, go to the bathroom, schtup the mistress.

Two Dix looked past the astrologer at his potential ally, the Dictator-for-Life and fellow whoremonger. "Glad y'all could come to the shindig, Max," Dix said without a note of irony, showing no hint of their earlier chance meeting at the Happy Fish. Dix proffered his catcher's mitt-sized hand and shook the dictator's with energetic pumping and added "good to see Republicans in the house!"

"*Republicanos.*"

"Say what?"

"*Republicanos.* People from La República are *republicanos.* Not Republicans." *Este jueputa todavía no entiende.*[4]

"Sure you are, har har." The ambassador turned to the First Lady and greeted her, "And how are you Mrs. Manhands? You're looking purdy as a picture. That tiara, are those sapphires?"

"No! *Señor* Ambassador. They are not! They are amethyst, they absorb energy from the universe and —"

"Is that so, I'll be goddammed! Look Ivana, a tiara made of … of something…." *Christ on a crutch, this dame is off. Cheap cut glass and universal energy, Goddang!*

Dix happily spotted Wulther and called to him over the hubbub of cocktail conversations. "Wulther, please. Drinks for the dictator and his, for Mrs. Dictator." Thus, America's Ambassador to La República handed off the leader of the country AND his wife to the bartender Wulther. A diplomatic coup.

Wulther, La Capital's most prolific mixer of cocktails, had been borrowed from the city's only five-star hotel, the Hotel Cinco Estrellas, to minister over the blending of drinks for the night's soiree. Dressed in a white jacket and juggling a silver shaker over his shoulders, Wulther oozed cool, calm class. Making his famous daiquiris and passing them around on a silver tray, the mixologist's mere presence diluted some of the tension building at the party.

Entering the reception behind the Mandamáses was Rafael Izquierdo, La Capital's diminutive mayor and owner of properties throughout the country including, it was rumored, the Happy Fish. Embassy events were not his cup of tea but as a public official he

---

[4] This son of a whore still doesn't understand.

was obligated to attend and deal with unpleasant people like the Dixes. Approaching them, Izquierdo beamed like a true politician, "Your Excellency, *Sra.* Dix a pleasure to see jou again. Mrs. Dix, jou look I don' know how jou say it in English, but we say "*Estás pero para comer enterita.*"[5] With that lascivious turn of phrase, Rafael Izquierdo, mayor, landowner, and closet communist grabbed Ivana's black-gloved hand and seductively kissed the inside of her wrist. *¿Coño, guantes con este puto calor?*[6] One thing was certain, Izquierdo was a paragon of *republicano* gallantry.

"Oh my, Mr. Eeezkeydo, how you go on." Ivana, though out of Apalachicola lo these many years, could still blush on cue, something every good southern gal learned at Gulf Coast Girls Academy. She added, diplomatically, "So nice to see so many prominent Republicans here tonight." Izquierdo, exasperated, sighed, "*Republicanos,* madame Mrs. Ambassador. People here, we are called *republicanos.* Republicans are like Goldwater, McCarthy, Palin. We are *republicanos.*"

The ambassador was hovering nearby, seething. *What's that commie saying, and what's with the wrist-kissing shit?* He jumped right in. "Goldwater? McCarthy? Fine men! Yes, it's men like them and myself committed to the fight of godless communists, is that not right, mayor? Har-har." Izquierdo flinched unobserved, made his apologies, and moved on to disengage from the uncomfortable conversation.

"What's all this talk about communists? Red bastards undermining American Interests and freedom." It was Steve Steele in his guise as Chief Pilot for Kiwi Airways (We'll Get There!) and dressed appropriately in his summer wool uniform: a close-fitting jacket with gold buttons and four stripes on each of the cuffs, pants

---

[5] Good enough to eat whole.
[6] Gloves in this goddam heat?

with creases as sharp as a Smith & Wollensky steak knife. His elegant feet were shod in high-gloss Florsheim wing tips he had admired in a photograph of Richard Milhous Nixon. An aviator's short-billed cap sat jauntily upon a gorgeous head of masculine hair. Tonight, the pilot chose to maintain his top-to-bottom Pan American Airways look by not removing his expensive gold-rimmed aviator Ray Bans.

Seeing the opening left by Izquierdo's departure, Mandamás moved in to join the two like-minded freedom fighters as they shook hands. "Gentlemen, we must meet in private. I have serious news that concerns us all. It's about the communists in Aguacate Province." The last sentence was whispered conspiratorially.

Steele and Dix tensed up like a teenager's prom night boner. Fueled by a few cocktails and a belly full of those little sausages on toothpicks, they were ready to fight communism right there, goddamit! Mandamás had their full attention.

"Let us meets, *señores*, after dinner over cigars. Ambassador, you can break away, *sí?* And we can meet on the Porsche."

Dix, bewildered, asked "You came in a Porsche?"

Que pendejo. "No, ambassador, I came in my limousine!" Adding proudly, "It is a Cadillac! Made in *La Yunae!*"[7]

"But you said Porsche, we would meet on the Porsche?"

Eyes rolling to the high ceiling, Mandamás clarified, "Porchut. We meet outside on the porchut. We talk about *comunistas*, we esmoke cigars." When stressed he tended to lose the American accent he had cultivated at Gluteus House, the athletes-only dormitory where Mandamás had spent his halcyon college days.

Others streamed in, grabbed a daiquiri from the ever-efficient Wulther and proceeded with cocktail hour behavior. Klaus

---

[7] United States in the local argot.

Von Klaus, a reformed Nazi, owner of La Capital's five-star Hotel Cinco Estrellas, was clicking heels like he was still in the bloody Wehrmacht and chatted with Tirso, a local Korean shopkeeper who, because he was Asian, was known as "El Chino."

"I am telling you that Riefenstahl's seminal documentary did not exaggerate." Klaus clicked his heels again in agreement to his own position on the matter of German documentary cinematography. Tirso, not listening, was daydreaming about Carl Yasztremski's shot at the Triple Crown back at Fenway. Tirso, an MIT graduate, was an ardent Red Sox fan.

In another klatch, Father Flynn, a defrocked Canadian prelate and longtime resident, held up his empty yet still frosty daiquiri glass for inspection, "You know Ugarte, I am usually a Canadian Club man, but Wulther's daiquiris are growing on me." He drained the remaining drops of the tropical elixir with great pleasure to the satisfaction of his drinking partner, Ugueth Ugarte. Ugarte was a daily regular at the Hotel Cinco Estrellas bar and considered himself an expert on all things La República. He had even penned the oft quoted (by him) and seldom read "History of La República," the seminal work on the history of the country going back to colonial times under the French. Ugarte was endured at times but mostly reviled for being stubbornly dogmatic about everything.

"That is because you are becoming one of us, *padre*, a *republicano*," replied Ugarte. "We drink rum of course. Which is why we are so virile. Not that that should be of any use to you. But we *republicanos* are famous for our virility. I made mention of that fact in my recent article in El Día newspaper, perhaps you may have seen it," replied the reporter.

"No, Ugarte I did not!" *Bloody Fishwrap!* The local paper was not a Father Flynn favorite; he preferred The Gazette from his native Montreal. Shifting to another subject, the priest asked, "What do you make of the disappearance of your goal tender, your so called "Wall," Ugarte?"

Other conversations, some laughter, and the tinkle of glasses were an indication of a successful cocktail party well underway. The hostess was so pleased that she became engaged in conversation with Gregorio, who was kind of interesting for a monk. Listening to the mystic's elaborations on early vaudeville kept her entertained while her husband Two Dix slipped out on the porchut with the dictator and the handsome, but intense, pilot.

⧗ ⧗ ⧗

"Here, *señores*, these are the only kind I smoke. I have them brought in especially for me by Esteeve Steele, Kiwi Airways' best pilot! Thank you *Capitán* Esteeve." Mandamás bowed his head toward the pilot.

"You are most welcome, Generalíssimo," Steele replied while withdrawing a long Macanudo from the dictator's hand-tooled leather case.

"Mr. Ambassador? A Macanudo?"

"Damn, don't mind if I do. I usually favor the 'Empresario' but I'll try this …?"

"'Dictador,' Ambassador. A little richer than the 'Empresario.' I think you will like it."

The three manly men commenced a ritual of Zippo lighter opening, snipping, clipping and licking, puff-puff-puffing, and smoke blowing. Each nodded in turn to the other and signaled satisfaction with the phallic symbols firmly clenched in their jaws, once again comfortable with their sexuality.

"*Señores*, we have a problem here in our country. We are a peaceful country of laws and orders. We love freedom and we love the *Yunae*, the USA, but there are these *hijo de puta comunistas!*" Man-damás allowed his voice to taper off dramatically while he held the Americans with his eyes. "I have it on good authority from our agents in the field that there are *fidelista* forces forming in our Agua-cate Province." He paused for effect and puffed his ginormous ci-gar.

"Commies? I heard something about a sleeper cell in the east. A cultural indoctrination center of some sort. Generalíssimo, just lend me some good men, and I'll lead them. We'll bring awe and shock to those leftist enemies of American Interests. They'll be sorry they messed with —"

"Alright, Steele, that's enough. Let's make sure before we act. You don't hunt deer with a bird dog son." Dix's speech was peppered with colloquial American hunting references that seemed to work somehow. "Generalíssimo, is there more to this situation?"

"Indeed there is, gentlemen. Indeed there is."

Seeing he had their attention, Mandamás wove his tale right out of the pages of the book he was reading, "Behind Every Tree!" A gift from the ambassador himself, he kept the volume by his bed-side as a sleeping aid. Full of chicken-little prognostications and Domino Theory posits, it warned of a communist invasion that threatened American Interests. Prompted by the CIA man's remark he began, "*Sí*, it is true, there is an esleeper cell, deep in Aguacate Province. They're funded by Moscow through the Jeeves Bank on Threadneedle —"

"What in God's holy name are you twittering about, Max?"

Steele cocked an eyebrow, raised his cigar-holding hand, and looked at Mandamás as if to say, "May I?" The dictator nodded.

"Mr. Ambassador, let me brief you. Here's the scenario. A communist sleeper cell —"

"Son, you have got to stop taking gibberish. You sound like that Rosemary chick with the crystals. No offense, Max."

"None taken."

"Okay, let me give you the deets in layman's terms, Mr. Dix. Here's the background. It's KTKO. See there's —"

"KTKO?"

"Need to know only, Ambassador. This is highly classified information. I assume you have 'secret' security clearance."

"Of course I do, why I raised nearly $5 million in the last month of the campaign! If that don't buy me some kind of clearance, then where is our country headin'? Why I told the President himself —"

Gritting his perfect teeth, Steele interrupted. "Mr. Ambassador, sir, the commies?"

"Oh right. Continue."

"Back a while ago, an elite force from Corinto, that's the nation to the north, invaded Aguacate Province. You've heard of Aguacate Province have you not, Mr. Dix?"

"What do you take me for? I ain't no freshman at the senior pig dance. Har har." *Aguacate as in guacamole? Christ's cousin, what next?*

"Well, these Corinto elites, backed by those eurocommies in Whitehall[8] poured over the border from the Aguacate Province, which was theirs at the time if you'll remember your history, Mr. Ambassador."

Two Dix remembered no such history. In fact, Two Dix never read any history. He only read books that were interesting. The last book he read was "Bass Fishing Secrets" by Bill Dance. Yet he nodded with conviction and took another satisfactory inhale of the Macanudo Dictador he had been fondling and fingering in his ham hands. *Goddammit, that tin-pot Mandamás sure knows his cigars!*

Steele was gaining momentum. "Well, they were repulsed, sir, by an even **more** elite force of *republicanos* under the supreme

---

[8] Demonym for Britain's Defense Ministry.

command of El Generalíssimo whose Macanudo Cigar you are now enjoying."

The generalíssimo gave a modest bow of his slightly over-sized head and waved his Dictador cigar in front of him like a windshield wiper and added, "It was thanks to the efforts of one man, Mr. Dix. A true hero of the nation. Brayan Buenaventura was his name. He repulsed the invasion and sent those sheep-fucking *hijos de sesenta mil putas*[9] back to Corinto, pardon my French."

"Hot damn, that's what we need here to fight these commies, a national hero! Let's get this character back. He should be the lead dog in this hunt. Where is he now?"

"I am sorry, Señor Ambassador. He is unavailable. He is very dead. In the cemetery. For you see, Mr. Dix, brave Brayan Buenaventura was the only casualty of the Guerra de Los Aguacates. He was run over by a Jeep, and that killed him very much."

"A Jeep?!"

"Not one of ours, sir, a Land Rover." Steele was careful not to let this detail sidetrack his story. "So, as you know, La República received the province of Aguacate along with some furniture under the conditions of the treaty known as the Guacamole Act. But, most importantly, sir, the Shrine of The Virgin of Aguacate, the patroness of La República which was in Corinto is now in La República."

"Well, don't that just beat the band? Y'all see Wulther anywhere? I could use some more lubricatin'."

Max cleared his throat and posed the question, "Do you think these godless *comunistas* are the ones to have enticed our goalie to defect, Señor Esteeve?"

Steele rubbed his chin thoughtfully with his non-Macanudo hand, "My thinking is as follows: a) there's a nest of Reds in Aguacate Province, 2) they're involved in some indoctrination —very

---

[9] Sons of 60,000 whores.

dangerous indoctrination — c) they got money from England, probably from the pinkos in the Labour government, d) they hate America, and 5) they are godless, so they also hate the Virgin!"

"No one hates virgins son, you just got to wait 'em out. Anyway, where are these commies?" Dix asked, not entirely following the thread.

Mandamás offered, "Behind every tree, it seems. *Señor* ambassador, we need support from the Republicans to fight this evil!"

"Well, what do I have to do with it? You're the head of the whole goddam country full of Ray-poo-blee-canos! You're a fucking dictator for chrissake!"

"Republicans. Señor Embajador. We need the support of Republicans."

"Now you lost me, son. I feel like I'm fishin' for bass without my Ugly Stik if you follow me."

Again Steve Steele signaled to Mandamás. Again Mandamás nodded. "If I may, Mr. Dix. What the generalíssimo is referring to is support from the United States Republicans. Not La República *republicanos*. Sir, with your permission I will take this to Langley! I'm flying Kiwi Airways Flight 2 to the States tomorrow. I'll go to Company HQ right away."[10]

"Alright, son, I'll call my contacts. We need a bigger tackle box for this job. There could be thousands of them poised and ready to sap La República's vital fluids. Generalíssimo, leave it to the United States, we will come to your aid! We never forget our allies!"

"I am most grateful. To both of you." *It is so easy to fool these stupid gringos!*

---

[10] Steve Steele, CIA operative had never been to Langley. "The Company" was the insider's term for the secret agency and one that Steve liked to throw around. Plus, he was dying to see the insides of CIA HQ.

"Oh, there you are! Three handsome men! Come back and join the party. Put those nasty things out, that exotic Mr. Gregorio is going to read my fortune in crystals. Come darlin', Steve, Mr. Dictator…"

Chapter 8

Tirofijo Hatches a Plan

Meanwhile, in another part of the city …

La Capital, La República's largest and most cosmopolitan city, was known for its gastronomy. The city boasted many restaurants that served regional delicacies from soups to salads, from beef to *baleadas*. This was a given. La Capital, however, was not lacking in international fare. The city was proud of its numerous restaurants famous for their unique preparation of succulent dishes including fowl. They seemed to be everywhere.

There was, in fact, a KFC less than dozen blocks from the *Escondite*, and it was there that Tirofijo, mouth watering, was headed. On foot and not in the comfort of his red Mercedez Benz 280SL because, in the new reality of La Capital, driving was impossible.

The intersections were jammed with cars immobilized by traffic lights which were all stuck on green. Everyone was free to move, yet no one was able. "The irony!" Tirofijo groused aloud to no one as he walked alone instead of driving his cream puff Benz. On the way to the KFC, he noticed a red 280SL only a block away stuck in traffic. Unmoving. He wondered if it was the same one from the parking lot a few years ago.

Inside the chicken place there were only two persons in line ahead of him. A couple, perhaps on a date. They received a red-and-white bucket of chicken, paid, and slipped out the door. Tirofijo stepped up to the counter and examined the colorful back-lit display of offerings above. After taking some time to choose his chicken, he ordered confidently, like a regular. "Two pieces of chicken, extra crispy, and cold slaw."

"Coleslaw, *señor,*" sneered the pimply-faced epicene youth smiling insincerely from behind the counter.

It is a general rule that crime bosses are not to be corrected, much less by a fifteen-year-old in a red and white paper hat with a matching apron. Tirofío leaned over the counter and growled, "That's what I said, *baboso!*"[1]

"No, *señor*, you said 'cold slaw' it is pronounced 'coleslaw.'" He (or she) then grinned like it said to do in the manual, "The Coronel's Guide to Customer Satisfaction." She (or he) had read it just that morning.

Tirofijo just wanted his chicken, not a lesson in English from this, this …

The youth confirmed, "Ok, so that will be two pieces. Extra crispy. With **cole**slaw." There was a snide emphasis there, Tirofijo knew there was, but he let it go. He just wanted his chicken.

"Yes," he managed to say through gritted teeth.

"White or dark?"

"*¿Qué?*"

"Your two pieces of crispy chicken. Would you like them white or dark?"

"Is that not racist?" Tirofijo hissed while he stared back.

"*Señor,*" she (or he) said, "we have white meat and dark meat, which would you prefer?"

"Dark, I guess."

"Spicy or Original Recipe?"

"*Puta madre,* will this ever end?!"

"We just want you to be happy with your order," quoting again from the manual.

---

[1] Drooler.

"Do I look happy to you?!" He replied nearly reaching over the counter to choke this individual, but he demurred lest it be a girl and what would that do to his reputation?

"Spicy," he relented.

"And to drink?"

Qué chingadisima madre. I may never eat!

"Coke."

"No Coke."

"No Coke?" Tirofijo asked.

"No Coke, Pepsi."

"Ok, Pepsi."

"What size?"

One hundred years later Tirofijo sat at a booth by a window in the empty restaurant eating his crispy chicken, coleslaw, and sipping a 32-ounce medium Pepsi. He looked out and noticed the red Mercedes had not moved. No one had moved. Traffic was at a standstill as always.

Except a kid on a small noisy motorbike with a lime green box mounted behind him. He had no difficulty with the traffic as he wove deftly between the stalled cars and buses. He could go where others could not on his cheap Chinese motorbike, wearing a waterproof outfit, and transporting a green box.

La República's thug of thugs took another bite of coleslaw and thought, "This is interesting. The kid on the piece of shit *moto* can go where the Mercedes cannot." He watched kid make his way to the KFC and park just outside the door. In he came with the green box the size of a big Christmas present. After handing over some cash, quite a bit of cash, he signed a receipt, and the cash and the receipt went below the counter into something Tirofijo could not see. The boy opened the top of the box and loaded it with takeout chicken, coleslaw, corn, and other delicacies of Kentuckian cuisine. He closed the box. He left the restaurant.

Outside, using a complex arrangement of ropes and elastic bands, the delivery kid strapped the box to the rack on the rear of his Chinese 60cc Poontang motorbike. Just as he was about to climb aboard, he saw the man. A chill went up the delivery kid's 18-year-old spine as the man stepped out of the shadows.

"*Hola, mae*," the man said with a voice trying to be friendly but not succeeding.

The boy swallowed hard. "*H-h-hola.*" His eyes darted to the lime-green box on his motorbike. Did this stranger want his dinner or something more sinister?

"Do not worry, you are not in trouble. Do you know who I am?"

Por la Virgen de Aguacate, I am dead. It is Tirofijo!
"*S-s-s-sí.*"

"Quit stuttering, I am not going to hurt you. What were you doing in there?"

"My job?"

"Are you asking me or telling me?" Tirofijo challenged him impatiently.

"My job, *señor.*"

"Ok, tell me … what is your name?"

"Potro, they call me Potro."[2]

"Ok, Potro. Let's pretend I am **not** who I am," he gave the delivery boy a crooked smile, "I am your little brother, and **he** is asking you what you do at work. Explain it in such a way that he can understand."

"I-I-I cannot do that."

Tirofijo, oozing patience from a tank of patience that read E said, "Why, Potro? And stop stuttering!"

"I do not have a little brother."

---

[2] Colt.

"Your sister — never mind, just tell me, without stuttering, what you just did."

"Okey. Well, I brought the money? The chicken money? From the deliveries of the chicken? You see people they call in to OverEats!" he said this pointing to the OverEats! logo on the back of his rain slicker and the side of the box.

"¿Y?"

"I take it to them. You know the chicken and the cole-slaw—"

"Cold slaw."

"*S-s-sí*, the cold slaw. I ride through the city, I deliver the food, they give me the cash, I bring it back to the restaurant, I give it to them, they put it in a bag with my receipt, then —"

"Stop. You bring the cash. They put it in a bag? Not the safe?"

The kid was a little out of breath, but he was excited that Tirofijo was taking such an interest in his job.

"It goes into the safe later? But it is in the bag all night."

"Then what?"

"Then I fill up the box with more chicken and cole, uh cold slaw, and do it all again?"

"And how many drivers does this KFC have?"

"I am the only one, *Señor* Tirofijo. But there are other drivers for other KFCs and Pizza Huts. We all wear the same uniform!"

Tirofijo now recalled seeing the green-garbed kids motor-biking through the city around ambulances, buses, on sidewalks running down nuns and old ladies. He hated them with their liberty in the increasingly horrendous traffic. But he was interested now.

"How many *tucanes*, Potro, would you say that you bring in a night?"

"Ay, *mucho, señor.* Many."

"How many?"

"Many many!"

Tirofijo was out of patience but didn't want to scare the young man away. "I remind you, young Potro, of who I am. Now, how many?"

"Well like a normal day like today … many, I mean 3,000 *tucanes* or so. On a normal day. Sometimes less. But tomorrow maybe 5,000 or more?"

"Tomorrow?"

"*Sí, señor*, tomorrow is the big game! La República meets Corinto in the fútbol grudge match. This time we are going to beat those *jueputas*. Our new goalie, Gómez!? He will stop —"

"Stop! Back to this chicken business, Potro. How much do they pay you?"

Proudly, "I make 400 a week PLUS tips. Enough for me and my *madrecita*, plus a little for my motorcycle payments and, if the Virgen is good enough, there is enough left over to take my Carmencita to the movies, she loves Cantin —"

"I'll pay you 1,000 *tucanes*. Each week. You come work for me. One thousand and maybe you do not work every day. You take Carmencita out twice and do something nice for your mother. What do you think?"

Potro did not hesitate. "*Sí, señor* Tirofijo! I will come work for you, but first I must make these deliveries and return my Over-Eats! uniform."

"You keep the uniform, and you keep the cold slaw and you drive me to my *Escondite*, my secret lair, to talk details. I'll get on the back and give you directions."

"I know where it is, *señor*!"

"Let's go then! By the way, Potro, that's an unusual name. Why do they call you that?"

"Because I am hung like a horse."

Chapter 9

Behind Every Tree

"Behind Every Tree" by Charles Foster Kane II
From the book jacket:

Eldest son of the famed publisher, Charles Foster Kane II is a great patriot who shares within the covers of this volume the peril faced by patriotic forces south of the border where Leninist-Trotskyites have made their beachhead. Kane is a well-respected chronicler of communistic chicanery.

A graduate of the prestigious MidAmerica A&M with a degree in Accounting, Kane gained notoriety as a young staffer in the U.S. Department of State's accounts payable division. Shortly after he began his tenure there, he sensed the department was rife with Reds. It didn't take long for him to unearth pinko nefariousness as his suspicions led him to discover dubious documents, dangerous to democracy. He tells us it was during a routine examination in the basement of the Foggy Bottom offices, that Kane II found some papers jammed in a broken-down shredder. Those documents, now safely locked away from the prying eyes of pinko paper pushers and journalists, have revealed the many dangers we are facing from the Russian and Chinese communistical influences south of the border.

Kane II has meticulously poured through these documents and writes about the findings in this remarkable book which should be required reading throughout America. This not-for-the-squeamish analysis of atheistical armies massing on our borders will keep you turning the pages long into the night. The remarkable first chapter of this book, Chapter One, was published in the respected conservative monthly, The Right Revolution magazine, and earned him the McCarthy prize for Amerikan Letters. He was lauded at the Congress of American Interests held annually in Genesis, Georgia.

The author is more recently an adjunct professor of American Studies at Billy Joe Bob University in Okeechobee, Florida. He is also a visiting professor of American history at MIT (McCarthy Institute of Tautology) in Thousand Lakes, Minnesota. Kane II makes frequent appearances on "Red Talks," a lecture circuit sponsored by Plush Velvet.

⧗ ⧗ ⧗

From Chapter One:

The traitorous communistic forces threatening American Interests are predominantly dark-skinned bad *hombres* who easily blend into the shade. Getting their orders direct from Nikita, they are spreading atheistic communism to our neighbors, ready to cross the Rio Grande River. Hordes of them with their Little Red Books, beards, and religion of immoralism ready to sap our great nation of its precious bodily fluids.

Now is the time to act, oh Defenders of Freedom. There are many of you I've been told. Men (and women, I suppose) who have bravely volunteered to hunt communists and communistic sympathizers in allied nations like La República. You are defending America from infection of the socialist disease and keeping us protected from the perils of land reform, universal health care, and public golf courses.

However, as you venture abroad to flush out infestations of Reds skulking around: Know your surroundings! The rebels hide like cowards using foliage as their cover. I have compiled massive evidence based on extensive research into botanical camouflage that is employed by the left. This is cowardly, come out and fight, you Bolsheviks!!

Be aware of two trees in particular, the Guanacaste (*Enterolobium cyclocarpum*) and the Ceiba (*Ceiba aesculifolia*), which are commonly found in these Leninist-infested republics. They offer good cover. Both species have large trunks and branches that can hide Trotskyites, especially the thinner ones. A simple "walk in the woods" could prove fatal. So beware. They ARE Behind Every Tree.

In my research, which was extensive, I came across a very worthy initiative. You won't read about this in the so-called news. Edward R. Murrow, that Leninist lackey laboring in the halls of CBS (and we know what THAT stands for!),[1] has moved the report to the bottom of his inbox.

I am referring of course to "Project Paul Bunyan," a secret CIA initiative to cut down Ceiba trees in the region. What happened to Project Paul Bunyan? It met the axe! That's what happened. Communist sympathizers in the state department that hate America and pinko elements in the so-called "Democratic" congress joined forces to defeat the initiative. Funds were never approved, leaving communistic elements free to continue to hide behind these trees threatening our way of life and God-given right to teach the Bible in schools.

Here's what the Leninists in the State Department claimed, among other filthy lies. Ceiba trees are "protected" in La República because they are considered sacred by the indigenous tribes there. What a joke. This is another Red ruse, a plain falsehood propagated by Moscow's anti-American printing press known as The New York Times. I ask the reader, how this could be true if nowhere in the King James Version of the Bible is the Ceiba tree mentioned? So how can they be considered sacred?

---

[1] Communist Broadcast System.

The government of La República should be encouraged to remove Ceiba trees and replace them with bamboo. It is very hard for a communist, no matter how skinny, to hide behind a bamboo tree. This would protect American Interests by making it easier to identify Maoists and Stalinists.

⧗　⧗　⧗

Also from the book:

Look closely, communists are everywhere.

They are clever rascals, masters of disguise. My very extensive investigation has churned up a list of no fewer than 57 famous persons who are secret members of the international communist and communist-sympathizing organizations plotting against America and her interests. People like Brigitte Bardot, Terry-Thomas, Topo Gigio, Cantinflas, and Liberace. Also Roger Maris who may be a Russian double-agent using the New York Yankees as his cover and colluding to break the great American Babe Ruth's record. The list is very long, believe me.

Communists communicate in hidden code with their moles, agents, double agents, and others in their network of spies. These codes, I have found through my readings, are well hidden in so-called works of art. All art is suspicious, especially foreign art with all those virgins and naked babies. Modern art is the worst. Two of the main culprits are Frida Kahlo and Dalí, foreigners who don't even speak English, are known for their outrageous paintings and facial hair. I have spoken to operatives in a top-secret department at CIA who have cracked the code used by these hirsute pinkos to transmit their movements. I cannot reveal that code due to being sworn to secrecy, but it has to do with the use of eyebrows and mustaches. That is all I can write at this point.

There are other artists who have been revealed as enemies of our country. It is by now a widely held fact that rock musicians who profess free love and all that jazz are closet communists indeed. And speaking of jazz, I have it on good authority, that jazz musicians are also using complex codes for transmitting anti-American, anti-Christian messages. How else would you explain so many ridiculous notes? Also let's not overlook screenwriters, directors, and actors determined to infect our democracy with their so-called cinematic art. Recently, it was uncovered that some of the more famous quotes in "Casablanca" were secret signals. Our true enemy was revealed to be Claude Rains. This is something else you won't read in the New York Crimes newspaper.

I implore your vigilance in your own community where communists may have infiltrated to preach their poison. There is a mountain of evidence and rumors in our Nation's Capital to know that we need to be on the *qui vive*, ever alert to suspicious movements in American cities and towns and villages from coast to coast.

In my next edition I will also detail the threats posed by teachers, librarians, TV weathermen, and Avon salesladies. It's frightening.

Chapter 10

Steve Steele in Miami

A few days later, in *La Yunae* …

A very excited Steve Steele was in Miami in a taxi headed for Little Havana. He was home, in a way. Although he liked to say he was from Miami, he actually lived in Miami Lakes which was a community pretending to be Miami. In the cab ride from the airport, the pilot had been thinking about the assignment to topple the rebel forces in Aguacate. The assignment, which because of HIS sharp eyes and ears, was brought to the agency. HE was the one looking out for his nation's interests in forgotten La República. It was HE that was in the front lines of the War Against the Red Menace. Fighting the battle for Sen. McCarthy and Goldwater, those great Americans. "This meeting should be in Langley, at Company Headquarters," he said to the plastic separation between driver and passenger.

Ever since joining the CIA as a low-level agent, he had heard and read all about "The Company" flagship HQ, the state-of-the-art spying facility hidden deep in the McClean, Virginia woods. Not hidden exactly, because it was a 15-minute cab ride from downtown DC. Still, the romance of spy headquarters in the woods was intriguing.

Steve Steele, a very minor cog in the organization, longed to see the collection of tools that were on display along with artifacts such as Ho Chi Minh's jock and actual clippings of Castro's beard. He pictured himself, once he had routed the Reds in Aguacate province, regaling the other agents in the HQ bar with his hair-raising tales.

For now it had to be Miami.

The driver slammed on the brakes, causing Steele to collide painfully, face first, into the hard plastic partition separating cabbie from customer. A nasty welt rose up immediately on Steele's forehead looking like a small horn. "We be here, mon. The Marsaylaise. Be ten dolla, dude." He stepped out of the beat up green-painted South Beach Yellow Taxi and passed $10 through the open window into a sweet-smelling cloud. The driver was in there somewhere and a hand reached out of the cloud to grab the bill before tearing back out into traffic.

The Miami heat was unbearable as usual. Similar in temperature to La Capital, but dissimilar in humidity, grit, smell, and everything else. The air was like an unclean sandbox. Steve Steele remembered that he actually hated Miami, yet he lived there at least half the time flying Kiwi Airways' only route: Miami to La Chingada Airport and back. Opening the door to La Marseillaise, the famous restaurant on Miami's Calle Ocho, Eighth Street, in Little Havana, the aviator welcomed the Arctic refrigeration within. La Marseillaise was a Mecca for true food lovers: intoxicating smells of slowly roasted pork, frying onions and garlic, sizzling fish, chicken, *yuca frita*, *maduros*, *tostones*, and other epicurean delights of Caribbean provenance. When one of the cooks lifted the lid of an out-sized 30-quart tureen, a humid cloud of steam rose to the ceiling and hovered like a tropical storm. Underneath was revealed a sea of perfectly cooked white rice, each grain proud and plump. And the noise! Every hue of Pan-Latin profanity was slung with glorious gusto. Loud conversations were peppered with delicious vulgar jokes, lids were slammed on bubbling saucepans, oils were spattered, pots were banged, steam hissed, and orders were shouted back to the kitchen with colorful obscenities.

Steve Steele paused inside the entrance and touched his forehead tenderly. "Fuuuck it hurts!" Looking around at the restaurant and soaking up the atmosphere calmed his nerves. With his schedule he didn't get much of a chance to come to Little Havana and enjoy the atmosphere of places like La Marseillaise. Slowly taking in the *mise en scene* he was unaware he was breaking the cardinal rule of the Cuban cafe: standing still. Standing still in La Marseillaise was discouraged, and *gringos* specifically were not permitted to linger.

"Ecueme!"

A filthy wet broom smacked into the side of Steve Steele's very expensive brown Florsheim broughams. He had recently purchased them at Burdine's in the 163rd Street Shopping Center. Sure to make a good impression on his CIA handlers. The mop sloshed around his feet some more, and Steve looked down at the dirty medusa's nest at the end of a stick. At the upper end, a pair of veiny dark brown hands swung the stick back and forth as if he were Wayne Gretzky angling for a shot. But it wasn't The Great One, it was a tall, lanky, one-eyed bony man who looked straight at Steele like a cyclops. *Probably a raft person.*

None too pleased, Steele squared his shoulders, "Watch it, *hombre.*"

"Casey Estengel, he manayes," the mopper said, still staring.

"What?" *Yeah, definitely came by raft.* It had slipped Steele's mind that there was a password and counter sign protocol. Real spy shit.

"Casey Estengel," this time a bit more emphatically. "He manayes."

"Manages? what, the restaurant? No, I'm looking for —" *Oooh, the fucking password. What was it. Dammit! I am going to meet with these top operatives, and I can't remember the countersign? Not good.*

Steve Steele hated baseball. He was in trouble.

"Oh wait! Yes! Ed Kranepool?"

The mopper raised an eyebrow and repeated, "Estengel manayes!"

"Oh, right. Ed Kranepool has four balls."

"Jes, jou walk now. Turd boot on the right."

Many informed sources[1] have said that the most spies in the world can be found in three places: West Berlin, Hong Kong, and the main dining room of La Marseillaise on Calle Ocho. Any casual observer could glance around the room and judge for themself based on the display of Ray Bans and cheap shiny suits.

In the third booth on the right were two such agents torn from the pages of a le Carré novel. The G-men blended in perfectly with the other clientele, wearing matching dark glasses and staring straight ahead. They also sat on the same side of the booth as if they were on a first date.

Our Man in La Capital approached the booth, "Excuse me, but are you?"

"Mantle swings both ways." This came from the agent on the right, on the inside.

Steele, more alert now, replied with confidence, "Pepitone is a putz."

"Sit." It was still the man on the right talking. His partner, on the outside seat said nothing and continued to stare straight ahead.

"No names," added the man on the right as Steve slipped into the booth and faced them both.

"What's wrong with your face?" he asked. Steele dabbed at his head horn and said, "Nothing, just a flesh wound."

Satisfied, the man said with a slight nod to his twin, "This is Agent Blue. I am Agent Orange."

"I'm Steve Steele, but you know this —"

---

[1] Who they are is classified. For security reasons.

"No names, Steele! We know who you are. Don't we, agent?"

Agent Blue, more sphinx than human, nodded.

"Sorry, I'm a bit nervous, I didn't expect to meet here. I thought —"

"Don't think, Steele, you're not cleared for that. Does he have clearance to think, Agent Blue?"

"No."

The sphinx speaks!

"You have something for us? Wait, quiet. Here comes the waitress."

An old Cuban woman with a set of yellow and black teeth that looked like kernels on an ear of Indian maize, stood with a small pad and pencil stub in her hands. Just in case, she had a back-up pencil behind one ear. "Gwatchuwant, *amor*?" She looked at Agent Orange as if she knew he was the talkative one.

"*Arroz con pollo*, a side of *maduros suaves*, some *yuca frita*, and a Pepsi."

"No Peksi, Coke."

"Ok, Coke then."

She rotated her ample hips and faced Agent Blue. "An' jou?"

"Same."

She pivoted, this time toward Steele. Before she could ask, Agent Orange said, "He's not eating."

"*Por qué, mi amor*? Dis is the best restaurant in Miami. Look at the pictures of famous peoples on the wall who ate here. There ees *El Papa Juan 23*, Mother Teresa, she likes the *tostones*, and the great author Charles Foster Kane Dos!"

"He's going home, his mother is waiting."

"Hokay, jour loss *mi amor*."

After she took their orders and left, Agent Orange nodded to the hungry airman. "Continue."

Steve Steele, back on solid ground, explained the situation in re the sleeper cell, the existence of a new operative in the Aguacate Province called "Supremo Comandante," the threats to American interests, communists behind every tree, et cetera. He seemed very well versed on the situation.

Blue and Orange looked at one another. Blue gave a short nod. Orange turned to Steele. "Pay attention. Here are your orders. First, you are to report to CIA immediately!"

"Langley?"

Blue and Orange said nothing and stared back.

"Not Langley. CIA, you know, La Chingada International Airport[2] Mister Pilot."

"Oh," was the sheepish reply.

"Second," Orange continued, "a C-46 aircraft has delivered a Jeep, a radio receiver, several crates of M1s,[3] uniforms, boots, and other materiel already waiting for you in the Kiwi Airways hangar. You are to take possession of said materiel and by no means are you to allow this shipment to fall into the wrong hands. Do. You. Understand?"

Steele nodded. He liked the sound of the word "materiel."

"Third, this code book." Agent Blue removed a small yellow booklet from inside his jacket as Orange continued his instructions. "We are using a cipher code. You're familiar with cipher codes Mr. Pilot?"

Steve Steele had never heard of cipher codes. "Yes, of course!"

---

[2] IATA code: CIA.

[3] M1 Garand is a semi-automatic rifle used by U.S. Army in World War II.

"Good. Ciphers will be sent by cable, and you are to refer to the codes in here," he thump-thumped the small yellow booklet that was cleverly disguised with the title "Handy Phrases in Albanian."

"Right, but will the messages be in Albanian? I don't speak Albanian."

"Of course not, what gave you that idea? As you know, the cipher code just points you to a message in a book that I will give you. I will have an identical copy of the book, so we are on the same page. Your orders will be encoded in this," he reached under the seat and used both hands to haul out the Oxford Library edition of "The Complete Works of William Shakespeare (Fully Annotated)."

"They had a run on King James Bibles at Brentano's, so we had to go with the Shakespeare. Evidently there's a convention in town. Rev. Grope's Glorification, Jubilation, Something. Big run on bibles at the bookshop. There's a bass tournament too. Grope's Fish for Faith. Might be worth checking into, don't you think Agent Blue?"

Agent Blue remained sphinxlike.

"Anyway, Brentano's is bereft of bibles." Orange cracked a smile, amused by his own alliteration.

"So Steele, listen up. Keep the book on your person and don't let it out of your sight, understand? And we'll need it back. When Operation Green Avocado is completed."

"Operation Green — wait, I return the book?"

"You're not cleared to keep it. Is he cleared to keep it Agent Blue?

"No," said Blue still staring straight ahead.

"But it's just a book, right?"

"No." From both.

"Fifth, funds will be wired to you from the First Trans-Caribbean Bank of Broward."

"Is that safe? Using a public bank, won't that compromise our cover?" Steve had hoped to be carrying the cash smuggled into the lining of his jacket. But the romance of being a low-level operative of the Company was just not there anymore.

Blue said, "No."

Orange then clarified that it was a "Company" bank.

"Oh. How do I get the cash? I need cash to pay my gang, uh, the elite corps I have recruited. Dollars if possible. Small bills."

Undeterred, Orange continued, "Six, contact our operative, Agent Weiss. He owns a hotel in La Capital. It's a five-star hotel."

"Klaus Von Klaus, the Nazi?"

Blue, with a smile, "*Jawohl.*"

"Seven: you will approach Klaus alone."

"Of course, I wouldn't think of approaching him —"

Blue, frowning, "Alone."

"The password is 'Afghanistan' and the countersign is 'Bananistan,'" Orange declared.

"Who says what?" Steele asked absentmindedly touching the throbbing bruise on his face. It was a legitimate question.

Agent Orange frowned, "It's simple, flyboy. The password is 'Afghanistan' and the countersign is 'Bananistan.'"

"But what am I, the password guy or the countersign guy?"

Orange looked at Blue, "He's the password guy, right?"

Blue nodded.

"Okay, Steele. You're the password guy. You say 'Afghanistan' he says 'Bananistan' —"

"Let's call the whole thing off," Steele giggled.

"Impossible, we would have to kill you."

"A joke! Just a joke. You know the song? 'you say tomayto I say tomahto, let's call the whole thing off?'"

Blue was humming along, then said, "No."

Orange continued. "He will hand you the envelope."

They gave another stony stare at the pilot from behind the CIA-issued specs. After an uncomfortable 30 seconds, Blue concluded the meeting. "Go," he said.

"That's it?" Steve asked looking from one set of black orbs to the other.

Blue nodded.

Steve Steele wedged the twelve pounds of English literary genius under his arm and slid out of the booth. As he stood he got a glance at the adjoining table. It also had a book. It was Plutarch's "Lives." Walking to the front door he saw books all around him on seemingly every table: "Rise and Fall of the Roman Empire," "The Complete Hoyle's," complete works of Twain, Thackeray, Tolstoy. Everybody had a book. Then he felt something wet and stringy around his ankles. Looking down he saw the filthy, soggy mop give his Florsheim's another once-over. He stepped out into muggy Miami and saw nothing through his fogged-up Aviator Ray Bans.

Meanwhile, the old Cuban lady had returned to the booth. "Who ordered the *arroz con pollo* and a Coke?"

Chapter 11

Piojo

Under the cover of a zinc-plated sheet, the kind used for roofing on auto repair garages, car washes, pre-owned tool shops, key makers, money changers, and makeshift barbers sat a skinny kid reading. The zinc offered excellent protection from the merciless tropical sun as well as the deluge of the upcoming rainy season. The kid was around 13 or 14, he wasn't sure himself. Propped up in the beat-up recliner, he sat absorbed in an adventure comic; slowly turning the pages, mouth agape at the gaudy colors and action scenes.

Piojo, Tirofijo's right hand in his criminal enterprises, had recently discovered and become enamored with adventure comics. So much so that instead of working as Tirofijo's loyal dogsbody, he chose to spend hours reading through the stack of worn-out pulpy books at his feet. He had found these entertainments in a cache dug up when foraging in the Arboleda neighborhood among the detritus of the moneyed classes. The street urchin had been picking through a promising pile of household garbage, pushing through a strata of orange peels, eggshells, and coffee grounds when he saw the cover of "Captain Freedom and the Soldiers of Socialism." Although he could read, he wasn't sure what "socialism" was exactly, but that mattered little to the boy staring at a drawing of a man, a *gringo*, with square jaw, aviator glasses, camouflaged from neck to ankle, firing a massive weapon that spewed flames and oblong bullets off the page.

He picked up the remarkable piece of literature and found another, similar volume below it. There were more. And more. Piojo furtively took his new collection to his beat-up chair under the zinc roof.

The reading habit took him to new heights — his imagination soared over the streets of La Capital to a world of good guys and evil-doers. Rather than spend his day enforcing Tirofijo's tax system, Piojo spent the day in the company of his new hero, Captain Freedom, while sitting comfortably in the old chair. He turned each page slowly and read, with great interest, plots unfolding on newsprint; cheap colored ink was staining his hands.

Captain Freedom fought the forces of communism wherever they could be found. He defended the American way of life. Piojo wasn't quite sure what the American way of life was but if Captain Freedom thought it needed defending, **then by the Virgen de Aguacate it needed defending**. Piojo was deep into the adventure titled "Captain Freedom Behind the Iron Curtain" where Captain Freedom, his hero, was engaged in destroying something called immoral religion preached by a man named Lenin — a balding man with a beard, mustache, and a lot of clothing.

Piojo wasn't too sure about immoral religion, he wasn't the least bit religious, but he knew he hated the communists. He knew from his readings that communists were always fat men in cheap, ill-fitting suits with skinny black ties and thick, unfashionable eyewear.

To Piojo they were too much like the men he had to deal with on his rounds in La Capital. Self-important, parsimonious, cruel men who never parted with a single *tucan* that Piojo could use to buy a *café con leche* in the market. But Captain Freedom was onto their devilry and stymied their nefarious efforts to threaten American Interests and the American Way of Life. That theme was the constancy of Captain Freedom's many adventures around the globe which took him to places that looked a lot like La República. Piojo dreamed of the day Captain Freedom would come to La República to fight the *comunistas* with Piojo at his side. Piojo assumed there were *comunistas* to fight somewhere in his country.

No one knew the real name of Tirofijo's lieutenant; he was always called Piojo, or "louse." When asked why he was called that, Piojo would just say, "Because I make people itch." Though it was unflattering to be referred to as a tiny insect, he didn't fight the nickname. There were far worse things he had to bear in his urban poverty.

Just as no one knew his real name, everyone could agree that he was like many others on the streets of La Capital. An unwanted child, a product of adult indiscretions, an embarrassment passed off to the Sisters of Perpetual Emotion who cared for the city's sins. There Piojo shared the cramped spaces with others of his ilk and legions of lice, learning to pray and read biblical passages with other boys whose futures were like the rainy season: long, wet, and miserable.

Raised by the *hermanitas* until he was too bored by the life inside the church, Piojo escaped during a tradesman's delivery of sacramental wine and took two bottles with him. Able to exchange the red wine, labeled "Que Syrah, Syrah," for a place to sleep and a warm *pupusa*,[1] it was his start to a new life in La Capital. The city became a private kingdom where he could wander unfettered, free. Life had doled out so many other cruelties that Piojo, being a realist, focused on those he could control or do something about. His day-to-day needs consisted of a safe place to sleep, food, and dry clothes. The boy often went hungry, or wet, or sleepless. Over time

---

[1] A stuffed cornmeal cake. Part of La República's national cuisine.

he developed a patina like old pewter which he wore like a gray uniform.

One morning Piojo was walking along Arboleda, a street in a district of the same name lined with embassies and estates. Piojo had no business there but liked to make it part of his daily walk as he admired the mansions with their fragrant flowers, trees, and expensive cars. As he ambled down the shady street, he caught a glance of a long tree branch that reached over the high wall from the grounds of the American Embassy.

The branch was drooping under the heavy burden of ripening mangoes, some already turning yellow. The sight made Piojo's mouth water. According to the immutable laws of the street, these mangoes were fair game to any and all who happened to walk by; so Piojo removed his shirt and fashioned a basket which he began to fill with one large mango after another. In his excitement he failed to notice the man standing behind him.

"*Qué haces, mocoso?*"[2]

The kid nearly shit his chinos and jumped a foot straight in the air like Elmer Fudd after a Bugs Bunny sneak attack. His makeshift basket lost all shape and a dozen purloined mangoes fell to the ground. Turning, he saw a menacing looking man who was grinning in a friendly way. "Let me help you," the man said and began to pick up some of the mangos that had rolled into the street. Piojo slipped back into his shirt and turned intending to run.

"Do not go. *No te asustes,*"[3] He said, producing a plastic bag. The two of them began loading the fruit into the bag although Piojo was still wary.

"There. All good. I am sorry I made you jump!"

"T-t-t-that is ok, *señor* …?"

---

2 What are you doing snotnose?
3 Do not be afraid.

"Tirofijo," Tirofijo said and watched the boy's eyes for any sign of recognition. There was none but he saw something else. The boy's eyes betrayed an intelligence, an ardent desire. *This kid must stay deep in the belly of the street not to know who I am.* Tirofijo recognized himself in the visage of the homeless miscreant as he looked the waif up and down, taking in the filthy clothes older than the boy himself. It didn't seem so long ago when Tirofijo was extracting a living from the same streets, possibly eating fruits from that very tree.

"Are you any good with that?" Tirofijo pointed to the old slingshot poking out of the back pocket of the boy's chinos.

"*¡Sí!*" Piojo said proudly almost as if he was issuing a challenge to make him prove it.

His wish was answered.

"Hit that," Tirofijo said pointing down the street to a lone metal garbage can. Piojo looked at the can and gave a nod. Carefully, he bent over and picked up his round of ammunition, a golf ball-sized dirt clod. He looked back at Tirofijo who saw something else in the kid's eyes, something he liked. Confidence and determination. This boy was not yet beaten down by life in the streets; he wished to prove himself to Tirofijo.

Piojo handled the slingshot expertly, he loaded it, raised his arm, pulled back the elastic and let fly the dirt clod. After a pause of one or two seconds, there was a solid pong of hard earth against galvanized metal — the clod had found its mark. Piojo did this with tremendous aplomb and had not taken his eyes off Tirofijo for a second in the process.

"*¡Coño!*" Tirofijo stood impressed. Even he couldn't have pulled off such a shot. He felt a need to protect this boy, this version of him. The boy could benefit from a father figure and be useful to Tirofijo in some capacity. He tossed the idea around for a few minutes while Piojo began picking up more avocados from the side-walk.

Convinced, Tirofijo looked at the young Piojo and leaned in to ask, "Do you want to work for me? I need someone who is good with *la gomera*.[4] I can give you a place to stay whenever you want, and food, some walking around money too."

Piojo saw the opportunity for career advancement and didn't hesitate with his response, thus becoming the thug's constant companion. To seal the pact, Tirofijo made great ceremony of presenting his new associate with "Goliat," his own prized slingshot. Piojo accepted it like Cú Chulainn receiving the belly spear. With great reverence.

It was Piojo who used his slingshot skills to enforce Tirofijo's extortion racket. No one wanted to have a window shot out or their customers peppered with dirt clod artillery, so they paid. He was also the crime boss's man on the street. His eyes and ears. A trusty Sancho.

Piojo made the streets of La Capital his dominion, his barony. He traveled freely about on buses, avoiding payment by hanging on to the rear bumper, holding the emergency door handle, out of sight of the driver. It allowed him to travel anywhere within minutes. This coverage was useful to Tirofijo's financial pursuits and Piojo was rewarded with room and board and, more importantly, kindness.

The gamin had also proven his mettle as the "Assistant Director" to Tirofijo, writer-director-producer, of his short film 'A Scene from Café Kasbah' in hopes of getting noticed by Hollywood studio bigwigs.

There had been none more loyal to Tirofijo than Piojo.

---

[4] A slingshot.

Recently, however, Piojo was seduced by literature and Captain Freedom became his newfound hero thanks to his discovered library of comic books. It was a difficult thing to ignore his duties with Tirofijo, who began to grumble about Piojo's absences. However, the sudden longing for adventures like those in the pulp comics drew him to Captain Freedom. He had just finished re-reading "Captain Freedom Behind the Iron Curtain," immediately picked up "Captain Freedom Behind the Bamboo Curtain," and settled in. It was hot under the zinc, but Piojo didn't mind. He wiped the sweat off his brow and left a red, white, and blue streak of ink.

Chapter 12

Paola's Palace Protests

Part-time prostitute and full time PTA president, Paola Labios had political ambitions. Unlike many of her countrywomen who took things as they came, she was affronted by the absurdity of the authority in control of her beloved little country. Specifically, Paola was up to here — fed up with the laws coming out of the Presidential Palace like tsarist ukases; not the least of which were the worship of the color amethyst, the wearing of tiaras, minutes of silence in observance of solstices, elimination of red lights, and the teaching of crazy cosmology in the schools.

Paola, a former Jehovah's Witness who left the religion after learning that they did not celebrate birthdays (Paola loved getting birthday presents), was angry that her kids were being taught the twaddle of the First Lady's pseudo religion. Every classroom had undergone an interior redecoration — gone were the multiplication tables. Gone were the nice maps of La República, provided by the Auto Club. Gone were the walls covered with cheery subjects like the alphabet, colorful dinosaurs, geometric shapes, pictures of farm animals, the flora and fauna of the world around them. All of that gone! Now the children had to gaze at a wall of charts called Universal Concepts of Chrono-Astrology. Concepts such as "Color Vibrations" and "Keeping it Green," "The 10 Cosmic Commandments" and other drivel that had to be memorized. A lot of time was spent with color wheels, prisms, and (of course) reading crystals. Precious little time was spent looking through the classroom's microscope, doing maths, or acting out plays.

Yunior, La República's leading bibliophile, had shared books with Paola during his occasional visits to the Happy Fish allowing her to amass a small library of leading authors. She had actually waded through most of the works of Jean-Jacques Rousseau and was introduced to concepts foreign to *republicanos* who had long ago submitted to the yoke of authoritarianism. She was a political autodidact, learning on her own about democracy, the rights of man, and other concepts. Her reading of Rousseau lead to Jefferson and Madison and Hamilton and the U.S. Constitution and the Federalist Papers. Her brain filled up with 150-year-old revolutionary ideas that excited her. *What if La República* … ran through her mind in between PTA meetings, taking Axl and Slash to school, and sessions at the Happy Fish.

Nothing intrigued her more than the concept of separation of church and state. She followed the beliefs of Jefferson, Franklin, Madison, and the rest of their mob. Thus she became a devout deist. Now thanks to *La Bruja's* imbecility, the Chrono-Astrology religion had taken root in the country's kindergartens, elementary schools, academies, and its only yeshiva. This was troublesome to Paola as a devout deist, mother, and PTA president.

One day her eldest son, 12-year-old Axl, came home from school at Colegio James Monroe (Slogan "Manifest Destiny!") and said "Mami! Today I got a gold star! I recited the 12 vibrations of the color blue! By heart!"

"Very nice, *mijo*. What's six times six?"

"I do not know," he shrugged and walked away.

So Paola organized a march. A small group of angry PTA mothers, who carried signs, well one sign, denouncing the absurdity of forcing the ridiculous religion or any religion into the classroom. As La República's leading deist, Paola felt strongly about this and led her group of a dozen or so mothers to the gates of the Presidential Palace in full view of Mandamás, his wife, and that creepy guy in the robe. No one paid Paola's group much attention. Except Mandamás, of course, who had picked out his favorite from the Happy Fish from his office window across the expanse.

Feeling she had a chance to start making a difference in the political landscape, Paola organized another group protest demanding order in the streets, reinstating the transit police, putting back the old red lights. Also demanding pedestrian crossings. This demonstration got a bit more attention and even a small article *El Día*, La República's small daily newspaper. "Protest at the Palace" was the modest headline over a two-column inch item in 9-point pica type. No one paid much attention to the news report .

Then there was the protest against the forced wearing of tiaras, amethyst colors or crystals. Again a small, but angry, group of *manifestantes*[1] marched in front of the palace. "Enough already," was the common theme of the four or five placards. There seemed to be a few more curious onlookers than before. Among them Juanita, the town gossip and owner of the coffee shop in the market.

Still another exhibition by the PTA ladies and a few of Paola's friends from the Happy Fish was the demand to stop the ridiculous practice of silent observances for equinoxes, solar flares, full moons, solstices, and other *estupideces*.[2] Few seemed to pay heed to these acts of civil disobedience, but there was talk. Gossips in the market, wags in the bar at the Hotel Cinco Estrellas, maids in the kitchens of the wealthy — all were talking about Paola the *puta* and her Palace protests.

Paola, never in doubt of her own convictions, was surprised by the reactions, however. Beyond the gossip, for there was always gossip, the people were responding to the acts of civil disobedience in front of the Palace. Despite the dangers of challenging

---

[1] Protesters.
[2] Stupid things.

the authority of the dictatorship, *republicanos* seemed ready to make a difference. They were tired of stupid laws being enacted, she felt. There was so much more to be gained. There were protests to be done, of course, in the name of human rights. But Paola felt this should lead to something more important for La República, for the future of Axl and Slash.

Even though the growing number of protesters and passers-by was a dangerous threat to the status quo of the regime, there was no movement on the part of the Mandamás dictatorship. So Paola decided on something bigger, something never dreamed of in La Capital.

That day, Paola Labios was joined in front of the Presidential Palace by a rather LARGE, rather loud, and very flamboyant group clad in colorful costumes. There were minstrels, cats, a *chupacabra*, Disney princesses, La Virgen de Aguacate, and even Frida Kahlo. Someone had rigged up a phonograph and "How Lovely to Be a Woman" came blasting out of a pair of speakers. A mannish-looking Ann-Margaret was dancing up a storm in a silky red dress. It was civil disobedience in the guise of a carnival parade.

A larger crowd showed up just to watch as Broadway had come to La República and the *capitalinos* couldn't resist bopping to the catchy tunes of "Bye Bye Birdie." The local press even rushed a photographer to the scene. Paola was leading something anathema in La República — a demand for gay rights. In between album tracks, she bellowed demands through a discarded Department of Public Works orange traffic cone repurposed as a megaphone. The music and chanting carried across the palace grounds.

"Paola, how can you do this to your *capitán*?" The puzzled generalíssimo said to the plate glass window as he observed the ridiculous display a mere 100 meters from his office. "I understand the school thing, and the green lights, and the silent solstices, but gay rights? What is that? Is that Tomás over there dancing? There are no gays in La República! She knows that! We are hung like a horse. Maybe in El Corinto …"

Paola lowered her megaphone as "Put on a Happy Face" was queued up on the record player. She met the leader's gaze from in front of the elaborate art nouveau iron gates and across the Presidential gardens. She knew exactly what was going through his brain, and her look was unwavering. Máximo Mandamás did not like that look. It was not the seductive look of a courtesan. Max's mind wandered as he was reminded of a line in a movie. *That's a lean and hungry look,* he thought. Snapping his fingers to remember. *Like that guy in Rome in that movie with Charlton Heston. He does something … something. Something not good, but what? I'll have to look it up.*

A door opened behind Max who welcomed the interruption. When he turned around his spirits plummeted even further — it was Mayor Izquierdo for his scheduled appointment. He had a soft spot for the old lefty, but not now, *por la Virgen.* There was too much going on: this thing with Paola gays at the gates, the harangues from his wife, even the fable he had fabricated about enemies in the Province of Aguacate. It was too much for a man who just wanted to play tennis. Mayor Izquierdo's presence only meant bad news.

The Dictator-for-Life heavily lowered himself into his large leather chair and gestured to one the overstuffed, stiff backed chairs in front of his desk, "Rafael, *un placer.* Sit, please."

The mayor sank into one of the guest chairs and wasted no time. "Generalíssimo, I fear you will not think it a pleasure after I relate to you what is happening in La Capital. As the mayor many people seek me out with many complaints. I never bother your excellency with these minor things as you are busy with affairs of …. well, affairs of state. As you know I have been working hard to maintain order and — is that Paola?"

Without turning to the window, Máximo responded, "Yes, Rafael, every day it is something. I am powerless to stop her. You know how she can get."

Izquierdo nodded appreciatively, not taking his eyes off the spectacle of a prostitute leading a protest at the palace.

"Today it is about, believe it or not, gay rights."

"Gay rights? But your excellency there are no homosexuals in La República. We *Repúblicanos* are hung —"

"Yes, yes I know. But continue, Mr. Mayor."

"Maybe in el Corinto, those *jueputas*, but in La República? *Que pendejada*."[3]

"I agree. But you were saying about complaints and such." Max rubbed his temples.

"Well, it is like this, Generalíssimo, there is a crime wave in the city and some of the businesses, businesses that pay much in taxes as you know, are yelling for immediate results. I tried to appease them with the usual threats, but it is beyond my powers to —"

"My friend, we have always had a certain amount of crime. This is not new news. Why do you bother me with such trivialities when we have many other problems facing our great nation? Look out the window, there are gays at the gates! Then there is the matter of *comunistas* in Aguacate. Not to mention that *menso* goalie, *El Muro*. Did you know he defected to El Corinto? Also, Tirofijo and his own system of 'taxes' or Piojo and his band of delinquents. They are always up to something, and —"

"Not Piojo, Generalíssimo. It is another thing all together."

Mandamás feared this other thing would be serious, something he would have to confront Rosemary with. And that he did not want.

---

[3] What a stupid thing.

"Something new. There is a man, a boy really, on a motor-cycle dressed as an OverEats! delivery driver, you know all in green and —"

"Over eats? What is over eats Mr. Mayor?"

"OverEats! A food delivery service for people. They deliver food to the house."

"Ah, OverEats! I understand, continue."

"He is robbing the Pizza Huts and the KFCs, all of them! And he takes the money from the deliveries and escapes into the streets like any other OverEats! driver. He just weaves in and out of traffic and melts away. It is a very effective way to steal money, and the owners are complaining."

Mandamás was quick to understand the situation, "He is stealing the coronel's chicken money?"

"As always *mi líder*,[4] you come right to the crux of the argument."

"*¿Qué* crux? *Mierda*! You are the mayor! Use your police, you imbecil! You have the tools to catch this miscreant. So catch him. Knock him around a little. I mean, do not be a maniac about it, just send a little message. He will stop."

"I cannot. I mean, they cannot. The police, they cannot. Our streets are so clogged with traffic the police cannot get through. They have tried to catch this thief, but you know the traffic lights are only green. Why, just yesterday I waited and waited and never got my order, my Caesar salad, and —"

"Caesar! He stabbed Caesar! Lean and hungry. Jajaja. Go on, mayor."

Izquierdo felt that Mandamás was losing touch. *Caesar? What the hell was he talking about?*

"We need a miracle, Generalíssimo!"

"Yes I know."

---

[4] My leader.

Chapter 13

The Ambassador Makes a Call

Güicho, son-in-law to the most powerful person in La República, sat in his office trimming his toenails. The clipper, a gift from the *gringo* Esteeve, was a fine device, hand-crafted in Bessemer, Pennsylvania and one of Güicho's proudest possessions. He particularly enjoyed the satisfying CHIK sound it made when cutting through his thick *republicano* toenails. Güicho ignored the pinging noises the nail bits made as they were fired like tiny bullets around the tiny space, strafing the lampshade and other furnishings.

He was working a difficult angle on his right pinky toe when the phone rang. The interruption startled him and caused him to flinch and cut the teeny tiny nail very short. "¡*Coño*! Who could it be?"

Picking it up on the second and a half ring, he answered. "Office of Máximo Mandamás Generalíssimo and Dictator-for-Life of La República, Güicho Gómez speaking, how may I direct your call?"

"The Ambassador is here to see the generalíssimo." It was the guard in the Palace reception. Güicho loathed him.

"Which ambassador?"

"The Ambassador! You ball licker! *The* Ambassador."

Güicho knew exactly who it was, he himself had set up the appointment for the generalíssimo. Still, he couldn't resist. "Which country!? *Idiota*! We cannot have *comunista* countries calling on the president."

"*La Yunae*, Los Estates United."

"Send him up."

A few minutes later a winded and red-faced (there was no lift) Richard Dix, was ushered into the office of La República's head of government. The dictator had once seen a photograph of Mussolini's offices at the height of his power and sought to emulate the style of furnishings and decor right down to the long, long walk of shame visitors had to make to reach his desk.

A heavy-footed and sweaty Dix clumped down said walk of shame as purposefully as possible. He surrendered to one of the two overstuffed hard-backed chairs in front of Máximo's desk. One thing about overstuffed \hard-backed chairs is that they are made for looks, and not for sitting as they provide no comfort no matter what acrobatics are performed. It was not seemly for such a high-ranking member of the American party in power. The Ambassador was ill-pleased.

"Generalíssimo, good day!"

"Welcome to my humble offices, *señor* Dick. Nothing like jour White House I yam sure, we are a poor country as jou are aware. But always fighting the *comunistas* as jou know —"

"Yeah, yeah. Look here, Max I came to deliver —" Dix squirmed uncomfortably in the awkwardly straight-backed chair. He dithered in delivering realizing his host seemed to be looking down at him. *Is that greaseball standing?* The dictator was not standing, only enjoying the advantage of having his chair resting on a slightly raised platform that had once been used on a movie set, right there in La Capital. It gave him an advantage he was enjoying while looking down on the winded *gringo*. "Jes, Mr. Ambassador. Jou came to deliver…?"

"Uh, is it safe to talk? Top-secret stuff —"

"Excellency?" A smooth, lilting voice interrupted in from somewhere behind the ambassador. A tall lissome blond woman poked her head through another door. "*Älskling*, it is time for your massage, *ja?*"

"Not now, Inga. Jou were saying Mr. Ambassador? Oh, is it safe to talk? But of course it is safe, this is my palace. Go on."

Inga? "My people, back at the, uh, State Department, tell me everything is set for operation Green Avocado —"

"Jes. What is that?"

"The code name. Tip-top priority. Along with Castro's exploding *arroz con pollo.* Amazing stuff. Hand grenades the size of grains of rice. Mixed in with the chicken. One bite and KAPOW!" The ambassador illustrated Castro's violent death by rice by slamming a fat fist on his excellency's polished desk.

"And?"

"And? And no more communism in Cuba, excellency. Things go back to normal: mafia casinos, twice-nightly shows at the Copacabana, girls galore, American Interests restored!"

Max was not interested in exploding grains of rice, at least not yet, and wanted the red-necked diplomat to get back to the subject at hand. "I was asking about us. Operation Aguacate? Our poor, still NON-communist nation. What about us?"

"Oh! Well, my people say they have delivered the goods and the cash. Materiel and dollars. Our best man is recruiting a team of contras to carry out the mission. Yeah, this should be over in a few days, Generalíssimo."

"Very good news, Señor Deex! Güicho!"

The son-in-law, who had finished his pedicure and was listening to the two men while putting on his socks, left his shoes by his desk and came in shuffling on little cat's feet.

"Sí, *suegro?*"

"Generalíssimo, idiota!"

"Sí, Generalíssimo," the son-in-law replied with a muffled click of his heels.

The despot turned to his guest and asked, "Would jou like to celebrate the successful start of this operation, *Señor* Deex?"

"Yes, of course."

"Güicho, Bring the American a cigar and a shot of rum."

"Very kind of you, Generalíssimo," said the ambassador quite impressed with his own self. Güicho ran out of the room to fetch the cigar and rum. He quickly appeared with a tray on which was a hastily clipped cigar that looked like a botched circumcision. Alongside it was a glass with the finest local rum. Dix mouthed the end of a cigar like Richard Dawson on a prom date and puffed mightily while Güicho held a Zippo lighter flame just under the tip. A satisfying number of toxic clouds were released, and the contented Ambassador looked up through the smoke to find the generalíssimo had left.

As Güicho retreated, walking backward and bowing to the Ambassador, Mandamás stage whispered from beyond the door, "Güicho keep the Ambassador entertained, I shall be … indisposed." The ambassador and gentlemen's club empresario found himself alone. He shrugged and took a manly puff of his freshly lit Macanudo followed by a strong pull on his tumbler of Ron Aniversario.

Two Dix looked out the window and enjoyed the view where bunch of women seemed to be burning brassieres. "It's that that chick from the Happy Fish," he said and swallowed his Ron Aniversario.

Chapter 14

La Chingada (IATA: CIA)

Kiwi Airways Flight 1 was on its base leg a few minutes outside of La Chingada International Airport. The airline's chief pilot was behind the stick ruminating on his personal situation instead of concentrating on the upcoming approach. Pilots shouldn't ruminate on their personal situation, particularly when flying an antique airship into a notoriously bad airport. Evidence of other pilots who had ruminated and failed to pay attention were strewn below in a debris field that had examples of every major commercial aircraft flown since WWII. A DC-2 here, a C-47 there, props, engines, fuselages, wing parts, landing gears, tail assemblies; it looked like the aftermath of an earthquake at the Revelle[1] showroom.

Steele's own aircraft was the proud flagship of the Kiwi Airways fleet, a newly refitted Douglas Aircraft DC-4. In its heyday the DC-4 had been famous the world over for its reliability. It was well past its warranty, however, and decommissioned. As the flagship aircraft, the rusty relic was born again to fly the only route of Kiwi Airways. It was a great improvement over the DC-3 Steele had operated before that could rattle a filing loose when taxiing. Today the newer vessel had all four Pratt and Whitneys churning up the horsepower, purring like panthers, hardly leaking any oil.

The ship was held together by the thoughts and prayers of the passengers aloft and the earthbound citizens in its flight path below.

---

[1] A manufacturer of plastic scale model aircraft.

The approach to La Chingada's only runway was quite scenic. Smoky slums sat on hillsides left and right, hugging the airplane's approach as if they were chaperones at a *quinceañera*. Passengers could look out their windows and appreciate the living conditions of La Capital's poorer residents as the proximity allowed for a detailed inspection of the homes. One resident, a Mrs. Mool, met their gaze with a silver-rimmed toothy smile as she hung clothes out to dry: jeans, unmentionables, blouses, and a worn Lakers jersey snapped in the breeze.

"Buckle-o your beltos, everybody," was the announcement yelled through the curtain from the cockpit. The handful of passengers nervously buckled-oed their beltos and prayed to the Virgen of Aguacate to watch over them just this one time, *por favor*. The landing was a rough one, but successful as there were no deaths reported.

A rickety set of stairs mounted on the bed of a WWII-era Citroen truck was pushed to the side of the old bird. The truck had no engine, and the pushing was managed by one man, José "Pepe" Gómez, stair master, air traffic controller, and baggage handler. He gingerly climbed the stairs, pried open the unwilling door to shout into the cabin, "Welcome to La Chingada, La República's International port of entry. Please watch jour estep."

Steele saw to the unloading of his unofficial cargo. It was a light load. For local crime king Tirofijo there were five boxes of Macanudo Dictadores, 25 cartons of Marlboro cigarettes, a case of Zippo lighters. He looked around for Tirofijo's errand boy Piojo who usually took delivery of these items.

"Peppy, watch this stuff I gotta go to the hangar."

"It is Pepe, *Capitán*. **Pepe**. Your 'delivery' is in the hangar also. The boxes are marked 'top secret,' right next to a Jeep. I think the Jeep is for the museum, *verdad?* Jajaja."

Steele stomped off to the hangar, the bump on his forehead throbbing mercilessly, the Shakespeare volume with its annotations and secret messages weighed heavily in the crook of his arm. He thought angrily to himself, *What kind of crapshit operation is this? Christ in an oxcart. Now I gotta find some men, no time to train, really. A battle-hardened cadre of anti-communist counterrevolutionaries is what I need. What's a cadre? Twelve, I think. Where can I find a dozen men willing to go into the jungle to fight a small army of Cuban-trained guerrilla fighters? Where?*

The enormity of the task began to panic the pilot-agent.

Once at the hangar, the pilot looked around for his contra communist cargo.

"Hola, señor Esteeve," someone chirped into Steele's right ear far too loudly. The pilot nearly had an accident in his freshly pressed pants uniform. "Piojo! What the hell? Why weren't you at the plane taking delivery of the contrab — uh, the goods for Tirofijo? What are you doing sneaking around here? Don't you know this is top secret, amigo? Toppo seecreet-o!"

"Jes, I can see that." Piojo replied as he watched his gang of street terrorists crawl over the boxes and crates with odd labels like BAND UNIFORMS — TOP SECRET. A couple of the gang were even in the Jeep. "*Brum-brum*,"[2] said the one behind the wheel as he was pretending to steer wildly around imaginary bomb craters.

"Tell them to stop, Piojo."

Piojo turned to his small gang and barked, "*Dejen de joder, coño y pongan atención babosos.*"[3] They jumped off the Jeep and the crates and assembled in front of Piojo. Steele was impressed. These street urchins acted as a unit. *As a cohesive unit! A cadre? Perhaps. All they need is a man like me, like Major Steve Steele, to lead them to glory. Or something.*

---

[2] Spanish for vroom-vroom.
[3] Stop.

"Piojo, let me ask you something."

"Sí, capitán!" *Respect, I like that. And he's at full attention! This could work.*

"Piojo, do you hate communists?"

Never one to miss an opportunity, Piojo responded, "*¡Sí, mi Capitán!*" Piojo had never met a communist, was only vaguely aware of them through his readings of Captain Freedom. They were bad people was all he knew.

"Are you ready to fight for your country?

"*¡Sí, mi Capitán!*"

"Are you ready to lead your band, uh, gang, uh brigade, yes your brigade, against the communist insurgency forming in the Avocado Province?"

"Aguacate, *capitán.*"

"What?"

"Aguacate Province, *capitán.* Avocado is what *gringos* put on their toast in *La Yunae.*"

"Whatever. Are you willing?"

"*¡¡Sí, mi Capitán!!*"

"Okay, then swear on this, this…" *Why isn't there a bible when you need one?* "This! Swear on this!"

"The Complete Works of Gweelyam Echakespeer?"

"Fully annotated, yes. Swear to uphold the Constitution of the United States of America and follow the orders of Major Steele by the grace of God?"

"*¡¡Sí, mi capitán!!*"

"Major."

"*¡¡Sí, mi mayor!!*"

He set the volume down with authority on one of the crates marked "SCHOOL SUPPLIES — TOP SECRET," turned to Piojo and said, "I now put you in command of the Brayan Buenaventura Bri —"

"Brayan Buenaventura!," the cadre gasped as one at the mention of the national hero and only fatality in the Guerra de Aguacate. Buenaventura had achieved mythical status for his bravery against the forces of El Corinto, those *jueputas*, even though no one was quite sure what exactly Brayan Buenaventura had done other than die a glorious death. They looked at one another and stood with great dignity waiting for the handsome *gringo* with the gold-rimmed Ray Bans to continue.

"As I was sayin', Piojo, you are to lead these delinquents, sorry, you are to lead the Brayan Buenaventura Brigade. The mission, Operation Green Avocado, is top secret, you understand. Can anyone drive a Jeep?"

"I can," Piojo lied.

"Good. You will drive the Jeep. I will ride in the back seat. We will lead the Brigade to Aguacate Province. We defeat the communists in the commune there. We will return in glory."

"…"

"Tell them, Piojo."

"*¡Chicos, vamos a hacer una fiesta de la chingada!*"[4]

Steele winced, not sure of the translation. "Uh. Ok. Good, I guess. Anyway, there are uniforms in the boxes, put them on cheekows. Piojo, take the Jeep around to the refueling station, fill it up and charge it to the Kiwi account."

"*¡Sí, mi Capitán!*" Piojo responded, adding a sharp salute.

"Major!"

"*Sí, mi Mayor.*"

Steele smiled as he saw his cadre rifle through boxes looking for uniforms and his second-in-command grind through the gears of the Jeep in incorrect order and jolt his way to the refueling station. *If those suits Agent Blue and Agent Orange could see this, then they*

---

[4] *Guys, we are gonna party!*

would realize they weren't dealing with a child. We should have met in Langley goddammit.

When Piojo returned, Steve was thinking it was time to contact Agent Weiss back at the Hotel Cinco Estrellas. Weiss was supposed to have the cash and further instructions. Steve was very excited to be a CIA operative in charge of his own operation. This was big stuff!

"¡Mayor!"

Steve jumped out of his broughams. "What the hell, Piojo? Don't do that."

"*Perdón, mi mayor.* The Jeep is full of gasoline, my men are looking for their uniforms, what are my instructions?"

"Ok, you and your men will bivouac here, we will meet at oh eight hundred hours."

"*¿Qué?*"

"You and your hombres sleep-o here, comprende? I will be back at 8. Las owe chow."

"AM or PM?"

Fuck me to tears. "AM of course. We move out in the morning."

"Will jou bring breakfast, *capitán?*"

"Breakfast?" *Weren't they getting a little ahead?*

"Napoleón said an army travels on its estomak. *Capitán.*"

"Major for the love of — never mind. Ok, I'll bring breakfast. Eight o'clock. AM."

"*Baleadas, por favor.*" The request came from within the foursome that was busy using a crowbar to open one of the crates marked "School Supplies."

Steele rolled his eyes and signed, "Ok, *baleadas,* sure."

"From La Tuerta,"[5] one of them yelled out to general agreement from his peers.

Steve Steele nodded as he and Mr. Shakespeare left the hangar and walked to the terminal. He mentally ticked off a to-do list: *Go through immigration, grab a cab to the hotel, get the cash, sleep, back in the morning. Oh, and get the baleadas, and THEN come back. There should be a cable from Orange at the hotel with further instructions. Maybe get something to put on this welt.*

He smiled and thought, "I have found my cadre."

Inside the hangar Piojo smiled and thought, "I have found Captain Freedom."

---

[5] One Eyed Woman. A well-known establishment in La Capital known for her warm, pillowy *baleada* breakfasts with black beans, avocado, eggs, chorizo, and chiles.

Chapter 15

Orders from Klaus Von Klaus

Steve Steele left the hangar and went to the terminal to proceed with the formalities required to officially enter the country.

"Welcome to La República, what is the porpose of jour visit, *señor*?" An official dressed in the uniform of an officer in the Ugandan Navy put his hand out, opened palm up. "Passport please." The pilot placed his world-worn green American passport in the hand, glared at the official, and exhaled. He was tired, stressed. "You know me, officer Gómez! Three times a week I come to La Capital. I fly that bird behind me. Every time you ask what is my purpose? My purpose, admiral, is to fly the fucking plane!"

"Please *señor*. I am doing my yob. There is much talk of *comunistas* coming from Corinto. Our goalie has defected. Many things are happening. I must be vigilant. I, Garcilaso Gómez, stand as the first defense of the nation. *Viva el Generalíssimo!*" The last point was added rather loudly by the customs officer just in case anyone was listening.

Whomp-whomp went the large stamp on the red inked pad. Whomp-whomp went the large stamp onto an empty page of Steele's passport leaving a blurry red image of the generalíssimo.

"Jou may proceed."

Terminal Uno of La Chingada was Central America's answer to a North African medina. Everything was for sale at outrageous prices unless you negotiated them down to a fifth of the asking. Steele hustled through the concourse like Amos Alonso Stagg cutting though a Princeton defense.

"Sunglasses, señor?"

"Lava lamp?"

"Jumper cables?"

"Feelthy peectures?"

"*Alpargatas?*"

"*Lotería?*"

"Tours, would jou like to visit the museum, *señor?* Or the overlook? We have a fine overlook."

"No grassyass, compadre."

He finally reached the curb and gave a big sigh of relief seeing the familiar figure of William, La Capital's cab driver *nonpareil,* and his semi-reliable Buick taxi. "William! So glad to see you."

William stepped back, dropped his right shoulder, feinted with his left, side-stepped to avoid a shot to the chin, and did a rope-a-dope against the front fender. Steve didn't seem to notice.

"Good to see you, *capitán.* To the usual place? The Happy Fish?"

"No *amigo,* my beautiful Paola ... she hates me now. I am banned it seems."

William, dodging an uppercut, fought the steering wheel like Ahab giving chase to Moby Dick. "You need to branch out, *jefe.* Find some other sparring partners." As an ex-boxer and contender for La República's middleweight crown, William tended to use boxing apothegms.

"To the Hotel Seenko Estreyes, my friend. Hey, I thought I'd see you behind that new Impala. Kay paso?"

"No can do. Too many *tucanes, señor* Esteeve. Perhaps next year, I have to save. To the hotel, then."

Steve rested the volume of Shakespeare on the seat next to him, making sure it was secure because inside amid the annotations were the cyphered instructions he would need to carry out his mission. He wondered if he would receive the codes in invisible ink, just like in the spy novels. A message was written using someone's pee, and then ... Steele couldn't remember any details past getting a message written in urine. Fortunately, the codes would come via telegraph, presumably dry and sans urine.

The leader of anticommunist cadre continued to day-dream, riding the springs of the old Buick like he was posting on a horse in a dressage competition. Outside the filthy window was a blur of tire shops, *yonque* yards,[1] muffler repairs, and nail salons. He liked La Capital and now after leading his hardened cadre against the godless communists he would probably become a national hero! Wouldn't that be great? What would Paola think of him then? She'd have to take him back. If his mission weren't a top secret-type secret he could tell her now.

"Here we are Mr. Steele. Let me know if jou need another ride, the overlook perhaps?"

"Thank you, William, this will be fine."

"What is that?"

"It's a book. The Complete Works of William Shake-speare."

"Fully annotated?"

"Uh, yes."

"I'm very impressed Mr. *Piloto. Buenas noches.*"

"And bwaynas to you William."

Steele took his tome along with a small suitcase and entered the Hotel Cinco Estrellas; walking directly to the front desk where the officious owner and manager Klaus Von Klaus met him with a Teutonic clicking of the heels. "*Herr* Steele, how good to see you." The former Wehrmacht *Oberstabsveterinär*[2] Klaus stared at his guest, who stared back for a few seconds. It was an uncomfortable silence. *Why doesn't this kraut give me the password?*

---

[1] Junk yards.
[2] Veterinarian.

The hotelier put a fist to his closed mouth and emitted a muffled grunt. *What the hell, that's not the password! Shit on a shingle.*

Klaus emitted a low whisper, "You first."

Steele looked at his Central Intelligence Agency contact and uttered, "oh … riiiight, yes. Uh, Afghanistan."

"Bananistan! Welcome to the Hotel Cinco Estrellas, the best hotel in La República! Here are your 'messages,' Herr Steve," handing him a thick envelope.

"Messages? So many?"

"Yes many 'messages.' Many." He winked at his guest conspiratorially.

"Oooooh, I see." Steele slipped the bundle of cash into his inside jacket pocket. "Do I have any messages?"

"I just gave them to you."

"Yes, I know. But do you have any mess-a-ges? Please check."

Klaus Von Klaus never denied a client, so he looked around: at the high ceiling, on the counter, under the phone, behind the phone, beneath the desk blotter, in the guest registry book, and in the pigeonholes behind the desk. "*Nein.*"

"I'll be in my room, should any messages come for me."

"*Jawohl, Herr* Steele. Here is your key, your usual room. And this came for you." He handed the flier a small yellow envelope.

"What is this?"

"A cable."

"But I asked you if —. Never mind. I'll be in my room."

"*Jawohl!*" CLICK

In his usual room, Steve Steele laid the volume of Shakespeare on a tiny writing desk only slightly larger than the book. The desk creaked in protest. Tearing at the yellow envelope, he opened it and took out a flimsy slip of yellow paper. It was a cable! In cipher. Steele's heart raced. *This is real spy stuff!* The cable read:

B 83xJ

"What the hell is that?" He asked the curtains. They maintained radio silence. Then he remembered the little yellow book and took it out of his pocket. After a frustrating 20 minutes of spy work, the result was "Bottom, Dream, IV s 1" followed by a number. Our Man in La República rose to the task and opened his Shakespeare and looked at the table of contents. *Shit on a stick. Plays AND sonnets. This is gonna take all night.*

But good karma intervened and he lit upon the play "A Midsummer Night's Dream" he remembered reading long ago. As a young boy Steele's grandmother had gifted him a set of Child's Golden Classics, slim volumes of the great works of literature abridged for children. He recalled the name of his favorite character: Bottom. *That's in the cipher! And that's gotta be Act IV, Scene I. I'm pretty goddam good at this!* Ten minutes later he found the play *why is this fucking print so small?* and the line.

I must to the barber's, monsieur; for methinks, I am marvelous hairy about the face: and I am such a tender ass, if my hair do but tickle me, I must scratch.

Ignoring the part about being an ass, probably a barb from Agents Blue or Orange, Steele slammed shut his book, hefted it under his arm and rushed out of his room on his way to the *peluquería*.[3] He trusted Klaus would send him to the right one.

"Klaus," Steele called toward the empty front desk immediately after the elevator doors opened. "Where is the barber shop?"

The German's head popped up from behind the counter and in front of the honeycomb of boxes, one for each room, each with their key. Alertly he straightened to attention. CLICK! "*Herr* Steve. Very simple. (Pointing) Out the front door, turn right. Go

---

[3] Barber shop.

200 meters. Turn down, then left where the blind lady sold cigarettes, then 35 rods and you are there." CLICK

Steele, having many years' experience in La República, actually understood these local directions and made haste. Once out
the door, however, the full effect of the midday sun of La República
hit him in the face like a wet boxing glove. *I need to get to the barber
but goddammit it's hot! If only —*

"Taxi, Mr. Steele?"

Chapter 16

The Dictator's Wife

One of the perks of being a dictator in La República was that you got to live in the colossal Presidential Palace. It was built by the French governor during the country's brief period as a French colony. A magnificent baroque edifice with many rooms, stables, two kitchens, gardens, billiard room, an oda, Turkish-style bath, smoking room, Mandamás's Brobdingnagian office, tennis court, vomitorium, and many other refinements. With careful planning and knowledge of the palace's complex layout of stairs, rooms, hallways, Murphy doors, false walls, and other hidden secrets, a Dictator-for-Life could avoid his wife for days at a time.

Mrs. Mandamás was none too pleased to be left to her own devices all the time and was grousing with Gregorio, mystic and advisor. Rosemary, the *primera dama* of La República, had a natural instinct for politics, manipulations, and harridanism. She also held a black belt (7th-dan) in husband hectoring. But it was not always thus. In her youth Rosemary Romero had been an ordinary girl: thin, pale, taken to shyness but a good student at Politechnical School for Boys and Girls. She earned prizes for her poetry.

Like many of the girls of her station in society, she spent Saturdays in the plaza with other girls strolling around the central fountain enjoying the cool shade of the trees. Gossip was the currency of the *paseo* and the girls, along with their aunts and married sisters who followed three or four paces behind, took note of any of the boys' glances. The boys, in turn, also ambled around the fountain but in the opposite direction. There was a lot of sizing up for potential hookups and even possible marital partners. The slow

Saturday marches were the first step of courtship in a centuries-old tradition brought by the conquistadors.

One Saturday, in Rosemary Romero's last year as a student, the teenager spotted a very upright, strong looking young man of her age. He was dark and athletic. Rosemary was not put off by the young man's unfortunate acne and thought to herself, I should have that man. Over the next month she observed him and confirmed her instincts that the tennis player Máximo Mandamás would be a suitable suitor.

Her Tía Justa, the official Romero family chaperone and advisor in matters of the heart, persuaded the young girl not to move too quickly, to allow time for her intended to develop "desperate longing." She often said this with her vibrating fist clenched in front of her navel. Things moved slowly in Rosemary's pursuit of love and soon her tennis player had gone to represent La República at the Olympics! What a great honor for him, his family, and all *republicanos*. It was not long after that he was offered a scholarship in *La Yunae* to play tennis at someplace called MidAmerica A&M to learn Accounting and Marketing.

Upon hearing this news, Rosemary burst into her room, flung herself on the bed and exploded into tears. Her aunt followed in her wake and sat on the bed consoling her with gentle endearments and advice. "*Paciencia, sobrina.*[1] She said. There is still much time."

"But Tía Justa, what if he falls in love with one of those *putas* in *La Yunae*. You know how they are with their white skin, blond hair and long tanned legs."

---

[1] Patience, niece.

"Niña, your man is a *republicano*! He will not fall for their charms. Besides, the *gringas* have no *nalgas*, no ass and *republicanos* they like their women to have good *culos*,[2] many curves."

Even though she was a good *republicana*, poor Rosemary did not have a very good *culo* and was devoid of the curves her aunt was speaking of. She would have to employ other means to attract her prey.

Mandamás had an unsuccessful academic career at Mid-America A&M and was back in a few months. He was more suited to the armed forces than the collegiate clay courts, so he returned to his promising career in the Armed Forces of La República.

"Now your handsome man is back, tired of the *putas* up north. It is time to invite him and his mother for tea as is customary in the best houses."

"*Sí, tía.* You are so good to me. I love you more than anything!" Rosemary squealed and jumped into her aunt's arms to hug her affectionately.

So it began, Máximo Mandamás and his mother came for tea. And coffee. And the opera. And the cockfights. And other genteel events of the social season in La Capital. But he made no overtures of love and never mentioned any future of them together.

"*Qué pasa*, Rosa?" Asked Tía Justa calling the girl by the pet name she had given her niece when she was young. "Tell your *Tía*."

The future First Lady burst into tears and buried her head in the older woman's enormous bosoms. "He does not love me, *tía*," came her muffled reply.

"Why do you say that? I see him always with you and the way he looks at you. Does he have the 'desperate longing'?" She added holding out her vibrating fist.

---

[2] Asses.

"Oh, yes, Tía I have felt the firmness of his desperate longing when we are dancing. But whenever I talk about **us** he just starts going on about 'tennis this,' 'the Army that,' or his friend Larree Muncie in *La Yunae*. And he looks at the other women too!"

"Does he take his 'desperate longing' to the Happy Fish!!?" Such a thought was shocking.

The girl continued to sob.

"Do not cry my princess, here is what you do..."

⧖ ⧖ ⧖

Some months later Máximo and Rosemary were united in hasty matrimony in a military ceremony. Soon after, the young lieutenant was mercifully shipped off to Aguacate province to maintain enforcement of the Guacamole Act against the enemy to the north, El Corinto. He left his bride behind where she gave birth to a child, their daughter. Away on military duty in defense of his country, Lt. Máximo Mandamás was unable to sit in the hospital waiting room while his young wife gave birth. Then, as the young officer rose in ranks Rosemary became more and more exigent that he should be aggressive and demand greater power and responsibility.

Máximo rose through those ranks rather quickly by means of steadfast sycophancy and sheer stupid luck. Since he was loyal and stole less from his superiors, he was soon promoted to Colonel and put in charge of rum, tobacco, and sugar exports. Then ruling dictator, President-for-Life Gustavo Garrapata, took the former Midwest tennis star under his wing and appointed him into a new position of *chargé d'affaires*.

"*Qué chargé d'affaires. Son mariconadas*[3] Máximo. You should be Vice President. But noooooo. You just sit back and let that *cara*

---

[3] Effete things.

de picha[4] Garrapata push you around! What about me? What about your family?"

"*Pero, mi amor.* He is the President. I must do as he says. Besides, it is a good job. I have very little to do and it gives me time to work on my backhand, the pro said that —"

"*¿Qué* backhand *ni qué* backhand? Something has to give." Rosemary squinted her eyes, deep in thought.

A few days after the conversation a lucky bullet found Garrapata's gullet and laid him out very dead at a ceremony honoring the president-for-life. Max fingered the assassin, who happened to be sitting next to him, and became a national hero. The assassin, who looked like one of his in-laws and seemed familiar to Max, was quickly executed without the inconvenience of *habeas corpus*.

Mandamás was immediately promoted to general by a ruling *junta* of aging generals and was soon sworn in as maximum leader of La República, to which Rosemary Mandamás nee Romero said, "I told you so." Max felt a bit of a spinal chill.

As leader, Max enjoyed the position of dictator and hoped that his people referred to him as "benevolent" since he didn't imprison or torture as many enemies of the state as had his predecessor Garrapata who was cruel and sadistic. But his wife would have none of that. She played on his insecurities time and time again.

"*Qué* benevolent, Max? You must be tough! They are laughing at you! You should harness the power of crystals Max, the energy of the stars to make the people obey to a new spirituality …"

Thus began the daily chivvying in the Presidential Palace aided and abetted by Rosemary's new advisor — the enigmatic Gregorio with his robes, foul beard, incense, chanting, and mysterious mumbling.

---

[4] Dick face.

☒ ☒ ☒

"Something is up, Gregorio. My husband has disappeared again somewhere in the palace! Probably with that Inga. *Qué horror,* such a white woman. But I think he is up to something."

"You vant I should find this *meshuggener*?" Offered the mystic.

"You know I cannot understand Tatar or Russian or whatever you are speaking but I need you to spy on my husband, see what he is up to. Ever since that cocktail party at the embassy he has been acting strange."

"*Mishegos?*"

"Mishi — *qué?* Just find him Gregorio. Change out of that cape and cowl. You look like a perverted version of *Caperucita Roja.*[5] Start at the Hotel Cinco Estrellas Bar; they are nothing but a bunch of gossips. You should learn more there." Gregorio's foreignness irritated Rosemary at times but she accepted it as part of his mystique.

"I will go find the *yenta.*"

"Not the *yenta* you Russian imbecil, the Cinco Estrellas."

Gregorio crept out of the room, leaving the First Woman alone in her chambers plotting like Lady Macbeth. "*Carajo.* I fear my husband's nature. Something is rotten with him and La República."

---

[5] Little Red Riding Hood.

Chapter 17

Luigi's Barbershop

Luigi's Barbershop was empty, devoid of customers. Luigi, sole owner and operator of the *barbería*, was a transplant from the North End of Boston with marinara running through his Venetian veins. He sat in one of the two barber's chairs in the shop reading El Día, the daily newspaper, to see what they were saying about the upcoming *fútbol* tilt.

He was halfway through the daily drivel Ugarte published under his byline and ugly photograph when the bell above the door to the shop ting-tingled announcing a visitor. The door opened and a handsome man in gold-rimmed aviator Ray Bans entered. Luigi appreciated the pilot's professionalism right away. Dressed in the pressed navy-blue uniform of Pan American World Airways, he wore a sharp-looking aviator's hat angled high on his forehead away from an angry looking purple protrusion. Judging on the sheer size of the logbook under his visitor's arm, Luigi surmised this was a very experienced pilot.

"Sorry to bother you. I was sent here by my 'Company'."

"Ah, Mister Steele! Yes, have a seat please."

After a bit of hesitation *he knows me?* Steve shrugged his shoulders and hiked himself into the empty chair, Shakespeare and all. Luigi snapped a fresh sheet open and laid it on the *capitán* like he was setting a table at the Cantina Italiana in Boston. As Steele settled into the barber's chair, Luigi began his prattle about a favorite topic: Boston sports. Like any transplant from Italy, he loved his soccer but missed his beloved Celtics and Bruins and, mostly, the Sox. Luigi took the liberty of filling in the pilot on Yastrzemski's chances for the Triple Crown of baseball; namely highest batting average, most homers, and most runs batted in. Steele tuned him out and took in the surroundings of the establishment: the jars filled with blue liquid and jammed with black combs; a poster of outdated men's hairstyles, a framed tonsorial license. Around the cloudy mirror he looked at faded Boston Globe color photographs of Yaz and Williams and other notables he didn't recognize. Steele lived in ignorance of such gods.

"Boston?"

"Born and raised, captain. Sox all the way!"

The barber bent over and began pumping a lever on the side of the chair which went up in short stages like William's taxi getting a tire changed. "You must go to Aguacate Province at the butt crack of dawn. There, at the check point, meet your contact. He will say, 'yon Cassius has a lean and hungry look,' you will answer with what's inside the envelope here," the Northsider whispered.

Taking the envelope under the sheet, the CIA operative alertly responded, "and?"

"And what? There is no 'and.' It's from your book, and the movie if I recall. That Heston was very popular here in La República. Anyway, those are the orders I am to give you. Word. For. Word."

Steele was confused by the reference but relaxed when he understood it to be more CIA code, probably from the book. He placed his hand over the Shakespeare tome under the sheet which had formed a big, very odd looking, cube in his lap.

"Butt crack?" Steele asked.

"I don't know buddy. Maybe it's code. I'm just the messenger, so don't shoot me, you know what I'm sayin'?"

"Yeah, code. In here." Steele lifted the book under the sheet. As he removed his hat to his lap, Steve laid his head back and rested in anticipation of a much-needed haircut.

The bell above the door tingled again, announcing a new visitor. Luigi, in one fluid motion, removed the sheet from Steve Steele, like a matador executing a two-handed *veronica*.[1]

"That will be 50 *tucanes*. Next!"

"Fifty for..." Steele was outraged at the price but had no choice but to maintain cover.

Fifty? What a ripoff. And not a snip! Ow, my goddam hat!

Turning to the new arrival, Luigi's face brightened at the sight of a fellow Red Sox fan. "Tirso! Man it is so good to see you!" The CIA agent recognized the Korean shopkeeper known as "El Chino" from the bar in the Hotel Cinco Estrellas.

What's that chink from the market doing here? Steve Steele did not trust Asians; he never met one personally but knew they were all just *a bunch of reds* and lingered at the door to listen in.

"Luigi! My friend! What do you think of this Yastrzemski?! He is something."

Luigi, not one to get too excited; after all they were talking about the Red Sox. The same Red Sox with the Curse of the Bambino. "We will see. We will see. It will take a lot to replace the Splinter."[2]

Steele tucked the small envelope in his pocket and moved on. He couldn't crack the code being spoken between the Dago barber and the Korean shopkeeper. Maybe it was in the damn book which was becoming a liability. Plus the fact he looked ridiculous carrying it around like a schoolboy.

He had his orders. *Butt crack?* And started to sweat immediately as he began walking back to the hotel. The precious Oxford

---

[1] Veronica is an elegant bullfighting pass.

[2] The Splendid Splinter. Ted Williams, the great hitting legend of Fenway Park.

volume was slipping out of his sweaty arms and hands. He needed
a —

"Taxi?"

It was William, of course. *How does he do this?* "May I take
you and your interesting book back to the Cinco Estrellas?"

Chapter 18

Paola Plots

Paola Labios, one-time paramour of Kiwi Airways' chief pilot, was having coffee with Tirso, aka "El Chino," in the market at Juanita Valdez' coffee shop. Juanita, a certified gossip hound whose only other vice was sex, joined the shopkeeper and his pretty friend.

Tirso's relationship with Paola was avuncular, not professional. He was not known to avail himself of the pleasures of the Happy Fish. At least not often. But he liked the girl. She was smart, took good care of her children, was a responsible citizen, and always called Tirso by his real name. They had become friends a while back when they were both involved in the version of 'Casablanca' dreamed up by Tirofijo. She was Ilsa Lund the love interest of Rick. He was the set designer.

The Korean had sought out his friend to give her the news of his visit to the barbershop. "So he left Luigi's with a big book and a look that said 'trouble.' Luigi was quiet about it, but I'm convinced that your *piloto* is working for the CIA."

"First of all, Tirso, he is not MY *piloto*. At least not anymore. We are no more!"

"Well, what happened, Paola?"

"That man, that *gringo*, that *hijo de su madre*.[1] I caught him trying to kiss Yettsy, you remember my friend from the Happy Fish, Yettsy?"

Tirso went a bit foggy-eyed. He certainly did. Remember Yettsy. "Yessss, I remember." The shopkeeper was definitely a

---

[1] Son of his mother. Paola was being uncharacteristically kind toward Steve Steele.

member of the Yettsy fan club even though he had never sought her out at the bordello. Nothing got by Paola who observed Tirso's momentary flight of fancy rolled her eyes and continued, "Well, before Yettsy went with her *americano*, she told me what Esteeve had done and then I broke it off. Anyway, Tirso, I knew Esteeve Steele was a CIA man. He told me."

"He did? Do they not keep that secret?"

"It was when he was, aaahh, most vulnerable. You know during …" Paola made the obscene, internationally recognized gesture for coitus.

"Coitus?"

"Yes."

"*Más café?*" Juanita did not wait for an answer and filled their cups as an excuse to listen more closely. "You know," she said, "I hear that Luigi never goes to the Happy Fish. Do you think he is a *mariposa*? At least that's what I hear."

Paola and Tirso looked up at Juanita with blank looks on their faces disbelieving her suppositions about the Italian American barber. It was just Juanita being Juanita.

Paola continued to enjoy her coffee despite her inner turmoil. This news about Steele skulking around upset her; he wasn't to be trusted. Meanwhile, a neighboring merchant, Chac Mool, quietly entered the small café and saw the trio sitting around a small table looking like plotters in the French Resistance. They turned their faces and looked conspiratorially at the shaman who nodded to each in turn. Chac Mool was a tall indigenous healer who sold salves, herbs, and tribal medicines from his stall at one corner of the market. He was well-respected in the city along with his mother who was known for her *fritangas*[2] and her laundry service. As a result

---

[2] Street food in La República featuring grilled chicken, fish, beef, rice, plantains, empanadas, and everything to go with.

Chac was always well fed and wore clean clothes. His daily garb consisted of Levi's 501 jeans, sandals made of rope and Michelin tires, an old Lakers jersey, and a colorful native vest.

"Chac, pull up a chair and join us. *Juanita otro café por favor.*"

"Thank you, neighbor." Chac and Tirso had neighboring stalls in the market.

Tirso continued. "Paola and I were talking about Steve Steele. We think he is up to something in La República. CIA maybe. What are your thoughts, Chac? What do the runes say?"

"The runes say nothing, Tirso. And I never argue with the runes. Oh! *Gracias* Juanita. But I do know something. Something serious."

"What??" The three said in unison.

Chac lowered his voice (there were ears in the market). "One of Piojo's boys, the one I let sleep in my stall sometimes, came to me all excited. He wanted to borrow some *ocotillo* cactus flowers. For his sore throat, you know?"

"Yes, we know! And?"

"And he said he was going to Aguacate to fight the *comunistas.* Piojo had organized the band as a brigade. A bunch of kids with nothing to do just looking for adventure chasing down some so-called socialists. It is absurd. They are going to be led by that *güero*[3] Steele. I am very concerned."

"I knew it!" Paola interjected. "This sounds very bad, anything else?"

"Sí, Paola," the shaman continued, "He said they had weapons. American guns! And materiel. He said it like that 'materiel.' I do not think the kid even knows what 'materiel' means. Then he ran off very excited. Those kids with weapons like that, they could get hurt. And the boys are fighting under the name Brigada

---

[3] *Gringo.*

Brayan Buenaventura, so they believe their cause is great. Who would do that to them? They are poor, ignorant, bored. This is no good."

"Brayan Buenaventura? The one who was drunk, fell off his horse, and got run over by a Jeep in the Guerra de Aguacate? *Por dios*, some hero. *Más café?*"

Paola thought of her own children, Axl and Slash, and pictured them on some lame-brained mission with weapons and under the command of Steele. Her heartbeat was quickening. Something had to be done.

Tirso wondered out loud to his friends, "What can we do? We must stop this *americano* before he gets any kids killed."

"Many of my tribe are in that area, I do not want them hurt in some stupid CIA lark! Every couple of years they think they have to mount some sort of purge, and our leaders acquiesce so to maintain the flow of *gringo* dollars. Now they are using helpless, homeless kids. But I have an idea. It will cost money for supplies and some money for my people to execute my plan, but I think it will work. But I need a lot of money fast!"

"How so, Chac?" Tirso asked.

"Materials, our own weapons, maybe a bribe or two. We can meet the *gringo* and his *gamines* and put a stop to this without anyone getting hurt. But I need money for that."

Paola snapped her fingers and got everyone's attention, "I know where to get it! I know where there is a pile of money. If I can get that money and give it to William, he can drive it over to you, Chac and then take you and the money to your *gente*."[4]

"*¡Deacachimba!*[5] Bring it to my stall before closing time in the market."

---

[4] People.
[5] Good.

There was a sharp, demanding knock on the shop door. The three conspirators and the coffee lady kibitzer looked at one another, chills running down spines, minds racing. They drew in their breaths all at once.

Had they been heard plotting against the CIA?

Who was knocking? Had the dictator ordered their detention? Was it the police? Would they be beaten? Arrested? Or worse, tortured?

Juanita asked the closed door in a shaky voice, "*¿Quién es?*"

"OverEats! I have your chicken and cold slaw."

Chapter 19

Back at the Hotel

Back at the hotel, Steve Steele felt that a cocktail followed by a light supper would be in line. He had a lot to mull over and one of Wulther's daiquiris would help in the process. He could hear the mechanical processes of the bartender's alchemy: the blending, the shaking, the clinking, the stirring, the pouring as he stepped into the cooler confines of the saloon.

Some of the regulars were in session and seem to be having a very heated conversation, Steve's Spanish could only pickup bits and prices.

"I am telling you, Ugarte. You watch. This new netminder, this Gómez kid, he is fantastic! They say he can stop everything. Even the penalty shots. We do not need that *cambia chaquetas*[1] Paredes!"

"Look Izquierdo, I want us to win. You know that. I am a loyal *republicano* and I want us to beat those *jueputas* for once. But Corinto always beats us. One-nil last time. They lost the war and the province to us. Now they are having their revenge. Maybe the Virgen is mad and still wants to be part of El Corinto and not La República. And I am with you my friend, as far as 'El Muro' Paredes goes, he can eat sand. Imagine defecting? Is he a *comunista,* do you think?"

Izquierdo, despite being a practical atheist, held the Virgen de Aguacate in high and respectful regard, responded tongue in

---

[1] Traitor.

cheek, "perhaps La Virgen likes this young Gómez and will intercede with the flight of the ball off the foot of a Corinthian *jueputa?* Jajaja."

"It is NOT to laugh, (switching to English) *Señor* Esteeve, what are jour thoughts on the matter? Perhaps the answer to our problems on the football pitch is in that impressive volume jou have been seen carting around. What is it, Cervantes?"

"Shakespeare. The complete works."

"Is it annotated?" Izquierdo was familiar with the Bard's work and fondly remembered watching Charlton Heston in a play on his Philips television.

"Yes, it is."

Ugarte, not wanting to lose a chance to pitch his own work, added "*Señor* Steele perhaps jou would be interested in my own volume 'The History of the Aguacate War'? It is yet to be annotated but many editorial houses have expressed interest."

Steve waved away the journalist *little creep* and stepped up to the bar, a daiquiri already iced was available and within reach. He lifted it like a chalice at the Holy Mass and as if on cue …

"Hello, sinners."

"Father Flynn!" Ugarte and Izquierdo greeted the defrocked Canadian priest, a popular fixture in the Cinco Estrellas Bar, as he entered and settled into his regular seat. The prelate turned to his drunken diocese like he was about to hear their confessions.

"Perhaps you can help shed light on a bit of religious dogma," Izquierdo asked benevolently but with a bit of irony. They were friends, on the same side of liberal causes but on the opposite sides of church issues.

"What is it my son?" Flynn had been defrocked but still held hard to his priestly habits of speech. "Thank you Wulther," he picked up a glass with two fingers of Canadian Club with its jaunty swizzle stick advertising the Cinco Estrellas Bar. Flynn smacked his lips. "Ahh, nectar of the gods, ehy?"

"Well, *padre*, Ugarte and I are discussing the match against Corinto. Ugarte thinks our new goalie will be able to block all efforts of the Corinthian eleven to score, thus ensuring a victory for La República."

"Oh, I know nothing of your *fútbol*. Hockey, ice hockey is the game for me, eyh. *Vive le habs*, eyh. Yes, it's the Canadiens of Montreal that matter to this poor priest," he replied before closing his eyes and taking a strong pull of Canadian Club.

Izquierdo, pushing on, said, "Well, it is a religious matter, your sanctity. I postured that the Virgen de Aguacate, whose shrine is now *republicano* soil, will take a liking to our young netminder and intercede in his favor by, perhaps, altering the flight of a ball kicked in his direction. Do believe that to be possible?"

"Yes, if she is approached with an open heart worthy of her indulgence," was the priest's secular reply as he eyed his glass and its last remains of sacramental whiskey.

"Has she been able to intercede on behalf of your hockey team? Up there in Montreal and with so many Catholics in attendance!" Izquierdo was getting the best of his Irish Canadian friend.

"Well not lately, that's for sure!"

Appreciating the priest's candor and good humor, everyone erupted in convivial laughter and had Wulther busy again behind the bar. Meanwhile another man had slipped into the bar in the priest's wake and ignored by the congress in session. The man appeared to be a traveling businessman, although a bit out of the ordinary, dressed in a heavy woolen black coat totally inappropriate for the local climate and an equally inappropriate black fedora. He looked more at home in Manhattan's diamond district than in the Central American tropics.

"Welcome *señor*, what can I get you?"

"Be a *mensch*, get me a Manischewitz." Gregorio sounded like he was right off West 47th street. There was little Wulther didn't know about the tipple, but he was stumped by the man's order. "I am sorry?"

"Any red wine, sweet. Thank you."

"We have a nice Concha y Toro, not sweet but a little past its prime?"

"That will do." The fedoraed foreigner paid for his wine and observed the goings on. He did a quick inventory. There was another foreigner, a priest. Two men seemed to be kidding him. Then there was the American with a stain on his face carrying a thick bible. *Possibly a missionary?* But no, as he finished his slightly turned red wine he looked closely … *Shakespeare? Oy vey. A spy no doubt. Something is rotten in the state of La República.* Just then the proprietor, Klaus Von Klaus, happened to step behind the bar to check on things.

"How are things, Wulther?"

"Same crowd jefe, except for the red wine at the end of the bar."

Klaus saw no one and only observed an empty glass with dark red lees along its sides. "Who?" The man in the fedora had left as quietly as he had come in.

Steele got up a bit unsteadily after a few daiquiris and a club sandwich. He had enjoyed exchanging pleasantries with another native English speaker even though Father Flynn spoke a peculiar brand with "ehy" thrown in now and again. *Must be a Yankee, or maybe a communist. Shit on my shoe, they ARE everywhere.* But it was time to go, so he said good night to the priest and made for the elevator in the lobby.

Back in his room at the hotel, the freshly showered CIA man got ready for bed. He put on his pajamas, a gift from Paola, with little blue and yellow airplanes. "For my *piloto*," she had said. Steele missed his Paola.

Sitting at the small desk, with the Annotated Works of WS pushed a bit to his left, Steve opened the yellow envelope and pulled out the paper within. "Another cable." He looked in the pocket of his jacket hanging neatly on the chair and pulled out "Handy Phrases in Albanian" for reference. Excited by the spy craft and his mission, Steele tackled the puzzle. He struggled with the cipher and finally came up with Caesar Act 1 Scene 2. Swearing out loud, "Jesus Christ, this is a pain in the ass," he opened to the Table of Contents and ran his finger down a list of histories and comedies. He went up and down the histories looking for Julius Caesar, one of the most famous people in history. He didn't find Julius Caesar. A couple of Richards. And Henries. "What a fucking lot of Henries!" Turning the page he came upon a list of tragedies and there found "The Tragedy of Julius Caesar."

"That ain't right. Should be a history. Crummy book." Thankful the secret code was not written with invisible ink; he popped the bit of paper into his mouth to dispose of it. He found the line in the play and as he chewed the cable he spoke the countersign aloud to commit it to memory. "He thinksh too mush, sush men are dangerush. Thish cable tashtes like shit."

His spy craft concluded, the captain, head pilot, CIA operative and ex-lover of Paola Labios slipped between the sheets and slept soundly. Three of Wulther's daiquiris will do that.

Chapter

Gregorio Reports

*D*ónde estará el ruso cabron?"[1] Rosemary thought out loud while she paced one of her rooms in the palace. Her apartments included a meditation center, bedroom, office, servants' quarters with their own *en suite* and occupied by Gregorio the bearded mystic of the steppes. Together they made up nearly the entire third floor in a wing well away from her husband's area of dominant interest. She had just left the meditation center where she made daily supplications to the pantheon of energies that resided in the many manifestations of color, particularly the blue hue called amethyst.

Amethyst-colored gewgaws hung from every conceivable part of her body starting with the bluish orbs on hooks run though the large gaps of her elongated earlobes. They looked like Dollar Store Christmas ornaments. Multiple strands of beaded necklaces hung around her veiny pencil neck, some reaching as far as her waist. Bracelets up to her elbows, many anklets, rings in the lobes of her ears, all the way up the helix including what is known as 'Darwin's tubercle,' through the nostrils, and on every skeletal finger. A sapphire-blue pair of dark glasses and an amethyst-encrusted tiara completed the look. The ambiance of room was equally jarring with its piped-in atonal space-age "music" that assaulted the ears like an audio root canal.

Rosemary stopped her pacing and sat at her desk to go over sales receipts for the mandatory tiaras all women were required to wear in public. The First Lady offered them at wholesale prices to vendors throughout the country. They were expensive, particularly

---

[1] Where is that damned Russian?

to teachers, clerks, municipal workers and other employees who had to lay out a week's salary to fulfill the requirement and keep their jobs. Men could not wear tiaras, obviously, but she and Gregorio were working on something. "Sales are down, that is very troubling," she spoke to her cat Ludwig. Ludwig did not respond. Ludwig was quite deaf.

A man in a black fedora and matching long woolen coat came running into the room and sat down in a wing-backed chair wheezing and gasping trying to catch his breath. He was not dressed for the climate, that was a certainty. The man got a suspicious up-and-down from the *primera dama*.

"We don't want any!" Rosemary said looking up at the intruder. Outraged, she added "who is letting you vendors think they can stream in and out of the palace?" The poor man was doubled over as he continued to gasp. He held up a hand in such a way as to say "Wait, I am out of breath ..."

"Well, speak before I have one of the guards arrest you for palatial trespass!"

The man took in a lot of air. After a few seconds he managed to say, "It (pant) is (gasp) I (pant)."

"I who, I? Speak imbecile!"

Another wheezy inhale and the intruder exhaled, "Gre (pant) gorio…."

"Gregorio, is that you? Why did you not say so? What have you found out? Excellent disguise by the way."

"I went to the bar at the Hotel Cinco Estrellas."

"Yes, yes?"

"I sat at the bar."

"Yes, yes?"

"Nobody recognized me."

"Yes, yes??"

"The priest and the newspaper reporter were talking about the Virgin playing football and —"

A roll of her eyes that sent vibrations through a sea of cheap glass beads was followed by, "Gregorio, get to the point. This is not Anna Karenina, *carajo*."

"I had a little wine, so as not to look suspicious, they had a nice —"

"Gregorio," she growled.

"I see this American, a good-looking *mensch*, vit that big book. Shakespeare. Used for cipher codes."

"Shakespeare? *Por dios*! And?"

"It was annotated! Vat a book, you should see."

"Forget the book, Dostoyevsky! What next?"

"The cherman, the Nazi owner. He showed up."

"Klaus Von Klaus? What did he say?"

"I do not know. I left."

"No matter, it is that handsome Steve Steele who is up to something. Yes, very good looking, tall, piercing blue eyes, broad shoulders. I like a man with broad shoulders." Gregorio was staring at her, mouth wide open. Rosemary ignored the look and continued on, "He is probably CIA. Something is happening, yes. That man and Max and that *pendejo* from the American embassy smoking cigars at the party. I do not like it. Go back tomorrow, it is Saturday and those alcoholics will be back, buy them a round of drinks —"

Gregorio certainly did not want to go back to the bar with Nazis lurking about. "I cannot go tomorrow, madame."

The First Lady angrily confronted her mystic who dared to refuse her direct order, "Gregorio, I remind you that you work for me and that your visa is up for renewal."

"I-I-I simply cannot." Gregorio's objection was hesitant, measured. He was desperately grasping for an idea, any idea that would get him out of returning to the Cinco Estrellas bar.

"And w-w-w-why can you not?" She mimicked. "Spit it out!"

"I am *shomer Shabbos*." Gregorio was stretching it, but it sounded pretty damned good.

"*Qué carajo?* What?"

"I-I-I must study the vibrations of color." The mystic was on a roll. "Tomorrow is a-a-a alignment of the ninth star of Maris with the right field of the Bronx continuum. Very rare, many mysteries within."

"Of course, Gregorio, continue your wonderful interpretations. They may reveal something." She placed her hands together as if in prayer, bowed to her advisor and said "*namaste*."

He returned the bow, "billimartin."

Chapter 21

Deployment Day

Steve woke up at a few minutes after the butt crack of dawn. Quite a few minutes, actually. He was in freshly pressed, but stylishly worn, desert camouflage suitable for a Central American interdiction were there any deserts in which to dict. There were no deserts, only jungles. Steele raised the issue with the salesman at Miami's leading Army-Navy-Coast Guard surplus store, but the salesman had assured him the outfit was "all terrain."

He had no identification other than the oak leaf on his lapels. Steele had promoted himself to the highest rank possible without creating outrage. After all, nobody cared about majors. A neatly folded red beret he had stolen from a sleeping paratrooper at the Miami airport was threaded underneath his right shoulder epaulet. With his mirrored aviator glasses he felt he exuded a professional appearance **and** panache if he did say so himself.

Exiting the elevator into the lobby of the Hotel Cinco Estrellas, Steve Steele in full undercover military regalia looked like a CIA agent in full undercover military regalia on assignment in Kabul. The Complete Works of William Shakespeare (fully annotated) under his arm like an American football added to his interesting choice of wardrobe.

"*Guten morgen.*" CLICK. "Your breakfast is ready *Herr* Steve, I know you must be off early this day on your mission — uh, errands."

Steve sat and dug into a repast of fresh warmed tortillas, *gallopinto*, fried cheese, *crema*, yuca, eggs, *plátanos*, cut mangos, pineapples, black bean soup, fresh papaya juice, and the best coffee in the world. It was enough food for three Americans. Which is a lot.

Finishing in a slight hurry, Steele nodded to the German: "Thank you, Klaus. I must eat and run." He hefted his book and walked out the door almost running over William who was standing directly outside.

"Good morning captain."

"Major."

"Major, good morning." William was nonplussed. A major or captain were much the same as long as they paid their fare. "William first to someplace called La Tuerta."

"Good choice señor. La Huerta de la Tuerta,[1] best *baleadas* in La República, and then?"

"La Chingada, the hangar."

William slipped a punch or two and they were off. The mission had begun.

⧗ ⧗ ⧗

Piojo was reviewing his troops. The Brigada Brayan Buenaventura, all 12 of them, were at a sloppy attention shouldering rusty M1 rifles. Some were on the right shoulder, some on the left. One boy's posture was correct in every way except he was facing the rear. Two of them had found cheap sunglasses and were saluting and addressing one another in Steele's gringo-speak. "Mucho expensive-o. Mi name ees Jon Wayne-o."

Nonetheless, they **were** lined up to Piojo's satisfaction. "*Hombres! Atención.* We await our *Capitán Esteeve* Steele."[2]

The boys looked expectant and admired one another in their camouflage fatigues that had been removed out of the crates marked "Costume Department: Do not remove." Although large,

---

[1] Garden of the One-Eyed woman.
[2] Men. Attention.

the gamins seemed not to mind — they simply rolled up the sleeves, pants legs, and secured the trousers with the belts provided (after making an extra hole). Stuffed copies of last week's "El Día" into the fronts of the dull black combat boots secured a better fit and provided insulation for their bare feet. From a distance, blurred by the rising waves of heat coming off the sunbaked tarmac of La Chingada International, they looked soldierly enough to Steve Steele who was peering incredulously through the filthy windshield of William's taxi. He nodded in satisfaction; they looked disciplined and their camouflage matched his own.

"Thank you, William."

"Anytime sir," he replied and motored out of the hangar.

The CIA man called to Piojo, "Corporal! Front and center!"

Aiming an index finger at his own chest, Piojo mouthed back, "*¿Yo?*"

"Yes, yo. C'mere."

Piojo, chest out, threw back a commanding look at his brigade and walked up to Steele. "*Sí, Capitán* Esteele."

"No names, Piojo. And it's major."

"*Sí, mi mayor.*"

"Help me out take these bags to the uh, men."

"The *baleadas*! Did you go to La Tuerta?"

"Yes, now let's feed the men!"

The men, ages 10-12, dug in like Napoleon's troops at the Battle of Marengo. Some thought it could very well be their last meal, but it beat the boredom and humiliation of living on the streets of La Capital. Besides, these were *baleadas* from La Huerta de La Tuerta and they looked at their major adoringly as they chewed gratefully. They might go to the wall for him.

"Men! Today we meet destiny head on!"

"*Chicos, hoy encontraremos nuestro destino.*" Piojo translated accurately.

"We are the Brayan Buenaventura Brigade."

"*Somos La Brigada Brayan Buenaventura, listos para chingar a todos!*"[3] Piojo added a little local spice to his translation and received a cheer from the "men." Steele liked the enthusiasm but was wary of what he believed was ad-libbing. His Spanish wasn't quite good enough to catch the nuance. He shrugged and carried on.

"Brave Brayan Buenaventura died for you in the war against El Coreentow!"

"*El valiente Brayan Buenaventura murió combatiendo esos lambehuevos de El Corinto.*"[4]

"Huevos? Eggs? What are you telling them, Piojo?"

"Not eggs, *mi* mayor. I tol' them Brayan died for their freedomses."

Steele looked at Piojo doubtfully but didn't want to lose the momentum. The continued, "Today we fight the communists to protect American Interests and our, uh, your freedoms."

"*Hoy vamos a mandar a esos hijos de putas a la chingada!*"[5]

"Did you just call them sons of whores?"

"No *señor, putas* is another word for strong person. Eets *republicano* eslang."

Putas was certainly a word Steve heard a lot at the Happy Fish; now he was glad to learn its local context and made a mental note to try it out on his next visit to the brothel.

The kids were charged up and ready to fight for anyone who brought them *baleadas*, especially from La Tuerta.

---

[3] We are the Brayan Buenaventura Brigade ready to fuck everybody.

[4] Brave Brayan Buenaventura died fighting those ball-lickers from El Corinto.

[5] Today we send those sons of whores to fuck all.

"Now we march!"

"Mayor Esteeve, we no march. We ride!" Piojo pointed to a wheeled contraption tied with a rope to the rear winch of the Jeep. It was the passenger ladder for Kiwi airways *sans* steps. Just the bottom which some decades past had been the bed of a Citroen pick up. Now unencumbered by stairs or engine it served as a trailer in which to haul the ragamuffins of the Brigada Brayan Buenaventura. Steele was pleased.

"Climb aboard, men," he pointed to the ex-Citroen. "Corporal, you drive the Jeep. I'll ride in the back of the Jeep." *And look like General George Fucking Patton! fighting Rommel in North Africa, by god!* "What's the matter corporal? drive!"

"I cannot see, *capitán*."

"Major, it's MAJOR! Remember that corporal Piojo or you will find yourself knocked down to Private Piojo."

"*Sí, mi* mayor. I still cannot see. The steering wheel is in the way. I am too chort."

Major Steele saw what the problem was immediately and provided an unorthodox solution. "You certainly are short, corporal. Here sit on this, it will raise you up. There! Good?" Steele hoped that he was not violating any regulations by using The Complete Works of William Shakespeare as a booster seat.

"Jes, now I can see mayor."

Everything was in place, ready to move out. Steve Steele felt that he had successfully completed the yeoman's task of organizing a hardened cadre. "I'm ready to lead my men into the glorious conquest of communists lurking in yonder jungle."

Thus the *Brigada* lit out to the Aguacate province: the boys looking sharp in their desert camo were pulled along in the Citroen practicing salutes, the CIA agent sitting upright in the back seat of the Jeep like George F. Patton, and Piojo driving with a clear view of the road ahead thanks to The Complete Works of William Shakespeare (Fully Annotated).

Chapter 22

Meanwhile at The Hideout

Tirofijo, like any good criminal king pin, had his own *Escondite*, or hideout. Being in a centralized location within walking distance of a KFC, possessing of ample space, it was ideal for a criminal operation. He enjoyed the central location with its proximity to the Happy Fish and easy access to the airport. And all the extra space? Well, he needed it to handle his bustling import/export business. On the import side there was contraband; items such as cigars, high-end liquors, Marlboro cigarettes, zippo lighters, perfumes and scents, dirty magazines, adventure comics, watches, handbags, etc. There was great demand for these items from the dictator and other domestic channels of distribution. The Hideout also offered space for his empty animal enclosures, beshat bird cages, and boxes of those mud figurines with the pre-Columbian erections.

Along the far back wall, the one bordering the street, was a curiosity; a makeshift soundstage with a faded painted version of Rick's Cafe Americain from the famous classic "Casablanca." The stage had been used only once in the production of a scene from that movie.[1] Tirofijo was the auteur of the cinematic work, the vignette he hoped would launch his career in Hollywood. It had not and the empty, unused stage remained as a testament. It wasn't even a stage *per se* as the riser had been appropriated by Mandamás to use in his palace office.

Tirofijo lived comfortably in the hideout as well. Years previous he had a full apartment installed including a master bedroom,

---

[1] See "The Kidnapping of Dennis Martin," Vol. 1 in the La República trilogy.

en suite, and an adjacent office. It was spartan, but met the criminal overlord's needs, particularly in the bedroom where the only furnishing was an imported mattress filled with water. "It is very *de riguer*," he assured Violeta who was not fond of boats or even the beach.

The space was part of Violeta's Sexx Shoppe, attached to the rear of her store and accessible from both her store at one end and the street at the other. It was a nice arrangement; before Violeta had given Tirofijo the heave-ho, the mobster had enjoyed free use of both Violeta and her warehouse. Now he no longer enjoyed any use of Violeta and there was the matter of rent on the warehouse. The cost of the two-year lease was not exorbitant, yet it was an added expense not included in Tirofijo's criminal enterprise business plan.

The head of said enterprise himself was sitting behind a desk the size of a regulation snooker table. Before him, on the other side of the table, sat a nervous young man in a green rain slicker. "You have done very well, young Potro," the thug told his young associate as he looked at the many stacks of yellow and blue *tucanes* — the stolen chicken money. He picked up a stack of the worn and filthy bills with pretty pictures of toucans and colorful reptiles, counted out ten of them and thought for a few seconds. Then he counted out two more.

Potro, the OverEats! motorcycle delivery boy turned OverEats! impostor and thief stared wide-eyed at the small stack Tirofijo placed in front of him. "One thousand, Potro, is your salary. The extra two hundred is a bonus for doing such good work. You were right about the big fútbol game. Take tomorrow afternoon off."

"*S-s-s-sí, señor* Tirofijo." The boy was so nervous, so excited, his hand shook as he picked up the stack of bills and shoved them out of sight before the boss changed his mind. He knew his mother would be very proud and his Carmencita, why he could take her out for *baleadas* AND a movie, one of those films with that man Bond or Cantinflas or both!

"Do not forget *muchacho*, leave the OverEats! uniform and delivery box. Put them over there. I'll see you tomorrow evening." The lad nodded, removed the rain protector and placed it in the corner along with the green box. He left out the back door to the street bumping into a beautiful girl with movie star looks and the smell of rain clouds. She flashed perfect white teeth. Her eyes were deep, dark, almond shaped — exotic for a *republicana*.

"I-I-I-I am so s-s-s-sorry. Excuse me, *señorita.*"

"Do not worry *guapito*, I am looking for Tirofijo. Is he in?"

"Yes, but I do not thi —"

Paola Labios didn't care about the rest; she just wanted to know if Tirofijo was there. She pushed past Potro, shut the door behind her, and stepped into the warehouse space. She knew her way around; Paola was one of the players in Tirofijo's ill-fated cinematic dream and had a good lay of the land. Also she had made a few professional house calls in the past. Once her eyes got used to the dim light she made her way back to Tirofijo's office where he had his back to the door and was putting the last stack of *tucanes* into an old safe with fading gilded letters that spelled out United Avocado Co.

"Hola, Tirofijo," she breathed huskily. Her scent filled the room in seconds and Tirofijo, hoping it was Violeta coming back to apologize to her strong and virile crime boss, swiveled his expensive desk chair around, not even bothering to shut the safe, and faced a vision. The vision was Paola Labios — sex-huntress. Often compared to Sofia Loren, the Italian film star, Paola boasted of legendary breasts that stood out even in La República where the women were very well endowed. The curvatures of her body invited his embrace. Her confident stance accented by a pair of broad shoulders. Tirofijo liked women with broad shoulders.

Great care had been taken in putting together Paola's ensemble: an outfit fit to seduce a hardened, experienced man such as Tirofijo. Starting with the tight-fitting bodice, its laces strained against the heavage of her cleavage. A short, SHORT skirt that ended many inches above her knees. And below the pretty knees were high shiny boots of Chinese plastic. Her long-tapered fingers ended with perfectly manicured nails in the French style, for Paola knew that Tirofijo liked the French style and all that they implied. Her coif was coquettish, much in the style of Veronica Lake in "This Gun for Hire," only black as a new car tire.

"*Me cago en* — Paola. S-s-so good to see you. What are you doing here?" Tirofijo was taken aback but not so much that the possibilities of this reunion didn't race through his head like a VHS tape on fast forward. He felt tumescence in his nether region.

"Ay Tirofijo, my Tirofijo. It has been too, too long. I cannot control my desires any longer." Paola strutted around the desk to the boss's side and hiked herself up on its corner. Her short skirt hiked up as well leaving Tirofijo ample opportunity to admire her thigh. He tore himself away from the view to look up at her. "You are looking very fine, Paola. VERY fine."

Paola observed the open safe from the corner of her eye and knew she had to distract her victim away from it. "Tirofijo, you know just what to say to a woman. You are a real man, a real *republicano*." Very slowly she opened a small black sequined clutch purse and removed a box of Marlboro cigarettes that she had cadged from her ex-boyfriend *that sonofawhore* Esteeve Steele. She took her time opening the top of the red and white box, peeled away a strip of protective paper foil, removed two cigarettes, and closed it. Tirofijo could not take his eyes off the girl's movements. It was a seduction played out by one of the great seductresses of La República. He felt a desperate longing as he watched her return the box to her purse and exchange it for a bright chrome Zippo lighter with the logo of Kiwi Airways (We'll Get There!).

The cigarettes, both of them, were held wetly but firmly in Paola Labios luscious Latin lips. Tirofijo stared at her, longing to lick those luscious lips. He heard the distinct sound, like no other in the world, of a Zippo lighter clicking open. It was a satisfying sound of machined metal. Simultaneously raising it slowly to her face and thumbing the roller to create a spark, the blue and yellow flame rose up to kiss the tips of each cigarette one at a time. There was a satisfying crackling sound like an outdoor wood fire. She inhaled lustily, breathing the North Carolina tobacco smoke deeply. After exhaling a long and luxurious bluish cloud she stared down at her target, and passed him one of the dampened, pre-lit cancer sticks. She had him.

"Tirofijo, let us not deny ourselves any longer. Violeta is in your past, this I know. And Esteeve, the pilot he has flown out of my heart. But *mi amor*, we have each other. We have always had each other, have we not?"

Ignoring the fact that Paola was always pay-for-play, Tirofijo was confident that his charm could not be resisted and was drawn in to the romance, "*Sí, sí* we always had each other. Let us go to —"

"*Mi amor*, let us not rush this beautiful moment. This will be our story! Let us … well, do you have any Ron Aniversario? I want to relax, feel the moment with two or three fingers."

"Two or three fingers? You want me to —"

"Of rum *baboso*, of rum! Let us raise glasses and drink a toast to our love!"

Tirofijo wasted no time in finding a bottle of the national liquor, Ron Aniversario in the second drawer of his enormous desk. Tumblers were not as handy, but he rooted around and found a couple of cloudy shot glasses. He placed all these on his desk and began unscrewing the rum bottle.

"Tirofijo?"

"Yes, my heart?"

"These glasses?"

"Yes?"

"They will not do. This is a special moment. One we will speak of all our lives. Do you think that such a moment would merit glassware that does not say 'I Swallowed in Saratoga'?"

Afraid to lose the "moment," Tirofijo began a panicky scavenger hunt for more appropriate glassware and found some lilac-colored champagne flutes (a remnant of the Violeta days). "Will these do, *amor del alma?*"[2]

"Oh, Tirofijo you know how to treat a woman," the girl said while leaning over and providing Tirofijo a view of the magnificent twin towers in downtown Paola Labios. Tirofijo shakily poured a measure of rum into each glass, perhaps a bit more into Paola's. They raised the glasses and in the time-honored fashion of modern lovers, stared longingly into each other's eyes. Just as they were about to sip the nectar of love, Paola gave a small yip and returned her flute to the desk.

"Tirofijo!"

"What is it, *flaca?*"

"I forgot to close the door. I came in through the back. I bumped into the young man. But I did not close it."

"I am sure it is closed. Let's drink to our love, *amor.*"

"Tirofijo, what if someone came in. Piojo or —"

"That *comemierda*[3] is gone! No one will disturb us, my queen."

---

2 My soulmate.

3 Shit eater.

"Still, I cannot, you know, if —"

Tirofijo was off like a shot to shut the fucking door. Paola quickly reached into her purse and removed a capsule of Rohypnol. She opened the capsule and poured the fine granules into the crime king's Ron Aniversario then returned the empty capsule into her purse just as Tirofijo reappeared. "Door is closed. Was closed I mean. Let us drink!"

"Sit, Tirofijo, come and let me admire the strong and virile man that owns La Capital. You are tough, but they say you have a heart of gold." Never one to eschew a compliment, Tirofijo looked down to peek at his lap in the neighborhood of his yonson. *Yes, she is beautiful, and I am a republicano. Strong, virile. Hung like a horse.*

She lifted the flute, knocked back the entire measure of rum, and slammed the glass back on the desk all without losing eye contact with her *conquista*.[4] Tirofijo felt a longing even more desperate than before and wasted no time in returning the gesture. He stared into her deepest dark eyes, picked up his glass, threw the alcohol down his throat.

"This rum is a bit off, my turtledove, let me get another bottle."

"Tirofijo, I cannot stand another minute without feeling the embrace of your powerful arms or your desperate longing for me. Sit in your chair, your seat of power so that I may admire you!"

He sat.

"Now, count to me, backwards from 100."

"Count backwards?"

"*Sí carajo!* Count backwards. It is very romantic; the French do it all the time."

Tired of the delay and ready for action, Tirofijo acquiesced.

"One hundred."

---

4 Conquest.

"Ooh, go on."

"Ninety-nine."

"Oh, Tirofijo, I am damp."

"Ninety —"

The man was out. He slumped a bit forward so Paola gently put his arms on the desk and rested his massive head on those arms.

Then she moved fast to the open safe.

"*Qué pendejo,*[5] he left it open." She removed the stacks of the colorful currency and placed them in a plastic bag she had brought along for the job. *It is a lot of money.*

Once outside on the street she waited less than 10 seconds for the rusty Buick with filthy windows to arrive. It soon rolled to a stop in front of the back door, emitting noxious fumes and coughing like a two-pack-a-day smoker. Paola jumped in the back seat.

"Perfect timing, William. Here is the bag of money. You know what to do, right?"

William ducked below the steering wheel for a second, then came back up, "*Sí.* Take it to Chac, then take Chac to Aguacate to meet his tribe!" Since nothing ever happened in La Capital, this was all very exciting to the taxi driver.

"This is for you, *querido* William," Paola said handing him a stack that she had removed from the bag. Paola had a soft spot for the older pugilist and wanted to reward him for time and mileage.

"Thank you! Paola, this is so much money! How can I ever thank you?"

"Just get the rest to Chac and get Chac to Aguacate Province. Here is my apartment, let me get out."

"You have a heart of gold, Paola! YOU should be the benevolent dictator! Jajaja."

The old Buick rolled away.

---

[5] What an idiot.

Chapter 23

On Maneuvers

Mayor Esteeve Steele and the Brigada Brayan Buenaventura were lost. The major consulted an old out-of-date map printed and distributed by the now defunct LRAC.[1] The map showed two bold red lines, one east-west and one north-south representing International Highway Two and International Highway One, respectively. Being as La República had only two major roads and only a handful of hamlets sprinkled around the country, the map was quite serviceable.

Republicanos had been proud of the fact that their small country could boast of having an auto club. "In Corinto there is no auto club," they bragged, often adding, "those *jueputas*." The auto club, a brainchild of Tirso who still maintained his membership in AAA,[2] did not count on many members; but its map of La República boasted wide readership. Every classroom had a map proudly pinned to a piece of wood nailed to the adobe wall so all the students could admire their country and its two highways.

Tirso no longer published the map and disbanded the small club after a cartographic conflict with Rosemary Mandamás. The First Lady had seen the map in schools and had a major fantod. It was while she was instituting her new age curriculum and giving away Astro-Cosmology (Cosmo-Astrology?) posters to perplexed professors; posters with colorful pictures of crystals, rocks, and whatnot that described their universal powers. She didn't like the

---

[1] La República Auto Club.
[2] The American Automobile Association.

maps; they did not conform to the color scheme that she had devised for learning centers. Principally she was against the red lines. She did not like them. The arteries of the national highways should be amethyst or possibly green, just not red. Communists are red. Roads are bluish, she felt.

Tirso had been summoned to the *Primera Dama's* offices in the Presidential Palace to discuss the issue of inappropriate map-page of La República.

"You are the man responsible? You are the printer of this abhorrent use of color on our national maps?"

Tirso, proud *republicano* felt that it might be better to play his Asian card. Silence and inscrutability, that's all she'll get. *Feita loca.*[3] Although Tirso WAS Korean, he was third generation and just as *republicano* as she. Nonetheless, the strategy he employed with the bizarre bitch was to play Hop Sing to her Mrs. Cartwright, bow deeply, say nothing.

"I will take that as a yes. *Mira*, Chino. That is what they call you, correct. Chino?"

Tirso bowed, "Collect." *Oooh, I am good at this.*

"Well Chino, we cannot have it. I am leading La República, without much help from my husband-for-life the generalíssimo, into a new universe of positive vibrations where we will harness the powers of crystals. Amethyst in particular. YOU UNDER-STAND." She shouted remembering Chino was a foreigner and one always had to shout at foreigners to be understood. "YOU UN-DER. STAND. CRYSTALS?"

Tirso bowed, "Clistals, yes me unnerstand."

"Good! Velly uh, very good. So, you will remove all the maps and replace them with new maps. The new maps shall have blue, amethyst blue, roads. Not red. BLUE UNDERSTAND?"

––––––––––––––––––––

[3] Crazy ugly.

Bowing, Tirso replied, "Broo. Yesssssss me unnerstand."

"You may go."

Tirso walked backwards and bowed two or three times. Victor Sen Yung[4] would have been proud. The maps were never reprinted.

⧗   ⧗   ⧗

Steele's fingers traced a bold red line from left to right. On the left there was a black dot marked "La Capital." On the right there was a black dot marked "Provincia de Aguacate." An emblem, also in red and just above the line indicated IH Two. The pilot looked up from the map spread on the hood of the Jeep. The Jeep had run out of road and Piojo had followed two faint tracks on the ground right into the forest.

"How in the name of Jesus H. Kennedy do we get lost when there's only one road!"

"Two roads, *mi mayor.* Highway One and Highway Two! Two roads!"

"I know there are TWO roads, Piojo. Goddammit. Where are we?"

"I think we are somewhere in Aguacate Province."

"I think we are in Aguacate Province," the major stated thinking it was his own idea. "From here we walk, gather your — where are they?"

"In the forest, mi mayor."

"What are they doing in the forest for gods' sake?"

"*Cagando,*[5] mayor. "The *baleadas* were very —"

---

[4] Actor who portrayed Hop Sing in TV's Bonanza.
[5] Shitting.

"Never mind, assemble your troops, rifles at the ready, we march in 10 minutes." Steele looked around like he had forgotten something, then remembered what it was and went back to the Jeep.

Walking toward the green canopy of the jungle, Piojo shouted to his brigade, "*¡¡Cabrones, dejen de hacerse la paja y reporten inmediatamente!!*"[6] The street miscreants turned hardened cadre emerged one by one with a great deal of shirt tucking, belt tightening, and loud bragging. After some searching for their discarded rifles, they tried to form two rows but remained bunched under the shade of a *guanacaste* tree. Piojo strutted in front of them examining each of his charges very carefully and pointing out an unzipped fly or unbuttoned shirt. Satisfied they were in fighting shape he addressed the *brigada*.

"*Chicos*, today we fight! Today we engage the *comunistas*, the *hijos de sesenta mil putas*,[7] in glorious battle to defend our nation, the generalíssimo, and American Interests! Are you ready, *cabrones*?"

"*Síí!*"

"Mayor Esteeve Steele, the Brigada Brayan Buenaventura is ready!"

"Very well, into the truck bed. Piojo, drive!"

After a lot of arguing and profanity the boys arranged themselves in the old Citroen truck bed tied to the Jeep with sturdy rope. Piojo got into the Jeep and balanced himself on the Shakespeare volume while Steve Steele regained his pose and determined expression standing behind the passenger seat. George Fuggin Patton.

⧗ ⧗ ⧗

---

[6] Cabrones, stop playing with yourselves and report for duty.
[7] Sons of sixty thousand whores.

After two hours, the Jeep tracks began to widen into a dirt road. Steele, standing, raised his left arm and made a fist. It was the signal to halt to anyone familiar with WWII-genre Hollywood fare. Piojo, driving, failed to see what was going on behind him. Steele barked, "Halt-oh! Stop!"

Piojo slowed to a halt. Steele peered down the dirt road. There was a shack ready to fall over at even the threat of a stiff wind. It was the checkpoint. "My contact!" Steve remembered he had to contact one of the Company's operatives in Aguacate. Steve, however, could not remember the countersign. *Something about danger? Stranger danger? No that's not it.* He de-Jeeped and signaled to Piojo to wait while he approached the shed slowly. As he drew near, a well-dressed officer wearing the uniform of an Admiral in the Laotian Naval Services stepped from behind the shed and demanded, "What is the porpose of jour visit to Aguacate Province!?"

Steele looked the customs official over. Despite the protection offered by his Ray Bans, he was partially blinded by the sun glinting off the man's many medals for valorous action. His torso looked like an Olympian athlete's trophy chest.

"For fucks sake!"

"Jour porpose, *señor.*"

"Officer Gómez you know me, Steve Steele? Pilot? Kiwi Airways?"

"Passport please!"

"We just spoke at La Chingada!"

Garcilaso Gómez, customs officer and CIA mole addressed Steve Steele, pilot and CIA operative *sotto voce.* Very spy like. "Tell me about Cassius …"

Steele was distracted by the infuriating exchange with the low-level bureaucrat, barely noticing the dirty Buick flying by on the main road.

Where did that road come from? Is that? No, couldn't be.

"Tell me about Cassius …"

"The boxer? Heavyweight. Changed his name and —"

Desperately, the customs man pressed on, "TELLLL me about Casssssius!"

"Oh, right the countersign! Uh, Stranger Danger? No?"

Garcilaso stared at something under Steele's arm. Steele followed the stare to the book. "Right! Shakespeare! Ok. Ok. Ok. Don't tell me. It's he's lean and dangerous?"

"Jou are getting warmer."

"Lean and hungry, that's why he's dangerous?" Steele said hopefully. Garcilaso shrugged. Close enough. "Jour no Charlton Heston, but jou and jour men may pass anyway, *señor*. Welcome to La Provincia de Aguacate."

"Forward, men!" Steele shouted back to his troops and Piojo to drive up and join him.

"¡*Vámonos, cabrones*," Piojo relayed and ground the gears of the vehicle looking for any low gear that would get it moving.

Chapter 24

William and Chac

During the one-hour drive over International Highway Number Two from La Capital to La Provincia de Aguacate, Chac and the driver chatted pleasantly about one thing and another. While the conversation was enjoyable, the ride was not. The Buick soldiered on but, after this run, would be a good candidate for extreme unction. Symptoms of its impending demise included a suspension that was a distant memory and seats whose springs screamed in agony. The less said about its engine the better.

Additionally the car body was so dirty and rusty that William, though he loved her, never washed the Buick for fear that the only thing holding it together was filth.

"So then Tirofijo gave that *gringo*, Dennis something … Dennis …?"

"Martin his name was. I picked him up at La Chingada. Drove him to the Happy Fish and around La Capital."

"To the overlook?"

"No, I did not take him to the overlook."

"A shame."

"Yes. But Chac, he took that film, the tape that Tirofijo made back to *La Yunae,* but nothing ever happened. Tirofijo was sure he would get a call from Hollywood. *Pero nada.* You know what I think?"

"What? Be careful there's a deep hole there!"

"Wow! Yes! *Gracias.*" William barely avoided the crater with no small amounts of wild maneuvers of the steering wheel which had so much play that it required a full rotation before engaging.

"I do not think he was an actor at all!"

The two were reminiscing about an incident in La República which was still being talked about in bars and salons around the city with many attendant theories and speculations.[1] Tirofijo had kidnapped an American named Dennis Martin, thinking he was Dennis Martin the actor. The man was just in the country trying to set up distribution of a drug called Stiffie! which made a man's johnson hard as sugar cane. Chac Mool was the only *republicano* that believed in the sales and profit potential of Stiffie!

"He was not," said Chac. "But he did look like one."

"What happened to Esteefi! the drug to make your manhood?" William illustrated the question with a tight fist held near his waist. "Hard as a cane of sugar," he added.

"I sell it in my *botica*, my stall in the market."

"With your secret Indian potions?"

"Yes, it sells very well. Mostly to women, married women."

"Why is that?"

"The men will not buy. You know what they say. *Republicanos* are hung like a horse!"

"*Jajajaja* ..." both men enjoyed a good laugh.

"Quiet, Chac! Look."

Through the window they saw a man, a *gringo* in desert camouflage arguing with a Laotian Admiral in front of an outhouse repurposed as a customs shed. The admiral was pointing to a very large book under the agent's right arm and making stabbing motions like he was murdering someone.

"We are just in time; my family hut is further up on the left. Drop me off, hide the Buick, wait before heading back."

------

[1] See "The Kidnapping of Dennis Martin," by the author. Available at finer bookstores.

"Are you sure? I can wait for you. Those boys have guns. They are young and crazy, who knows what that *loco* will do. It is going to get dangerous *miy broder*."[2]

"It is okay, William. These are the ancestral lands of my people, the Descalsos. We will be safe, but you need to drive back to La Capital before this ship sinks. Just park it over there under that hut on stilts, wait a bit so Steele will not see. Then head back to La Capital. Tell Paola, only Paola, that all is well." With that, Chac Mool took the paper bag with the wads of *tucanes* and began to get out of the car. After a second's hesitation, he reached into the bag, removed one of the stacks and handed it through the rolled down window to William.

"For you, *amigo*, you deserve something."

"Thank you, Chac, I am grateful." As Chac got out and began walking toward his family's hut, William placed the stack neatly next to the one from Paola. He drove through the stilts under the other hut and waited in the dark shade. When the time was right the Buick struggled to hurry home: William had urgent business in La Capital.

A small boy about five or six, dark and tall and very lean with bright intelligent eyes came out and smiled, "*Hola, Tío Chac.*" He ran up to his uncle and hugged the healer around the knees. "What did you bring me, *tío?*"

"I am sorry, Conejo.[3] Nothing today. I came on important business. You can help. Do you want to help your *tío?* There are men coming to Aguacate to hurt the men in the village, do you know those men in the village? The one they call Yunior, he is not old, but his other friends the *viejos* who are always together?"

---

2 My brother.
3 Rabbit. The boy's name.

"Yes, I know Yunior! He gives me books and pencils and paper and teaches me to write *en inglés*![4] I have seen his books. I know he is meeting with the others right now. They are watching the television! He lets me see it sometimes. They have cowboy shows, I know you do not like cowboy shows *Tío* Chac, but there is only one channel. Yunior says that in England that have TWO channels! What it would be like to live in a place with two channels on the television?"

"Slow down, Conejo," Chac said, stifling a laugh. He loved the boy's enthusiasm about everything and would normally let the kid go on but had other things on his mind. Chac was furious at Mandamás and others like him putting people at risk just to create a distraction from their incompetence and mismanagement. A lot was at stake, Chac feared. Not just the harm to Piojo's gang of street kids, but the other hapless victims in the CIA agent's self-aggrandizing mission — the kind old men in the club who often bought books, magazines, and school supplies for the children of the village.

"Go now, quickly, bring my brothers to our hut. Fast! Do not talk. Just tell them to come here. ¡*Vete*!" He watched the boy run to one of the huts and slam the door as he entered.

The door to his own hut opened and a woman who looked much like his mother Mrs. Mool stepped out. She wasn't smiling, however, and her old face looked wrinkled and worried. "Chac, I sense bad things. This morning the runes were troublesome. Why are you here? Are you …"

"*No tía, nada.* I am fine. *Pero* look there is a crazy *americano*, CIA (she gasped) coming with some armed men. Children actually. It is Piojo and his street boys —"

---

[4] In English.

As they walked together into the hut, she spoke with worry in her voice. "I know that Piojo! Poor child is always doing that Tirofijo's bidding. My sister says the poor boy worships Tirofijo. *Qué pena.* A great shame. And now what is Tirofijo up to with the CIA? This is the devil's business, Chac."

"Tirofijo is not involved, *tía.* For once. No he is in La Capital and very busy stealing chicken money."

Chac's aunt came up to him and held her arm way up (she was much shorter) to feel his forehead with the back of her hand. "*Tienes fiebre?*[5] Let me get some Vaporú[6] then you tell me about this chicken money."

"No fever. And no time to explain. It is worse now *mi tía.* Piojo and his gang have been armed with guns! And I fear they are going to attack Izquierdo Yunior and his friends. The man leading them is disillusioned enough to do so."

"Ridiculous, those *viejos* just sit around and read crazy stories and tell lies. Why would the *gringos* even care?"

"Yes, they are harmless, I know. But this *gringo*, the Kiwi Airways pilot is actually a CIA man (she gasped anew) and he is attacking Yunior because the *comemierda* says the old men are communists."

"*Sobrino,*[7] this sounds like boys, dangerous boys with dangerous toys, just wanting something to do!"

"Worse, I think Mandamás is behind it. He needs a miracle, a distraction to make himself look good. La República is a big mess thanks to that *bruja* he is married to with her crystals and religions. A defeat of a communist, eh, sleeper cell I think it is called, would

---

[5] Do you have a fever?

[6] Vicks VapORub. The go-to panacea from Puebla to Punta Arenas.

[7] Nephew.

make the *gringos* very happy. Happy *gringos*, happy dollars, happy dictator. But I have a plan to scare them away so that no-one gets hurt."

Five young men entered the hut, shuffling their feet and with a look of excitement on the faces. Rabbit had concocted some Cowboy and Indian fairytale to get them moving quickly and so they arrived a bit out of breath. All were obvious kin to Chac Mool: lanky, tall, athletic. Although similar in size and mien, they had different tastes in fashion. Chac Mool, himself, always wore a Lakers jersey, but with the other men in the room it looked like an NBA all-star game. The Bulls, Knicks, Celtics, and Spurs were all represented. The only outlier was Chac's rather heavyset brother, "Rocket," who wore a well-worn Montreal Canadiens hockey sweater. It had been a gift from a foreign priest that used to visit Aguacate Province. The quintet acknowledged Chac simultaneously with a silent nod from each. Chac was highly respected in the Descalso tribal village, and they sensed he was there on important business.

"*Hermanos*. We have little time. The CIA is coming to attack our friends in the book club. Something about *comunistas*, a sleeper cell, the usual nonsense. They come armed and are very near."

"*Qué chingados*? You mean The Culture Club?" Asked the Spur.

The Bull quickly added "Those are just old men. They help our kids with books and give to help the schools!" The men were incensed.

"*¡Mierda!*"[8]
"*¡Mierda!*"
"*¡Mierda!*"
"*¡Merde!*"

---

[8] Shit.

Everyone looked at the native *Descalso* tribesman in Canadien sweater. "Just practicing for the *padre* …"

The Celtic brought everyone back to reality, "What can we do? We only have a few blow guns and bows for hunting in the forest. We cannot fight *gringos* with guns!" The All Stars concurred heartily shaking their heads and making bow and arrow motions, mimicking being shot by M1 Garand rifles, falling to the ground, bleeding out. The All Stars tended to be dramatic.

Chac held up a hand to stop the histrionics and silence them. "We are talking about boys on an adventure. I think they will be easily scared if that *estúpido* Esteeve Steele doesn't have them shooting their rifles.

"Here is what you do …" Chac's voice faded as he gave instructions to his kinsmen and passed out the last of the chicken money, giving each a similar stack. They left one at a time on their errands.

"Conejo," said Chac, "let us go and tell the old men to stay inside where it is safe."

"I do not think they will go anywhere, they were watching a film and talking about Marx on the *televisora*."

"Really? A TV show about Karl Marx? *Puta madre,* maybe they **are** communists. No matter, let us go."

Chapter 25

Bar Cinco Estrellas

"Those *jueputas*! They did it again. Two-nil! And where my dear Izquierdo, was the great Gómez? The fabulous new netminder that would stop every ball coming off the feet of the Corinthians? Those goat rapers. You said he was a crack![1] He did not even show up!"

"He had diarrhea, Ugarte, from a bad *baleada*. How was I to know that a bad *baleada* would be to blame?"

"From La Tuerta?" Wulther piped in as he was pouring another two fingers of Canadian Club for the chuckling defrocked priest eavesdropping from his near barstool. Father Flynn was greatly amused by the conversations gleaned over a glass of Canadian Club, particularly when they involved the two most self-important individuals in La República. His only entertainment were the goings on in the bar of the five-star Hotel Cinco Estrellas and he was seldom disappointed.

"Of course not!" Answered an indignant Ugarte. "La Tuerta only serves the best *baleada* in La Capital. This is a known fact! I have even mentioned it in my column. And she doesn't wrap them in newspaper, either. *Qué asco.*[2] La Tuerta's *baleadas* are even blessed by the Better Business Bureau —"

Izquierdo would not be sidelined from the issue at hand, that of the ignominy of falling, yet again, to rival Corinto. "Enough with the *pinches baleadas.* Corinto, those sons of whores, beat us again. It is a disgrace. I tell you, a goddam disgrace!"

---

[1] Really good.
[2] How disgusting.

"You have seen nothing, Señor Izquierdo. There is a bigger disgrace in La Provincia de Aguacate!"

The statement came from the front door, which had been slammed open by a slim wide-shouldered figure with very nice breasts. The men, including Wulther behind the bar, turned their heads in one motion like swimmers in a Busby Berkeley number. They faced her and acknowledged her presence.

"Paola."

"P-p-Paola!"

"Paola?"

"*Sacre bleu*, Paola!"

"Yes, it is me Paola Labios, *chicos*, and this is a dark day in the History of La República!"

"Worse than October 27 —"

"Shut up, Ugarte! What are you talking about, Paola? Are they closing the Happy Fish?"

"No *pendejo*. Sit down. We have to talk. Wulther, get me a *gintoniq*[3] if you please. That Esteeve Steele …"

All of La Capital, it seemed, was aware of the falling out between Paola and the pilot. In the bar the men, except for Father Flynn, gave a series of low whistles and inappropriate catcalls at the mention of the (part-time) prostitute's ex-lover. A number of knowing looks and a few obscene gestures were exchanged. Father Flynn tried to appear disinterested by focusing his attention on his breviary.

"*Babosos!* Shut up. This is serious. *Gracias,* Wulther." Paola hardly knew where to start, everything had been happening so fast: her ex-boyfriend arming Piojo's street urchins, the talk of communists, Mandamás' distraction and vulnerability, her theft of the chicken money, the upcoming clash in Aguacate province.

---

[3] Gin and tonic.

She sat down and crossed her legs which, thankfully, were sheathed in a pair of Levi's jeans and not a miniskirt or there might have been a fistfight. As it was, the men still elbowed one another to sit nearer to her or improve their line of sight.

As Paola began her briefing, the men became respectfully quiet. She told them about Crazy Esteve Steele, his new sidekick the hero-worshipping Piojo and his band of street ruffians, the approaching attack on the communists in Aguacate, the impending peril at the hands of Piojo's *pandilla*, his gang of delinquents. She had everyone's undivided attention. This was big!

As he listened to the trollop relate events that would change *republicano* history, Ugarte mused on rewriting his "History of La República." He would add this exciting chapter, history he would witness firsthand. The opening paragraph was already written in his mind, even before learning the details forthcoming from Paola. He considered writing it in the first person.

Across the small table, Izquierdo worried about his son Yunior off in the province armed with only volumes of Penguin Classics, the paperbacks! And seated up on his usual bar chair, Father Flynn said, "Let us bow our heads and —"

"*Padre* … do not start. I think Chac may be able to stand up to this CIA *sinverguenza*[4] and his 'battalion.' They are only boys, after all."

"But Paola, you said they have guns and you know how that Piojo is? He WILL order to shoot if the pilot tells him to."

"In any case, *señores*," she continued, "we have to trust Chac. If the CIA man and his little soldiers are defeated, they must come back to La Capital. Mandamás will not have his miracle, his victory! He will have to resign!"

---

[4] Man without shame.

"And what will happen then? The *gringos* will come again! They will occupy every inch of the republic. They will bring protestants and missionaries and mayonnaise and make us put aguacate on our toast."

"Actually according to the Constitution of 1935, which is still in force, we can —"

"Shut up, Ugarte!"

"Let him finish, Izquierdo."

Ugarte began again, "As you may remember from my 'History of La República,' the conservative coalition backed by the church (he gave a nod to Father Flynn who returned it respectfully) argued that —"

"Ugarte, please. The 'Selecciones Reader's Digest' version if you will." Izquierdo snapped, then added, for effect, "men's lives are at stake."

An unhappy Ugarte gave the mayor a look and turned to Paola. "We are supposed to have a Prime Minister. If Mandamás resigns he can turn power over to an Interim Prime Minister until such time as a universal plebiscite can be convened as long as it is within 30 days or not during the feast of La Virgen de Aguacate, in which case —"

Paola raised her hand palm out. "Got it. *Chicos* we must move fast. First, we must isolate Mandamás from his insane wife and her so-called monk Gregorio. That is the only way to get him to resign — a one-on-one confrontation. If she is present, with all her witchcraft he will not dare defy her. On the other hand, if she is not there … well, I will get Mandamás to resign. I know a few secrets about him that he, shall I say, does not want Ugarte to publish in his column! He will sign." Paola Labios smiled proudly.

A round of guffaws, indecent hip thrusts, and backslapping lightened the mood again. They suspected what secrets Paola had stored away. She was going to make the dictator an offer he couldn't refuse.

Wulther, serving another round of drinks from his tray, asked, "But how will you isolate *La Bruja* Rosemary?"

"Consultations, *mae*. Consultations."

"*¿Cómo que* consultations ?" Came the men's chorus.

"That *pendeja* cannot resist giving her 'consultations' with her beads and crystals and that foreigner, that old Russian chanting '*oy vey*.' Those two live for that and asking her for a *consulta,* a spiritual consultation will feed her ego. I have a plan that will have her tied up doing consultations all day with my own brigade. Then I can get Mandamás alone and get him to sign on the line which is dotted."

Just then the door to the Bar Cinco Estrellas was flung open like a scene in a bedroom farce. Into the bar marched a dozen purple-clad women of various ages twirling amethyst-beaded necklaces and crowned with the cheap plastic tiaras First Lady Rosemary sold wholesale. The men stared. And stared. Paola announced, "Here is my plan! *Señores*, I present to you the Colegio James Monroe Parents Association!"

"Manifest Destiny!" the women shouted as one.

"*Mon dieu*, God save us all."

Chapter 26

At the Palace

They say leadership is lonely. Try being a dictator with a nagging wife, a crumbling country, a losing soccer team, rising discord, and a demand for rights, when all you want is to schtup your secretary and sneak in a set of tennis. That's lonely.

Máximo Mandamás, La República's Dictator-for-Life, supreme leader and staunch ally of the United States of America was down in the goddam dumps. He paced his office and looked out of his custom floor-to-ceiling Andersen windows, a gift from the United Avocado Co., and saw the gray-black skies that meant the rainy season was near. He needed to talk to someone who understood him. The talk with Paola at the Happy Fish had been unsatisfying. He would never be able to stand up to his wife's hectoring. He needed a sympathetic ear.

"Güicho!"

"*Sí, suegro?*" Responded the First Son-in-Law opening the door to his closet halfway as he leaned back in his office chair to look out.

"It is Generalíssimo! How many times —. Forget it. Just get me my friend Larree on the phone."

"Larry Muncie, *sueg* — Generalíssimo? In Indiana City?"

"Yes, imbecile! Larree Muncie. *Coño*, how many Larrees do I know?"

"Okay, let me try."

While the generalíssimo waited, he strode across a room the size of Madison Square Garden over to his little bar, the feeling of his brass spurs dragging fresh grooves into the polished wooden floor was very satisfying. At the bar he reached for the bottle of Ron

Aniversario Centenario, the good stuff, and poured a couple of shots into a crystal tumbler with a monogram, HCE, etched elegantly into its side. He pulled once at the drink and smacked his lips. "Ahh."

He walked back over to his desk, erect and soldier-like, and sat. And waited. And waited …

"¡Güicho!" *What is that incompetent son-in-law doing?*"

"¿¿¿Güichooooo??? *Deja de manotear tus huevos.*[1] Where is my call?"

"One moment."

Güicho went back to his phone and picked up the receiver.

"… you son of a bitch! How's it hangin'? I haven't heard from you in a coon's —"

"Please hold for El Generalísimo Máximo Mandamás …"

"Goddammit Karen. I told you not to pass the call until you have Max on the blower. I don't talk to underlings!"

"Hello? Larree?"

"Yeah, this is Larry. That you Max? Jesus Milhous Christ, what the hell is going on? I'm hearing things up here in Indiana City that I don't believe. Is it true about some kind of Rooskie monk your ball-and-chain hired to teach her some kind of new age shit? Really? People gotta wear quartz jewelry and such?"

"No quartz, amethyst."

"Amethyst. What kind of gay shit is that? And no red lights? Only green? And those crazy holidays? Who gives a rat's ass about the equa …. equo… uh, solstice? Max you're losing control. You are the dictator of La República and a staunch defender of freedom and American Interests, backed by the full faith and credit of the U. S. of A. You need to whip that horse, start riding it again."

---

[1] Stop touching your balls.

Mandamás, who was afraid of horses, didn't understand the homey American metaphor but was happy to hear a sympathetic voice. "*Amigo* Larree, so good to listen to jou talk. Jes it is bad may fren'."

"How come you're talking like that Max? All Republican like?"

"*Republicano*. Yes sorry. I slipped. Larree things might go bad here. There are *comunistas* in Aguacate Province and unless I defeat them I may have to not be so benevolent anymore."

"Communists? Communists are bad for business amigo. Like that Castro guy in… in… in, well I forget where he is. But like him. Bad for American Interests too. We here at Pills! have a lot of interest in La República, you can be sure of that. What do you need buddy? More Stiffie!² samples? I can send down more samples on the next flight! Make your cane pole sit up and take notice."

"No, Larree. I just need a friend to talk to. And maybe open up a bank account for me up there. My wife controls the money in the palace and —"

"Say no more, amigo. I'll do what I can and as far as a friend, well you got one here buddy. Call me any goddam time. I have to let you go; my massage is here. Karen, my God girl you look —" and he hung up.

Why is he letting me go?

"¡¡Güicho!!"

"¿Sí, Generalíssimo?"

"Get me that half-wit at the American Embassy!"

"Which, *señor presidente*?"

"Sorry, they are bound to have several halfwits. I mean *Dos Vergas*, Two Dix. The Ambassador."

"Right away."

---

² An E.D. drug manufactured by Pills!, Larry's employer.

Güicho held the heavy black Lucite phone receiver to his ear and dialed the Embassy's four-digit number.

"American Embassy, how may I help you? For Spanish say 'trays.'"

"*Tres.*"

There was a slight pause, but no clicks or buzzing to indicate a new connection. "Americano Embassy-o, *cómo* yo help-o." It sounded like the same voice.

"*Embajador* Dix *por favor.*"

"Uno momento."

After a pause and a few muddy clicks, another voice demanded, "Yeah, what?"

"Embajador Dix por favor, Máximo Mandamás, Generalíssimo and Supreme Leader of La República is calling."

"Speaking."

Güicho was always impressed at the efficiency of *gringos.*

"One moment, *señor* embajador," He pressed a purplish button. "Excellency, I have the Ambassador."

"What took you so long? Hello, hello —"

"Hello?"

"Hello? Who is this?"

"Richard Dix? Who is this?"

"Generalíssimo Max Manda —"

"Oh, yes, general. What's up?"

"Generalíssimo. I am concerned, ambassador. No word from our man in Aguacate. It is very quiet. Too quiet. I cannot say more, the wires have ears. And the palace is full of deceit and conspiracy."

"Christ in a Corvette, you sound like a Russian novel. That smelly guy in the robes is getting to you. Take it from me, *compadre,* you gotta clean house over there, get rid of that mystic with his beard, beads, and all that other shit. They don't take to that in Foggy Bottom[3] you know what I'm saying?"

"Yes." (He didn't.)

"My instructions from D.C. are to tell you to get your house in order, Mandomass. You're skatin' on thin ice; you ain't the only bird dog in the kennel. Don't make us go to Plan B."

Mandamás heard the threat loud and clear although the reference to bird dogs was puzzling. He did not like it and was about to object when Dix went on to say, "Me and the little woman are going up to MidAmerica A&M for homecoming this week. Big game against Purdue, you understand. I'll be back in a week and expect things are normalized. The President of the United States is behind you! God Bless America!"

"*Sí, pero —*"

"And trust the CIA man, that Steve Steele he's the real deal, tops in his field. Gotta run!"

"Why is everybody so busy but me?" Mandamás sighed into the dead phone.

The Dictator-for-Life leaned back in his large chair, symbolic of the trappings of power that were slipping away. Too much depended on that lunatic Steve Steele, the lukewarm support from his old pal, and the *gringo* Two Dix with his hard ass diplomacy like some kind of folksy Teddy Roosevelt. It couldn't get worse.

"Generalíssimo, your wife on line two."

---

[3] A metonym for the State Department in Washington, DC.

Chapter 27

La Brigada Advances

"I don't see a thing!" Major Steve Steele stood on top of the hood of a Willys Jeep overlooking a tall field of corn. The Brigada Brayan Buenaventura was lost again. Piojo, his driver and corporal in the elite fighting cadre that was poised to eliminate the scourge of communism from the Province of Aguacate, sat looking at the solid west to east red line on the auto club map they were using for navigation. It was one of only two solid red lines, and it clearly led to the town of Aguacate.

"Send a squad, three men, put eyes on the ground, do some recon, clock the enemy, one click to our Charlie." Steele was impressed by his own military sounding gibberish. Just to be clear he asked Piojo, "Are we clear corporal?"

"*¿Qué?*"

"Piojo, don't question your major. Just send a couple two three of your guys that-a way, see what's there." He pointed east. It seemed random to Piojo who relayed his interpretation of the order to his crack squad.

"¡Cabrones! *¿Alguien sabe la salida al pueblo?*"[1]

The boys, the "men," were huddled in the empty Citroen still attached to the Jeep, playing a dice game for coins and cigarettes. Two or three brown arms emerged from the huddle all pointing north. As Steele climbed down from the hood, leaving size 10 boot-shaped dents, he told Piojo, "Wake me when our recon reports back," and settled into his backseat throne with his officer's

---

[1] Anyone know the way to the town?

cap over his face, careful to avoid painful contact with the purple-turned-black injury.

The corporal, knowing an opportunity when he saw one, motioned to his crew to take a rest before leaning back to take a little *siesta* himself.

⧗ ⧗ ⧗

Chac Mool knocked on the door to Izquierdo Yunior's house. He could hear the book club discussion going on. It sounded like one of them was making some sort of point, the others were quiet. Were they really *comunistas*, these harmless old men? They could get hurt, foolish *viejitos*. Chac eavesdropped for another minute or so before realizing it was the television they were watching and since it was in English, Chac had trouble understanding all the words. *It is that film about Karl Marx; it must be coming from the El Corinto television station!* He pressed his ear to the door, a scratchy voice from the TV said, "I can see you in the kitchen bending over a hot stove, but I can't see the stove." The Cultural Commune of Aguacate Province broke into hysterical laughter. Chac knocked.

"Come in," came the chorus within.

⧗ ⧗ ⧗

"Mayor! Mayor Steele, wake up. We have a report from the field." Steve Steele woke, got out of the vehicle to stretch his CIA legs, and looked grim, ready to receive bad news. "What's the report, corporal?"

"The men on recon, they say we are to head north."

"How far?"

"Two leagues," was Piojo's confident response although he had no idea how far that was. Neither did Steve.

"Any casualties, Piojo?"

"No, mayor. All the men returned alive. Thank the Virgen!"

"Yeah, whatever." Steele climbed back into the Jeep and sat erect in the back seat and pointing like General Patton barked, "Let's move out!" They moved in a northerly direction right into the field of maize. They were closing in on the book club, just not right away.

⧗ ⧗ ⧗

Chac was never able to describe the scene to his satisfaction. It was a bit bizarre even by *republicano* standards. There in the room were half a dozen older men, plus the younger Yunior whom he recognized. All were dressed alike: baggy black woolen pants with wide white piping, white dress shirts, a loosely tied cravat that hung down to the waist, jackets with long tails in the back, black horn-rimmed eyeglasses, and a black top hat. But the distinguishing characteristics they all shared were a wide grease paint moustache and tremendous black eyebrows. Each also wielded a long cigar, a Macanudo.

"*Señores*," the native began, "you are in great peril."

"Chac Mool! What a surprise. Welcome to our club. The Cultural Commune of Aguacate Province. Sit down we are enjoying some Marx —"

"That's the problem. You know I do not care what your politics are, but the *gringos* are not tolerating communism. They have conspired with the Generalíssimo to root out Marxism in the Province!"

"Groucho," said Yunior.

"Harpo," said another.

"Chico," joined in the rest.

Yunior explained, "we are watching the Marx BROTHERS my dear Chac, not the Karl Marx you are thinking of." The book club had a very good long laugh at that and began stomping around the room bent over at the waist, raising and lowering their eyebrows while flicking imaginary cigar ash which caused another round of laughter.

⧗   ⧗   ⧗

Reaching the outskirts of Aguacate, Steve Steele suddenly raised his right fist and ordered "halt-o!" Piojo jumped on the brakes with both feet, the Jeep slowed to a stop two yards later, followed by the Citroen full of the hardened cadre which, lacking brakes, slammed into the back of the Jeep, pitching Steve violently forward. The CIA agent's face and Willys Jeep windshield met at precisely the wrong intersection on the agent's forehead. What was a purple and black bump on the mend, immediately transformed into an ugly black and blue lump the size of an avocado pit that rose up volcanically on his right temple.

The pain blinded Steve and brought him to his knees where he took a moment to gather himself and egest a soliloquy of swears so profane that it wilted the leaves off a nearby Guanacaste tree (*Enterolobium cyclocarpum*). After a suitable time, he stood up again, though quite unsteadily, and put one finger on his discolored bump and another to his lips, "shhhhh."

He heard laughter.

"I hear laughter," he said.

"Shut up, brigadiers!" Piojo whisper-shouted.

⧗   ⧗   ⧗

Chac Mool had finished giving the details of the situation to the book club who now looked very worried at the prospect of a bunch of children with M1 rifles and orders to shoot from a deranged and self-delusional minor CIA agent. They could be outside their club house at any minute. Temples were sweating, grease paint was running down in black rivulets like the mascara on a jilted teenage girl. The TV set was turned off.

"What shall we do?"

"I think we will be okay. As you know my village is but two leagues away." The men nodded as they seemed to know what that meant. "I have given them instructions to bring the tribal warriors —"

"You have tribal warriors?"

"Well not really, it is the midnight basketball league. Keeps kids off the, uh, street. Anyway *señores*, the 'warriors' are very tall. Should scare the shit out of the *soldaditos* so they do not shoot. We do not want any shooting."

"No!"

"No!"

"No!!"

"Say the secret woid and you win fifty dollars!"

"Emilio!"

"I am sorry, it is just what would Groucho say."

⧖   ⧖   ⧖

Steele's hand-picked collection of quislings, the hardened cadre, had formed a semi-circle around the entrance to the house. Armed children with guns ready to do the bidding of the major. *I'll get a promotion out of this, for sure. Then they'll have to fly me up to Langley, to Company HQ! Fuck! My forehead huuurts!*

Piojo looked alert. He mused, *Tirofijo will see how brave I am and take me back. Then I will get rid of that Potro and his moto de mierda.*[2]

---

[2] Shit-cycle.

"Come out and nobody gets hurt!" the major bellowed through an orange traffic cone he had found in the hangar and stashed in the back of the Jeep. "We know of your illegal meeting! The Generalíssimo has authorized the Central Intelligence Agency, that is me, to commandeer your literature and disband this sleeper cell!"

"Mayor Esteeve …"

"Be quiet, Piojo. Be ready to give the order to the men to fire. When I give the order."

"You order me? Then I order them? Why not just order them?"

"Because we have to respect the chain of command corporal."

"Ok, mi mayor! Except for one thing."

"What is it? Can't you see we are in the *dénouement*, Piojo? It is the climax, the resolution of a chain of events. It is the *dénouement*. It is French!"

"Ah, I see."

"What were you going to say, corporal?"

"Just that we have no bullets in the guns."

"Well, Piojo, take charge and have the men load their guns," Steve said patiently. *Do I have to do everything?*

"I'll wait."

"Mayor, we have no bullets for the guns. There were no bullets in the shipment."

"Fuck me!"

Out from behind the house and behind the houses on each side emerged what looked like barefooted fierce Yanomami Indian warriors decked out in NBA jerseys wearing plastic feathers, day glo paint, shields, spears, bows and arrows, and magnificent head-dresses. They were very threatening to the CIA man: tall and athletic, were grouped into fivesomes and ready to let fly their sharp weapons. As the warriors babbled angrily in some ancient tongue they raised their weapons showing fierceness and resolve to protect the old men inside. As any moviegoer will tell you, Indians with spears and arrows surrounded by huts in a humid rain forest spelled trouble; big trouble to Steele who hesitated to order a charge, advance, enfilade, or some such military-sounding maneuver.

"Put down those guns, *niños*. Throw them over there in a pile." It was Chac standing in the doorway and speaking to the hardened cadre of street children. "Piojo, come inside. You! *Gringo*! You stay here or my warriors will make you so full of holes with their weapons you will leak for the rest of your life."

Steele sat dispiritedly on the ground and waited, disgraced. So despondent was the failed major that he did not even notice the warriors were just adolescents and young men a bit older than his own hardened cadre; that their arrows were just wooden dowels used to mix paint, their shields *papier-mâché*, with broom handles for spears, and Authentic Apache Headdresses by Mattel. He had been defeated by a costumed cadre.

Inside, the dressing-down began. Chac was fond of Piojo and took a tough love approach with the lad. "Piojo, what is this! You put these beggars in danger! *¿Qué te pasa?* This is your tribe; you should be taking care of them. Instead you listen to that character, that *gringo* and his stupid ideas? What if they HAD bullets?"

Head down in shame, Piojo blubbered, "I know, I know. It is just that I was caught up in the moment. I wanted to do something big. Like Captain Freedom! And Tirofijo, you know …"

"What about Tirofijo?"

"He does not trust his Piojo anymore. He is more interested in getting that Potro and his *puto moto* to steal the chicken money!" Poor Piojo was close to tears. Chac softened his tone, "*Mira* Piojo. Come back with us. I do not think Tirofijo will have any more chicken money."

"You do not?"

"No I do not. You belong with him, not this fascist fanatic. He needs to go back to flying that airplane, you need to go back to *El Escondite*. Go back and tell your gang, they look up to you. You are their Tirofijo."

"Really, Chac?"

"Yes, really. Now go back and disband your brigade, I will take care of Steele.

Outside Piojo addressed what was left of the Brigada Brayan Buenaventura as some had run away. "*Chicos. Lo siento.* Our work here is finished. Let us go back to La Capital and … where are Brian, Bryon, Byron, and the other Byron?"

"They are staying, they say they miss home and their village is near," said one of the remaining gamins. "Do we walk, Piojo?"

"Anyone need a taxi?" It was William, who had been watching the proceedings from behind a *ceiba* tree unseen by the *dramatis personae*. He pulled up to Yunior's club house alongside the Jeep and its trailer. He was Buick-less. Instead he was driving a slightly used Lincoln Town Car large enough to fit Tirofijo's desk. As he watched the kids pile into the Town Car, Piojo grinned widely. It was a smile two leagues wide. The brigade arranged themselves on the floor and the faux leather bench seat. Piojo sat up front, next to the pugilist.

"Well done, William! Go to the Hotel Cinco Estrellas, give this note to Paola from Yunior. She must get the news of what has happened right away! Then take Piojo and the boys back to The Hideout. I will deal with … *con esta mierda*,"[3] Chac said waiving a long brown hand at the frightened *gringo*.

---

[3] With this shit.

William engaged the massive engine in his transport and drove away with the remainder of the former Brigada Brayan Buenaventura.

"Go home, *Capitán*. I'm sorry but you must take the bus. I will disband my legion of warriors, but you must wait here for the bus. You should be back in time for your flight."

"But my flight is tomorrow. What about the Jeep?"

"The Jeep is evidence of your treachery!" Chac then faced his costumed warriors and gave them a proud look, "Guerreros of Aguacate, I salute you! *Ciao chicos*, see you on the courts." The high fiving, low fiving, fist bumping midnight basketball league of Aguacate shuffled off to their homes, huts, and hovels. They looked magnificent in their get-ups which they refused to take off for days, even when engaged in midnight basketball.

"*Comuna Cultural*, I return you to your, eh, Marxism. I also suggest you change your name, you know how *gringos* are so trigger-happy and ready to kill the communists they think are behind every tree. Anyway, I must go too. It is time —."

"Time flies like an arrow; fruit flies like a banana," one of the Marxists quipped, causing a new eruption of slapstick stoop-shouldered marching around the room. The television was turned on anew, catching the signal from Voice of America, and showed the start of "A Day At The Races," a Marxist Classic.

Chac Mool climbed in and started the Jeep. He made a wide circle and raced out of town as fast as possible with the empty Citroen still in tow. Something caught his eye and he reversed the maneuver to return to the circle of huts. The Jeep came to rest at the stop where Steve Steele was waiting for the bus to La Capital.

"*Señor* Steele."

Steve flinched when he saw Chac behind the wheel of the Jeep. But Chac was smiling. Perhaps he had reconsidered and was going to offer the airline pilot a ride back to the city.

"You forgot this," Chac said, throwing down a very large object on the dusty road and then driving off with the Citroen behind him kicking up a cloud of dust. Steve Steele and The Complete Works of William Shakespeare (Fully Annotated) were left waiting for the bus to La Capital.

Chapter 28

William Returns

The Lincoln Town Car, a cobalt blue beast, boasted a 3.5-liter, V-6 engine generating the power of 365 horses. Possibly the most powerful vessel on wheels in all of La República. William, finally behind a wheel of a car as responsive as the girls at the Happy Fish, maneuvered the beast over International Highway Number Two like he was delivering life-saving cold cuts to a rugby team stranded in the Andes.

His charges, Piojo beside him on the front seat and the seven or eight street children who were oblivious to the meaning of what had happened in the last 24 hours, bouncing around in the back. They played with the electric windows until one stayed in the open position. Then they hung their heads out like dogs and shouted obscenities at cars, trucks, and pedestrians as they zoomed past. What a day! First the uniforms, then the *baleadas*, then the adventure with that *gringo*, those wild Indians, and now this?! Yippppp-peeeee!

William was happy to see them having a good time because he had often observed them in La Capital and knew their life on the streets could be cruel and hard. *I hope Tirofijo will take care of them.*

Piojo, up front, looked distractedly out the clear window. His brow was tightly knitted. He was thinking.

At the first intersection, William stopped even though the light was green and not wanting to get hit in his new car on its first day. The noise from the back seat had abated so he looked in the rearview mirror to do a quick check on the street urchins. They were gone. First chance they got in La Capital, they opened the doors and went back to the streets. William hadn't even heard them get out of the car. He was touched with a bit of sadness when he realized the kids had run off, he couldn't exactly tell why he felt that way. He drove on, with Piojo still sitting very quietly beside him leading William to wonder what was going through Piojo's mind.

Piojo was thinking hard, unsure of what to do. He didn't know what Tirofijo's response would be since Piojo had left him in the lurch first to curl up with the adventure comics and then off on his own adventure with Major Steele. His emotions were an admixture of regret, shame, despair, and even fear. Would Tirofijo send him back to the street?

They were close enough to Tirofijo's place to walk, so Piojo said to William, "On the corner, please."

Soon after leaving Piojo on the corner, the newish Town Car pulled up proudly, majestically to the front door of the Bar Cinco Estrellas. The ex-boxer got out, slammed the driver-side door which closed with the sound of a bank vault and looked at the beautiful product of America's love affair with the automobile, "*¡Que nave!*"[1]

He entered the bar where Ugarte, Izquierdo, Wulther, Paola, and a bunch of ladies dressed in purplish outfits, were sitting quietly. There was tension in the air. It was Wulther who first noticed William, "Did anyone order a taxi?" The assembled all looked up, first at Wulther and then the cab driver just inside the front door.

"William!" Paola jumped to her feet. She had not seen the man since putting the chicken money in his hands and sending him off to take Chac Mool to Aguacate. "*Estás bien?* William, why are you smiling? Did you get to Aguacate?"

"How is my son, how is Yunior?"

"Do I need to rewrite my History of La República?"

---

[1] What a yacht.

William waved them off and continued to smile. "Your son is fine Izquierdo; I saw him myself. Yes, Ugarte you will need to do a lot of writing, but not yet. It is not over. Paola, this is for you." The taxi driver handed Paola an envelope. It was the one given to him by Chac Mool just before he left Aguacate. It was from Yunior.

"It is from Yunior!" Paola began. She read on, holding the sheet and trembling with excitement. Her head began moving back and forth across the page like a spectator at a tennis match. "He says nothing happened to them in the book club —"

"*Gracias a dios*," said the communist mayor. He was an atheist but still believed in hedging his bets.

"He says that Chac Mool stood up to Esteeve Steele —" She suddenly dropped her hand with the letter and angrily spit out, "—*ese malparido, le voy a cortar los huevos.*"[2]

"Paola."

"What? Ugarte. What?"

"The letter."

"Oh, yes. Well listen to this. Great news everybody. It says that Chac and his band of warriors, armed with toy weapons, faced down the CIA agent, that is the son of a whore Esteeve, and disarmed his men. Disarmed his men? *¿Qué* men, William?"

"Only Piojo's band of beggars."

"Those poor boys," said Ugarte angrily.

"*Sí*, they were seduced by the adventure of it all." William clarified, "They are back safe. I drove them back myself. Well a few stayed in Aguacate to move back in with their families and I dropped Piojo near Tirofijo's Hideout. But they are all safe. Finish the letter, Paola."

"It only says, 'You must act fast! Do what you have to do!'" Paola lowered the letter to her side once again and repeated

---

[2] The bad man. I'll cut his balls off.

Yunior's directions. "We must act fast! This could be the end of the dictatorship!"

There followed what is known as known in literature as the pregnant pause. It started slowly, then began to expand, until … in a burst of excitement everybody started speaking at once, shouting speculations as to what needed to happen next! It was a happy panic in a place where nothing interesting ever seemed to happen. But something was about to happen, something that would change the course of history in the small country. It was Ugarte who was the first to sense the historical import of the moment at hand. He stood on his chair like a true statesman and held up a sheaf of papers that he produced from the inside of his English-wool jacket. "¡*Señores!* Ahem. ¡*Y señoras!* Our destiny is at hand. I have here the Constitution of 1935, which is still in force. It calls for the succession of power to an Interim Prime Minister to be signed by the current head of state, namely Máximo Mandamás. The interim Prime Minister's name to be entered here on this last page."

This came as a shock to the gathering. Time ceased to exist at that moment in the Bar Cinco Estrellas. Wulther stopped making cocktails, the Colegio James Madison Parents Association ceased breathing, Izquierdo was caught frozen in mid gesture, Father Flynn looked at his empty glass, William was barely moving. A bright yellow lizard looked up from a small dollop of spilled daiquiri it was sipping. You could have heard a pin drop.

This was truly an historical moment, the opportunity to shed the yoke of an oppressive dictatorship and replace it with … well with something, no one was quite certain. However, all were wondering the same thing, whose name should be written in? There was not a man in the bar who didn't picture their own name on the page, their own self in the Presidential Palace ordering the servants around. Who would be up to the task of cleaning house? Who would become the first Prime Minister of La República since the assassination of the last Prime Minister back in 1936?

Each potential candidate, from Izquierdo to Ugarte and even to Father Flynn, wondered if they would be the next leader of La República.

Chapter 29

Back at the Hideout

Tirofijo Gómez Gómez y Gómez, the roofied racketeer, woke up in a tepid pool of his own drool. He lifted his head off the desk a little too quickly and felt a pain in his head like his brain was trying to get out with a ball-peen hammer. He had slept like a dead man and lost a full day.

"What happened?" He said out loud instantly regretting it. It came out as a scream. A car passed on the street outside the hideout sounding like A.J. Foyt on the straightaway at the Indy 500. A fly was rudely walking very loudly across his desk. Swallowing hurt. Blinking hurt. Even thinking hurt.

Somehow the ruthless gangster managed to get to his feet and walk in a stooped-bent fashion. Just the thought of standing straight up frightened him. It felt like an hour later before he made it to the bathroom and, once inside, to the sink where he turned on the faucet and drank long and deep directly from the tap. It helped. Fully eight percent of his faculties were recovered.

It seemed like the return to his desk occupied another painful hour. He sat, flicked on his favorite lamp that was in the shape of a woman's leg in fishnet stocking. ¡*Coño*! The light speared into the back of his occipital lobe like a very frozen icicle, so he quickly flicked it off. The room was dark again (*ah, much better*) so Tirofijo rested his pounding skull on his crossed arms. ¡*Coño*! *Why is my desk wet?*

Rising again, a painful maneuver, he managed to make it to his bed and lay down. The waterbed's patented "motion of the ocean" gave him a bit of nausea but eventually the bed returned to calmer seas. He went over his last actions, what he could remember. It hurt to think but one thing lingered in his mind. Then it hit him.

"Paola!" He said out loud and sat straight up — an act which nearly killed him. The Rohypnol had made him dizzy and nauseous. Events of the previous night fuzzily projected in his head like an old black and white TV with a bad signal. He fell back on his bed which made him seasick on top of everything else.

Things became clearer bit by bit. *Paola. Her perfume and that blouse, and that skirt, oh those boots of Chinese plastic. Nails just like I like. And her tetas ¡por Dios! We smoked like lovers … then we … did we? I do not think we did!*

"Paola!" More pain, now mixed with anger. "*Esa puta*!" Still confused but now disturbed about something else that was nagging the back of his addled brain. He wasn't quite sure, but there was something wrong. Another bent-over walk to his office desk and there! *The safe is open! The chicken money! That trollop has taken my tucanes. Puta madre!*

Sitting at his desk once again, Tirofijo ignored the expanding tidal puddle of saliva as things came into focus. He had been seduced by Paola Labios and robbed. *Robbed! In this world you could not trust your friends anymore. Yes she is a prostitute, but is there no honor?*

Thump, thump, thump, squish. Thump, thump, thump, squish. Thump, thump, thump, squish. Tirofijo looked around his office to see what the noise was about. Thump, thump, thump, squish. It was Tirofijo. He had been drumming his fingers thinking of his next move.

"What is she up to? Where is Piojo? Oh my head." Once king of the underworld, such as it was, Tirofijo was now down to the felt, out of chips. No money for financing. Piojo, his most reliable confederate, his aide-de-camp, was missing. And the rent, dear God, the rent. Violeta was sure to begin pressuring him.

He still had his contraband business, yes, and there was a box of the indigenous mud dolls with pre-Columbian erections packed and ready for the gringo museums and art galleries. He had to get them on the next flight. *Where the hell is that pip-squeak Piojo?*

"Okay get a hold of yourself … maybe a little Ron Aniversario. What the hell are these? Champagne flutes?" When a man realizes the treachery of being roofied, he starts talking to himself out loud. He changes in other ways as well. He becomes wary and cynical, much more cynical. Such a change came over Tirofijo. "Never again trust a woman! I must steady my nerves." So he took a shot, maybe a shot and a half, straight out of the bottle of Ron Aniversario. To be safe.

"*Mejor*, I feel better. Just need a little more rest. Maybe a couple of Mejorales.[1] A little nap, then go to the airport with the box of horny little mud men."

Tirofijo went back to bed.

---

[1] Mejoral is a top selling aspirin.

Chapter 30

The Constitution of 1935

"**P**eople, people!"

Sounding like a movie director clamoring for attention during the barroom fight scene, Ugarte was slapping his hand and yelling. He held aloft the document that would change the fate of each and every one; it was the sacred Constitution of 1935, the one still in force, the one that had a provision that stated the government could be put in the hands of a Prime Minister (Interim) and wrest control from the grip of the Dictator-for-Life and, even better, from the bony hands of his wife. "We must act, gentlemen! Our nation's future is at hand, men," the journalist proclaimed, fully ignoring Paola and the other women in attendance.

He added, "La República needs a strong hand to take the reins and sail her up the river of prosperity, leading the march to a bright future." Not put off by the mixed metaphors of land and sea, all seemed to be in full agreement. All included the usual crowd plus the ladies group, Paola, a Shirley Temple, a martini straight up, a vodka cranberry, a rum and coke, and a Tom Collins. The place was packed.

"We need a confident man, a man like Garcilaso Gómez!" Ugarte proposed half-heartedly, secretly hoping someone would put his name, Ugueth Ugarte historian, journalist, patriot into the offing. "After all, his uniforms bespeak of a man of great importance," he added unconvincingly.

One of the regulars, the martini straight up, said "Do not be a pandering fool, Ugarte. Gómez is a nobody. We need a man who knows how to command people who is respected and well known in the community. A real man. Virile, hung like a horse. Tirofijo, for instance."

The vodka cranberry sitting at the end of the bar quipped, "That mafioso? Over my dead body."

"I am sure Tirofijo could arrange that." Returned the martini, smiling at his audience knowing he landed a good one. General mirth confirmed it and after a lot of laughter and nudging of elbows there followed another call for drinks. Wulther was at the ready; ice cracked, liquor blended, spirits poured. The men resumed slaking their throats while the women watched quietly; ignored in the proceedings. With renewed energy the men commenced different points of view and each being shot down in turn.

"A merchant is needed, commerce is the future, someone adept in business. Tirso could lead us." This suggestion came from the vodka cranberry who was miffed at being a foil for the martini.

"Tirtho? You mean El Chino? That ith outrageouth."

"Did he say 'outrageouth?'" one of the women asked.

The remark came from Izquierdo who tended to lisp when tipsy or extremely agitated.

"He ith a foreigner," Izquierdo clarified after pouring another daiquiri down his throat, ignoring the fact that Tirso was as much a *republicano* as anyone else in the bar.

Wulther volunteered his opinion while shaking a new batch of daiquiris (they were flowing like water during the summer rains). "No *señores*, it must be someone humble, a man of the people. Like Chac Mool."

The suggestion met with a nodding of heads and some tete-a-tete discussion between the bar patrons. In the corner Paola and her PTA kept out of the political fray and chatted quietly amongst themselves.

"A man of the cloth, *amigos*. It should be Father Flynn."

Honored, Father Flynn bowed to the Tom Collins sitting against the wall who had made suggestion and raised his breviary. "*Mon ami*, I —"

Izquierdo downed his fresh cocktail and cut the priest off. "He cannot! He ith a *gringo*."

"No he is Canadian I think," said the Tom Collins.

Ugarte, wanting to maintain the upper hand as the chief parliamentarian announced, "That is a type of *gringo*. Besides the Constitution of 1935 outlaws clergy in government."

"Thank you for that clarification, Ugarte. I think the man is right here." Heads turned in the direction of the rum and coke who had been sitting quietly, sharing a table with the Tom Collins. Ugarte looked hopeful.

"We are overlooking one who is amongst us who would be a formidable Prime Minister (Interim)." Added the rum-and-coke.

Ugarte straightened up, ready to receive the nomination from the rum-and-coke, followed by the accolades of his peers. The speaker polished off his rum-and-coke and said, "I am speaking of course, of Wulther," pointing to the bartender in mid swizzle.

"Wulther? As Prime Minister? Are you insane? Who will pour us drinks? Who will dispense daiquiris?" This comment was made with universal approval and nodding of heads. Who, indeed?

"How about William?" Someone offered.

"William? The strain of office would kill him. He is too nervous. No offense, William."

"None taken."

"Piojo?" Came a weak suggestion from the Shirley Temple.

"Have you taken leave of your senses?" It was Paola interjecting from her seat in the corner with the PTA. "A street urchin? Tirofijo's deputy would be beholden to the mafioso himself. You might as well elect Tirofijo. Anyway he is too young to vote."

This unleashed a hubbub of conversation, draining of cocktails, sounds of ice in empty glasses, and the reordering of fresh rounds of drinks. As Wulther distracted everyone from the debate and served rounds of daiquiris, Tom Collins, martinis, vodka cranberries, rums-and-coke, and one Shirley Temple, a strong voice rose from the chaos, "I nominate Ugarte!" Conversation ceased like the sudden closing of a spicket. Heads turned toward the speaker.

"Ugarte? You nominate yourself?"

"Well, yes. It was I, after all, that produced the Constitution of 1935 from the archives. It is I who is the most knowledgeable about the history of La República. Have you read my book?"

"Enough!" All eyes were on the tall indigenous man who had slipped into the bar quietly and was standing near the door with his hand in the air.

"Yes? You wish to speak?" Asked the journalist.

"I nominate the Mayor. I nominate Rafael Izquierdo!" It was Chac Mool who said this, pointing to the drunken closet communist and rumored owner of the Happy Fish. "I second the nomination," said the journalist resignedly. "Oh what a chapter this will make! The first communist Prime Minister of La República. Oh, the irony! But we must move fast," he added as he stepped down from the chair clasping the constitutional document to his chest.

Everyone was in quick agreement. Izquierdo was a known entity, respected, and a hero-by-proxy as it had been his son who had resisted the Brigada Brayan Buenaventura. "I humbly accept, *theñores*, what is our next thtep Ugarte? What does the Conthtitution thay."

"It is simply a matter of getting Máximo Mandamás to sign over the government to you, Izquierdo. There is space for your name, here. Just take this to the Presidential Palace, have him sign on the line which is dotted."

"He cannot go to the palace; he will be shot on sight. I heard the guards discuss this when I led the protest against the new tax on *baleadas*. They would kill Izquierdo, that is a fact." Paola spoke with alarm.

"Is that true, Paola?" The priest asked in dismay.

"Is what true, Father?"

"About the tax. On *baleadas* of all things. Because —"

"Of course, it is true. Also about shooting Mayor Izquierdo. Because of his communism. It is an order from the *gringos*. But I have an idea." Paola looked around the room and spoke in tones conspiratorial. "I will go. I will get the signature."

"How, Paola? That *bruja*, the First Lady, SHE will have you shot on sight!"

"No worries, I can enter through a secret side entrance that I used for, uh, well I used it before. I can slip through the secret side entrance past the surly security guard. The ladies of the PTA can go see La Bruja, get her to answer questions about Astro-Cosmology or Cosmo-Astrology or whatever. Once she gets going, she will not shut up. She will be distracted long enough for me to meet one-on-one with Mandamás —"

"Some one-on-one, huh Paola? *Jajaja?*" There followed some lascivious jeering and obscene body language.

"Shut up. *Babosos impotentes!*[1] Ugarte says it is just a matter of writing in Izquierdo's name and getting Máximo to sign."

"Rafael Ithquierdo Gómeth, if you please Ugarte."

"Yes, quite. It is just a matter of — just hand me a pen."

No one had a pen.

"I will get a pen from Mandamás," Paola said. Many heads nodded at the wisdom of this strategy.

---

[1] Impotent droolers.

"Paola, here is the document. You must put Izquierdo's name here," he pointed to a dotted line on the last page.

"Rafael Ithquierdo Gómeth, do not forget."

"Thank you Mr. Mayor. Then the Generalíssimo must sign here."

"Okay Ugarte, I think I have it."

"Good. Plus he must initial here, here, here, aaaand here."

Paola grabbed the document and looked at the ladies, her Parents Association, "Mujeres, tonight we ride into our destiny to protect our Republic and our kids at Colegio James Monroe, Manifest Destiny!"

"Manifest Destiny!"

Paola was unsure how her gambit would pay off, if *La Bruja* could be so easily duped or if might trigger Mandamás's dictatorial temper. Her first hurdle was getting to the Presidential Palace with her PTA. As the women turned toward the exit, William excitedly gestured to the door and said elegantly, "Ladies, into my taxi and we will away to the Presidential Palace."

"Oh, sweet William. We cannot all fit into your corroded car. We will find other rides."

"Look no further, Paola." William opened the door to the street, and the women beheld the cobalt blue Lincoln Town Car! Paola whispered to him, "William, did you steal …?"

"No, it was the chicken money," he whispered back. Paola looked up at the driver and giggled. "Let us go ladies."

Between the floor, the back seat, the front seat, and the opened trunk they managed to get twelve purplish parent activists and Paola into the Town Car. In the front seat, Paola Labios instructed the driver: "To the Presidential Palace, William! Drop the ladies off at the witch's entrance then take me to the dictator's secret side entrance, you know the one."

"Roger."

Chapter 31

The PTA Visits La Bruja

"Where is that bloody Bolshevik? *Shomer Shabbos*, my ass. I think he has flown the coop. He will not get far with that Esteeve Steele fighting *rojos*[1] in Aguacate. What a farce. Put-up job if you ask me. Max, and that flaccid foreigner Dix seeing *comunistas* behind every tree. Give me a break!"

Rosemary Romero, La República's first lady and top termagant, was livid. Her arguments fell on deaf ears. She was alone with her cat Ludwig and without the benefit of counsel. Gregorio, the fabled mystic, and his greasy beard had disappeared Friday evening to reflect on universal truths or something. "Probably at the Happy Fish, that horny Hun."

Alone with her thoughts Rosemary wondered why Gregorio abandoned her during a period of great cosmic need. She needed him as a sounding board; she had some ideas of how she might achieve the co-Dictator-for-Lifeship. She assumed Gregorio was a Bolshevik or Trotskyite or something that would know about such things. Totalitarian oppression and what not.

Bored, she considered taking a short walk to her husband's apartments. "Maybe I will surprise him fucking that Finn, Inga! That woman, so white and so blonde. I will have her deported." Ludwig was non-plussed.

There was a knock on her door. "Gregorio, can you see who — *coño*, never mind. I shall go myself."

She crossed the room making tinkling and jingling sounds like a cheap Chinese plastic wind chime. Opening the door, she

---

[1] Reds.

came face-to-face with a group of women dressed like herself. They all wore amethyst beads, purple robes, crystals, and bejeweled plastic necklaces. On their heads, they each sported *La Bruja's* own merchandise, the amethyst tiaras … *True Believers!*

"Yes, ladies?"

"We have come for a consultation, *primera dama*," said the one in the lead who barged past and into the room. As the others followed, Rosemary beamed proudly. *I knew it was only a matter of time.* "Of course, *señoras* come in. Gregorio did not tell me about our appointment. Still, come in and take a seat, there are enough chairs for everyone around the table. I am so delighted to see you. There are many who laugh at the power of amethyst and are now embracing the New Universe of Understanding the Energy and wisdom of Chrono-Astrology."

She grabbed a set of finger cymbals, a gift from Gregorio, *that jueputa where is he?* and ching-changed the brass disks above each of the women's heads in some sort of purification ritual. After going around the large oval table she took her seat at the head of the table, behind a large glass globe. "What is the subject of the *consulta* you wish to make?"

The leader of the group said, in all seriousness, "Tell us the story of the power of the crystals."

Another added, "From the beginning."

"Do not leave out a single detail. We wish to, er, learn," said another.

"Well, where do I start? How do I start?" Rosemary could hardly contain her excitement. These were true disciples.

"What I am about to teach you," she said, "you will not read in any book in any library. Well not yet, that is a project I am pursuing with Gregorio, to publish his, er, my findings."

"We would love to read about your findings and the wisdom you have accrued, *primera dama*."

Rosemary's ego swelled at this most learned interruption and continued, "I have learned much from scholars and mystics, through secret ceremonies and secret rites. I have found this to be true: that there is a power, a very great power in our universe —"

"We seek to know more. Tell us."

Not used to such eager acceptance, the dictator's wife lost her train of thought for a moment but then recovered. "That power resides in crystals of all kind, particularly amethyst. It all started in the Year 123 AD in Gaul when a young Roman pompatus by the name of Maurice found —"

"What did he find," one of the ladies politely asked while glancing at her wristwatch.

"I was about to tell you. Maurice found a small crystal. An —"

"Amethyst, I bet it was an amethyst. Was it an amethyst? Was it?"

"What happened next, Doña Rosemary?"

Such enthusiasm! Rosemary continued to weave her mythology to her captive audience, the earnest women of the Colegio James Madison Parents Association.

"What happened is a long story."

Chapter 32

Max Surrenders

While the Colegio James Monroe Parents' Association was keeping the First Lady busy "consulting" on the nature of amethysts, the universe, and the power of color blah blah blah, William dropped Paola Labios, part time *puta* and political plotter at the side of the current dictator's residence, namely the Presidential Palace. Paola blessed the memory of Governor Patek, old "Pizza Face," for having the vision to install the false wall hiding the secret side entrance of the palace.

Rolling up the Constitution of 1935 like a wallpaper sample, she entered the palace through the hidden doorway without bothering to knock. Paola channeled Anna Pavlova and walked quietly, *en pointe* across the "stage" of the main reception area. La República's prima ballerina found herself alone.

"*Hola?*" Her voice echoed through the empty lobby. She had expected Güicho at least, but La República's *charge d'affairs* was nowhere to be found, nor was the rude guard who usually watched over the reception area. "*Holaaaa,*" she ventured again.

Shrugging her wide shoulders, Paola took herself up the grand staircase and found a door with a large brass plaque that said: "Offices Of Máximo Mandamás Supreme Commander Generalisssssimo (sic) and Dictator-for-Life Of La República Do Not Enter."

She entered, pushing the door open with the rolled-up Constitution of 1935.

"Max? *¿Estás aquí?* It is meeee," She sing-songed.

"Who is there? Speak to Güicho, my *chargé.* ¡Güicho! ¡Carajo! Someone is at the door."

"He is not here, Máximo. It is just me, Paola."

The supreme leader of all *republicanos* nearly swallowed the Macanudo he was wet licking, preparing to enjoy a good two-hour tryst with his tobacco. He put the cigar down immediately and stood up, simultaneously hurrying to make a neat stack of his papers. Papers stacked, Max ran a hand rapidly down his shirt front, smoothed his hair, squared his shoulders.

"P-P-Paola. So good to see you. What do I owe for this, eh, pleasure." Max snuck a look at the other door to his apartments, the one his wife used when she needed to drop by with some criticism or other.

"She is not coming, Max. She is busy, I have seen to that."

"Paola, you think of everything," he said loosening his tie and welcoming the warm feeling coming over him. The fact that she was dressed like a civilian made him more excited. He felt a desperate longing in his dictatorial loins.

"Put that away, Máximo. I come to talk to you about the future of La República. This is your epiphany Generalíssimo, the culmination."

"What in the Virgen de Aguacate are you talking about? Look Paola, put your *palabras de domingo*[1] aside and let us, you know, let us make love like before, eh. Before *La Bruja* thinks it is time to chivvy me about red stop signs. She wants to make them green too goddammit."

"The jig is up, as the *cheles*[2] say, whatever that means. Anyway Máximo, your jig is up —"

"Yes, I know. That is what I have been talking about!" Máximo started loosening his belt like an over-served drunk at a urinal.

"Your plans in Aguacate are kaput!"

---

[1] Fancy words.

[2] Gringos.

"Kaput? Paola have you been talking to that Gregorio guy, because —"

"*Ay, cállate*[3] Max. Look those kids and that Esteeve Steele *idiota, hijo de puta, malparido, lambe huevo* —"[4]

"Tell me how you really feel."

"— asshole, licker of cat testicles, cocksucking —"

His face flushed crimson, Max blurted, "My God! Your English is making me so, so —"

"*Cállate, baboso* and put your clothes on!"

"Do not talk to me like that! I am the su —"

"—preme *pinche* Commander blah, blah, blah. I know I read it on your door. By the way it is misspelled. Who put your name on the door, Generalissssimo? Tomás, *jajaja*?"

"I told that goofball Güicho —"

"Never mind your stupid son-in-law!!! Shut. Up. *Mira* Max, I am here to depose you. You have to sign over the government to a new Prime Minister. I am … what? Why are you looking like that? Is there someone behind me?" She turned around, saw nothing. "*¿Qué diablos* are you looking at?"

"Your army, your troops, at least someone with a gun. How do you expect to depose a dictator without any soldiers? It is Revolution 101!"

"Be sensible. This is what is known in the history books as a 'bloodless' coup. Your distraction in Aguacate was a farce. There are no *comunistas*, just a book club. And that *pinche gringo* Esteeve Steele is coming back to La Capital in disgrace. On a bus. His army of *gamines* came back, thank God. They could have been hurt. They were armed! With rifles! American rifles! But they were repelled! The CIA will definitely pull the rug out from under your tennis

---

[3] Shut up.
[4] A lot of bad words about Steve Steele.

shoes *señor* ex-dictator. You have no one to fall back on not even at the American Embassy. Your friend Two Dix is in *La Yunae* giving the girls at the Happy Fish a break. You are finished!"

"You cannot make me! Here, I am going to sit." Lately confrontations like this made Max nervous and in need of a bathroom break. Sitting allowed him to ignore his urge to urinate.

"You cannot force me to leave. You have no right. Nyah, Nyah!"

Did he just say 'Nyah Nyah'? Paola rolled her gorgeous eyes and brandished the rolled-up document like a club. "Here is my right, Máximo Mandamás, nyah nyah nyah!" She unrolled it on the desk and anchored the corners with his Zippo lighter, a set of official-looking rubber stamps, a crystalline cube, and a tennis trophy. You just need to sign here and initial a couple of places."

"*Ja ja ja.* You may be sexy, Paola Labios, but you are foolish. Nothing can make me sign. Nada! What is that? Why are you making that motion with your hand. Is that some new delight —?"

Paola had her arm extended in front of her about waist high and she made a slight fist of half her hand, then followed by a curious flick of her middle and index fingers, almost like a snake's tongue. Then a little wiggle of the two fingers.

"I do not understand?"

Paola gave up and came right out with it, "Your piss has two streams."

Mandamás jumped to his feet and his undone pants, belt, and large buckle fell noisily around his ankles. He quickly bent at the waist to pick his pants up but banged his head violently on the edge of the desk cutting it open and nearly bleeding on the signature page of the Constitution of 1935. After reeling a bit and recovering enough to pull up and fasten the trousers and tuck one of his shirttails in, he tried to appear dignified, sat down and demanded, "Who told you that?"

Máximo Mandamás had never told ANYONE about his bifurcated urinary stream. Not his parents, his lovers, his wife (that witch), no one. It was his secret. In fact, he had taken such care to hide his johnson from prying eyes in the locker room that it was whispered that his dick was dinky. It was not. He was hung like a horse. A small one. But still.

The dictator's mother, a saint, was Jewish. This was an unpopular thing for a person to be in La República at the time. Still, she was a good Jew and wanted her son to be blessed by the thousands of years of traditions of the Jewish faith. Thus she held a bris, the Jewish rite of circumcision, in secret. There were no *mohels* in Central America, so the elder Mrs. Mandamás imported one. He was an honest-to-god *mohel* she found in the Manhattan Yellow Pages during a shopping trip to New York. Milton, that was his name, was working out of his family's gem-cutting business on W47th St. The family diced diamonds, Milton filleted foreskin.

What Max's mother did not know was that Milton was subpar, a mediocre *mohel* at best. There had been complaints of crumby clipping, shoddy workmanship. Anyway, she flew him down for the secret bris, and snip snip (no one heard the "oops") and he was done. The tiny, jagged flaw on little Maxie went unnoticed but the boy's piss went out in the shape of a "Y," which Paola had tried to mimic with her little fist.

"I saw it. At the Happy Fish. When you were at the *mingitorio*.[5] I saw," and again she made that curious "Y" with her wiggled fingers. "Micturating Máximo Mandamás! *Ja ja ja!*"

"But Paola …. You. Can. Not. Tell. Any. One. I'll be a laughingstock. No one knows!"

"And no one will know. So sign."

---

[5] Urinal.

"I know I can trust you Paola. Maybe we should, you know, eschtup to seal the —"

"Not on your life. That is in our past and I am no longer going back to the Happy Fish."

"But you are the Employee of the Month!"

"Shut up. Sign." He sighed and signed by her index finger, turning over control of the state. But not quite. "Initial here. And here. Again here. Good."

"Why is the line where it says 'Interim Prime Minister' blank? I demand to know to whom I am handing the reins of our great nation —"

"Stop speechifying Max, it is going to be Rafael Izquierdo Sánchez or Gómez, I forgot which. We did not have a pen to fill it in, but I will take this one back to have him enter his full name. Is this a naked woman floating in your pen? Oh, Max. Did you steal this from the Happy Fish?"

The dictator softened his tone, "I was a good dictator, do you not think? At least at first. They called me benevolent in the press, remember? They said something about the benevolent Mandamás' administration."

"It was a typographical error, Ugarte meant 'bedevilment.' Something about the public beatings and arrests."

"Those are part of the job. But Izquierdo, is he not a communist?"

"Maybe, anyway Izquierdo will only be an Interim PM until we hold elections."

"Elections?" The ex-dictator mused, "I was a good leader, my people worshipped me, did they not? They said I was without peer in the history of La República."

Paola looked at him and smiled, "Without peer is right. No one could match your record of indiscriminate arrests."

"And Paola, remember when I had those mother stabbers and father rapers arrested? Or was it the other way around? Anyway it was good that I cracked down on the mother stabbers. The father rapers. They said it was Máximo who wiped the town clean of mother stabbers and father rapers, sent them back to El Corinto, those *jueputas*. You admit it, *¿no?*"

Paola looked at the former Generalíssimo. *Is he weeping?*

"Yes, Max. That was good. But what about making the kids learn nonsense about universal vibrations of color. They cannot add. They cannot multiply. And, Max, you cannot even cross the street!"

"It was that witch! SHE made me do it. She forced me. Said I wouldn't be able to see our daughter again if I did not." He was maudlin now, his face awash with tears, his usually magnificent mane of hair a mess, and his clothes were suddenly soggy and damp.

"And do you know what my Paola? My dear, dear Paola. I do not think that girl is even mine. Or hers for that matter. All a ruse. All a trick to ensnare Máximo into a marriage he never … she was not pregnant, Paola. I do not care if anybody knows now. Not my child. Not my child."

"Whose then?"

"NOT MINE AND NOT HERS." He shouted at the common wall.

Paola was drawn in. "Whose child then?"

"Can you not see? By the way do you have a tissue? *Gracias.* A girl that fair. Blue eyes. Blond hair. And me? The one they called Buster Brown at MidAmerica A&M (Go Indians)? Those racist pukes! And my lovely wife, the chicken-necked *bruja?* She is darker than me! Do you not see my lovely Paola, my fragrant *xochitl?*[6]

---

[6] Flower.

"No." *Puta, pero this guy has issues,* she thought looking on with sympathy.

"She bought the child. From some *gringa* who did not want it, came to La Capital to visit the itinerate abortionist. She bought the child from the *machita*[7] to keep up the charade of being pregnant by me!"

"How do you know this, Max?"

"My mother done told me."

"Why did you not do anything."

"B-B-because … do you have another tis —? Thank you. Because I liked the idea. And she was beautiful. But then that *bruja* got in with the mystic and all this new universe *mierda* and changed the baby's name to Amatista, you know like all those ridiculous cheap crystals she has and turned the child against me. Long story short, my girl hates me, marries that do-nothing Güicho who spies on me I am sure. BUT NOT ANYMORE. Oh Paola, Paola, please."

"Please what?"

Weakly, looking up from his crossed arms where he had been resting his head, the ex-autocrat whimpered, "One last time …"

"*Vete al carajo.*[8] Look Máximo, maybe you should just go. Leave her. Leave La Capital. There is nothing for you here. Maybe in *La Yunae.* That man you mentioned, maybe he can help."

"What will my country do without me? Wait! You mean Larree Muncie, my old friend?"

"Max how should I know? If you are lucky you can take the Kiwi Flight Number Two tomorrow. I tell you what, you can spend the night here in the palace. Do not give me that look! Never!

---

[7] Blonde woman in the local argot.
[8] Go to hell.

Just spend the night here and be gone tomorrow or (she made the "V" sign) the world will know Mandamás makes two wee wees."

It started to pour down outside. The rains had come to La República.

Chapter 33

The Return of Captain Steele

The once Major Steele was back to being Captain Steele and chief pilot of Kiwi Airways. Due to fly back to the States in less than 24 hours, he waited impatiently for the one and only bus back to La Capital. He consulted his Bulova Royal Clipper timepiece, a sharp-looking self-winding wristwatch strapped stylishly to the bottom of his left wrist. It was the way PanAm pilots wore theirs, he thought, so it was the way Steve Steele would wear his. What a disgrace returning by bus. He consulted the watch and began calculating his ETA in La Capital.

Let's see, it's ordinarily a 60-minute drive but this is a bus, so with a few stops and a slower speed it'll probably take two hours to get back. A quick drink at the bar, shower, sleep, ready for a new day. I'll fly back to the States, back to my normal routine with Kiwi. Yep! Steve will be back! I might even get rid of this fucking book at the hotel, I can't leave it here with these commies everywhere.

Just then a bus, or what passed for a bus, rolled along the rock and dirt hard pan that served as a road during the dry season in the Aguacate Province toward Steve Steele. The yellow Blue Bird, a veteran of the Jonestown (South Carolina) school system, had a seizure and skidded to a halt in front of the CIA operative, steam rising from beneath the hood ornament of La Virgen de Aguacate. Close behind the bus was a dust cloud twice its size that passed over Steele like a veil of darkness. The vehicle itself was like a much larger and motorized version of the character Pig Pen.[1] It was the only bus to the capital, a fact confirmed by the crude cardboard sign in the

---

[1] One of the children in Peanuts, drawn by Charles Schulz.

window which said: *"Ruta Número 2. La Capital."* The obverse of the sign said, of course: *"Ruta Número 1. Aguacate."*

This must be it. Steve Steele was a quick study.

The *autobús* could have been the big brother to William's Buick; filthy, with blown shock absorbers, bald tires, and brakes that had a mind of their own. Since he had flown similar equipment as a Kiwi Airways pilot, the condition of the conveyance did not raise any concerns with the pilot. He was a bit apprehensive, however, when after boarding he saw a sea of quizzical brown faces staring blankly up at him. With them were enough livestock for a children's song: chickens, goats, a piglet or two, a rattan cage full of tropical birds, and a sleeping dog. *Is that a python?*

A woman with more gaps than teeth smiled at him and slid over to the window to give him room to sit. She patted the empty space coquettishly and looked at him in such a way that might put him off women forever. Having no other choice, he sat and carefully put the volume of sonnets and plays between them.

"Tenés que pagar por el libro."

Steele looked into the eyes of a kid standing in the aisle wearing a dirty T-shirt threatening Virginia was for Lovers. It was the child tasked with collecting fares from the passengers.

"WHAT." Steve yelled.

"Jou pay. Book costs money to ride. Jou pay."

"THE BOOK IS MINE. I ALREADY — WELL SOME-BODY ALREADY PAID FOR IT." Steele shouted at the boy in the time-honored American tradition of communicating with foreigners.

"JOU PAY. THE BUK PAYS." The boy shouted back. Meanwhile the bus had not moved, just in case the *gringo* was going to be a problem.

"OKAY AMIGO. HOW MUCH?"

"CINCO, I MEAN FIVE TUCANES. TWO FOR JOU. TREE FOR THE BOOK. JOU PAY."

"SON, I ONLY GOT DOLLARS. YOU KNOW? REAL MONEY? HAHAHA." Steve looked around expecting some sympathetic laughter.

"JOU PAY. FITTY."

"CENT?"

"NO SEÑOR. FITTY DOLARS. JOU PAY."

"WHAT? THAT'S ROBBERY"

"I AM SORRY, SEÑOR. I DO NOT MAKE THE RULES. NOW JOU PAY."

Steele peeled off three tens and four fives, leaving him just enough for one of Wulther's daiquiris which he now craved like a junkie at a methadone clinic. The bus started off, jerking and wheezing, with a good measure of diesel exhaust pouring in the open window. Steve stood up, his head pounding, leaned across his seat companion, and grabbed hold of the window's small latches. He worked the window latches back and forth trying to loosen them and thus raise the pane to cut off the flow of noxious fumes pouring in before they all died.

"Oooh, *señor*," the woman said delightedly as Steele leaned his hips across her upturned face. Focused on the task, he began to worry the stuck window with a vigorous shaking and pulling back with his shoulders, shaking and pulling back, shaking and pulling back. Each iteration caused him to drive his hips further into the woman's face. She didn't object and neither did the men, women, children, and goat passengers on Ruta Número 2 who were enjoying the scene with the crazy *gringo*. It was the most sex any of them had experienced in recent memory.

"IT'S STUCK," he shouted.

"Oh, *sí*. Very estuck *señor*."

Why is she so happy? It's like a WWI trench in here.

With the window not quite shut, the captain sat and consulted his chronograph once again. *Yikes! We burned up valuable minutes with that exchange. All over this stupid book.* He looked down and snarled at the Annotated Shakespeare. *Well we're rolling now, that's good. What the goddam hell?*

The bus stopped. It seemed it had traveled less than a minute. The driver rolled down his window and addressed a man standing in front of what looked like an upright coffin. He was dressed in the uniform of an admiral in the Mongolian submarine service. It was the checkpoint. "Just driving to La Capital, admiral."

Garcilaso Gómez looked suspiciously up at the driver, then suspiciously down the length of the bus, then suspiciously back at the driver. "See anything suspicious?"

"No, your excellency."

"What is your purpose on this road?"

"Just driving the bus, your worship."

"Cargo?"

"Just the usual *gente*, chickens, goats, a pig I think."

"A little pig?"

"Yes, your exaltedness."

"They grow up. Make good *chicharrón*."

"Oh, yes, mi coronel. And *chuletas*. Do you like *chuletas oficial?*"

"Very much! Have you had the *chuletas* at Mrs. Mool's *fritanga?*"

"Yes, your holiness. I always get *chuletas*. And *gallopinto*. Mrs. Mool has the best *gallopinto*."

"Yes, she does. You may proceed, drive carefully and arrive alive."

"*Gracias*, your eminence." And with that the bus driver cheerily drove through the checkpoint.

Another fucking ten minutes, we'll never get there!

While Steele fought off a hungry goat with its head buried in his lap munching on his shirttail, the bus continued to make short stops to deliver packages, to pick up packages, to flirt, to yell, to stop for prayers at the shrine of the Virgen de Aguacate, to buy lottery tickets (after grand deliberations over the numbers), and to make regular stops. He pushed the goat away from his crotch where the animal had eaten through the shirt with bovid determination and walked down the aisle of the bus toward the front.

"HELLO!"

"*Señor*, do not talk to the *piloto*. He has to drive the bus."

Steele was standing behind the driver trying to get his attention. "Peelowtow! Just like me, see? You're a peelowtow, I'm a peelowtow!" He pointed to the four stripes on his captain's sleeves before realizing he was still in his all-terrain desert camo. He became serious and said to the driver, "Look buddy, I need to get back to La Capital today if at all possible."

"*Señor*, let me translate."

"*Me vale.*" The bus driver said.

"He says he feels jour pain, he also hopes that jou enyoy the journey and wishes to help jou arrive promptly at jour destination."

"All that, really? Ok, no more stops then."

The bus driver looked back at Steele and grinned widely showing maize-colored teeth with one or two rotting kernels. Then he made the international sign for money by rubbing thumb and forefinger together in a greedy gesture.

"Moocho dinero-o. Okay, amigo." Steele reached into his pocket and pulled out three filthy single dollar bills. He had forgotten he had already paid with larger bills for the ride. *Shit!*

"Okay, I have something better. Hold on." Returning to his seat, Steve picked up the big book and brought it up front. The bus was tooling along. *This should help keep us on track.*

"Hey, little guy. Tell him I'll give him this book. This biiig book. Moocho page-o if he doesn't make any more stops. Big-o book-o. Tell him."

"*Dice el cabrón que te regala el libro sí paras de parar*"[2]

"*Pregúntale de que se trata.*"

"What is it about, *señor capitán?*"

"What is it about? Well, kid, it is an expensive book. Very expensee-vo. It contains every word written by William Shakespeare. Every sonnet, every play. The dramas, tragedies, romantic comedies, histories, everything."

The boy translated word for word.

The driver rubbed his chin, impressed. He was considering the offer … "*Pregúntale al gringo sí es la versión anotada.*"

"He wants to know if it is the Annotated Version."

"He wants to know *what the absolute fuck* if it's annotated? OF COURSE IT'S FUCKING ANNOTATED. *Sí* it's annotated-o!"

"Please be calm meester. He says he will take it. No more unnecessary estops. Now jou sit."

The book was handed over to the boy who put it in a Stetson hat box for safekeeping and stowed it behind the driver's seat. It rested there along with a gallimaufry of seemingly useless items. There were a small sewing machine, a bowling trophy with plastic gold-colored accents, several blunt knives, boxes of watches, rings, metal buttons, light switches, solenoids, a deck of Washington Senators baseball cards, and much more. Incredibly the driver was operating some sort of rolling flea market complete with fleas from the livestock on board the conveyance.

An astonished Steve Steele went back to his seat, removed a chicken, and sat back down. The bus started out again on what

---

[2] He says he'll give you this book if you stop stopping.

Steve Steele expected to be non-stop service to downtown La Capital. He could almost taste the limy goodness of a Wulther daiquiri. *It'll be icy cold; I don't care about the brain freeze. Then shower, bed. Get a good night sleep before tomorrow's flight. AND I got rid of the Shakespeare. Could be worse* — "What's that?" Steele looked up at the ceiling where there came a hard ping-ping-ping on the bus's roof. It sounded like they were under fire from an artillery regiment armed with Daisy BB guns.

He looked around and watched the passengers unpack as the driver eased the bus under a large, spreading Guanacaste tree. "Wait! No estop-o. We had a deal-o."

The driver's assistant explained, "We have estopped, mister."

The violence of the pinging began to escalate. Steve felt like they were individual needles in the brain.

"I know we have estopped! I can see we have estopped! We are not supposed to be estopped!" Steve yelled above the noise of the rain.

"But we must, the rains have estarted."

Kiwi Airways' chief pilot spittle-sprayed a string of vulgar, quite original, and colorful profanity that insulted the driver, his mother, his assistant and his father, the rain, the communists, the whole goddam country, and maybe even the Virgin but he was fortunately drowned out by what sounded like six million liters of water falling on the rusted, now leaking, bus roof. Looking around he saw that the passengers took no umbrage at the delay and instead had laid out a picnic, several picnics it seemed, inside the leaky bus.

Steve Steele, defeated warrior, fell into his seat again with a sigh of resignation. He was handed something warm wrapped in a newspaper. "*Baleada, señor?*"

Chapter 34

Back at the Palace

Rosemary Mandamás, nee Romero, First Lady of La República was alone in her apartments that night. No Gregorio, it was just her, Ludwig, and her crystals. Thinking ugly thoughts, she walked around in furious clockwise circles, but the exercise got her nowhere. She reversed direction — no help. Then she left her studio to wander the halls of giant building, footsteps echoing in the empty palace, her only company the ghost of the French colonial satrap.

"Gregorio … Gregorio! … Gregorio??!! Where the hell is that fucking Russian?"

Rosemary cupped her mouth and called down a hall, "Max? … Máximo? … Máximo Mandamás, where are you? Answer me!!"

Am I really all alone?

"Ingaaaa?" *God, what am I doing calling —?*

"*Sí*, Mrs. Mandamás?" *By God it is that Finnish floozie* "Are you still here, where is my husband?" She demanded, one hand on her hip and angling her body to get a good look behind the girl.

"In his room, I tink."

"Well, we shall see about that!" And with a jingle of glass beads and other accessories the First Lady marched down the hall to her husband's quarters, flung open the door to find him … "Packing? Are you going somewhere Max?"

"I am leaving, I decided the best decision for my country, for La República, is to resign. Yes resign! I have resigned from the office of Dictator-for-Life, and I am resigning from you, *bruja*." Mandamás acknowledged to himself that it was quite a fine little speech to an audience of one. Where was Ugarte to record this moment in *republicano* history? His visions of weeping countrymen begging him to reconsider had been interrupted.

"You may resign as Dictator-for-Life, *mi amor* but never as Husband-for-Life. We were joined in Holy Matrimony for better or for worse."

"I have had our marriage annulled, you witch!" It was a bitter bluff, but the best Max could come up with on the spot.

"Under whose authority?"

"Father Flynn," he lied.

"That *gringo*?

"He is Canadian."

Rosemary was wound up; she'd been holding back too long.

"Same thing Max, *baboso*. Anyway he is defrocked. Spends his day hanging out with those ne'er-do-wells, those good-for-nothings, those dipsomaniacs, at the Cinco Estrellas. *Gringos*, drunks and Catholics. Do not make me laugh. *Jajaja*! Anyway, what is this about resigning as dictator? If you are serious, then the job goes to me! I will rule La República. As your co-Dictator-for-Life it is only my right. I will finally be able to implement my plans without your ignorant interference. My purple pyramid of crystal will rise from the Plaza. A new branch of the military, I shall call it Astro-force, will guard our vulnerable borders armed with amethyst-tipped bullets that none will be able to withstand. You should see the uniforms I have designed! Purple braid, epaulets, spats, the works. Yes, it will be a glorious era of positive vibrations from crystal colors! Where is Gregorio, I need to consult with him as to the —"

"You are not co-Dictator-for-Life! Anyway, I turned over the rule of La República to an Interim Prime Minister. It is all there in the Constitution of 1925 or 1935, I forgot which."

"Hmm we will see about that. I AM *primera dama*, logically the mantle of power should go to me. I do not need a piece of paper to tell me anything different. If I have to, I'll rewrite the constitution as my first act, that is the way things are done in La República. So who is this Interim Prime Minister?" *This should be a laugh.*

"Rafael Izquierdo."

"That *comunista*? He will be shot on site. The palace guards have their orders. The *gringos* want him gone, and also that shiftless Stalinist son of his in Aguacate fomenting a red revolution."

Mandamás did not waste any effort telling his soon to be ex-wife of the defeat of the CIA and their elite forces in the province. "Izquierdo sent a representative to have me sign over the government. It was all very legal. I had to sign and initial in many places."

"A representative? Do not make me laugh. *Ja ja ja.* Who would dare?"

"Paola. Paola Labios."

"No really, who?"

"I am telling you it was Paola Labios. She made me sign on the line which is dotted."

"The *p-p-puta*? You turned the ruling of La Fucking República over to a communist because that p-p-prostitute?" Rosemary sputtered, unable to put the words together as she looked around for something to throw at her husband. Fortunately, for Max, everything had been packed away, including the tennis trophy which would have made a fine missile. This frustrated the Chrono-Astrologist and amethyst worshipper even more. "Did that cheap Dolores del Rio knockoff hold a gun to your head?"

"Y-y-yes, she did. She did hold a gun to my head."

"Liar, okay run away. *Cobarde*.[1] If you leave, I will take over as is my right. Forget the Constitution of whatever, it is only paper. I will be in my office managing affairs of state." Striking this final note, the former First Lady turned on her amethyst encrusted stilettos and called, "Gregorio! Where are you? Are you dead?"

Max closed the Bermuda-green Samsonite suitcase and put it by the others just outside the door for William in the morning. He had already packed his dictator-on-the-go kit: a case of Ron Aniversario, a box of Macanudo cigars, his English riding boots with their tiny spurs, and a newly re-strung Wilson Pro Staff Original tennis racket. He was ready to go.

He wondered, wistfully, if he would ever return to La República.

---

[1] Coward.

Chapter 35

Back at the Hotel Cinco Estrellas

Back at the Hotel Cinco Estrellas things were very quiet. The lobby lights were all out. Only the tinkle of glassware from inside the bar was audible. It was Wulther doing his final cleanup for the night, putting polished glasses on the racks and shelves. He liked to have everything in order for the next day: glasses bright and clean, bottles in their proper order, napkins stacked, and surfaces polished enough to hold his reflection.

It was his favorite time of night, Wulther enjoyed the silence and liked to play back some of the bar's conversations in his mind. Today was certainly full of interesting discourse. The defecting goalie situation. Ugarte and the Constitution that would change the lives of all *republicanos*. And the debate about who would lead La República. The future would be exciting. And what of the failed revolution in Aguacate Province? Would they try again?

Did they really consider me, Wulther, to run the country? Yes! But it is true, I am needed here, behind the bar, to serve the drinks. Still … Izquierdo is a good choice even if he was a communist once. He dresses very well and always leaves a good tip. He will make a fine Prime Minister (Interim).

Wulther hummed his favorite tune, "As Time Goes By," to make the chores more pleasant. *You must remember this; a kiss is just a banging on the door … what is that banging?* Looking up he saw a man standing in the rain in wet clothes, *a gringo* ? He was banging on the glass door street entrance. Wulther waved to the man and mouthed "we are closed" through the glass. He hoped the man would go away; he was wet, probably drunk, and, judging by the knob on his forehead, had been in a brawl. Klaus Von Klaus would not approve if Wulther let someone like that into the five-star hotel.

"Wullrr!" Said the man with his lips up against the sliver of space between the door and the door jamb.

"We are closed, *señor.*"

The man was insistent; he kept banging and yelling "Wullrr." It seemed he might even be crying.

Opening the door a crack, Wulther said, "We are closed, *señor.* It is late. You look like you've already had enough. Go home." In truth, Steeve Steel looked like ten miles of bad road.

"Wullth, goddammit! It's me! Steve Steele! I live here re-member?"

"This is a hotel not a house, *señor.* Oh, it IS you. What hap-pened to your head? Did one of Piojo's boys hit you with a dirt clod from his *gomera?*"

"Just let me in and get my key please."

"Certainly, *capitán.* I heard you had a bad time of it there in Aguacate Province. I'm sorry I have closed the bar for the night so I cannot make you a daiquiri. Can I offer you some Ron Aniversa-rio?"

"Bless you Wulther, but real quick."

The bartender took down a newly polished glass from the shelf and fished out a couple of ice cubes that were melting in the sink, dropping them with professional flair into the glass. He poured carefully, with an expert's eye measuring out two fingers of Ron Aniversario. After throwing down the two fingers of rum, Steve Steele started a hasty retreat to his room. He looked very pale and felt an upheaval in his stomach, something that was in there wanted out.

"God I'm sick, Wulther, must have been something I ate. Good night.

"Sí *señor* Esteeve. You look like you could use some esleep."

The *señor* raced up the stairs to his room. "Must have been that *baleada* on the bus, ooof."

Wulther returned to his ministrations. "*A sigh is just a sigh* …"

Chapter 36

Morning in La Capital

La República was a sleepy, contented nation that just wanted to be left alone like a middle-aged American on Thanksgiving — a brain full of football and a belly full of tryptophan. For some in La Capital it was a day like any other, children played recklessly in the streets dodging cars, buses, motorcycles, and wagons. In the market customers haggled over the price of chicken. Throughout the city beggars begged, vendors vended, hawkers hawked.

The pleasant weather of the city took on an entirely different aspect during the rainy season. A fact of life in the tropics, the arrival of the rains marked the passage of time like baseball's spring training. Cool, breezy mornings gave way to monsoon-like afternoons and torrential evenings, events as consistent as a Swiss watch.

There were benefits to the rains, however, as they nourished the crops that *republicanos* relied upon to eke out their existence in the hemisphere's second poorest nation. Coffee bushes, tobacco plants, avocado trees were nourished while cows, goats, pigs, horses, *et al.* all drank lustily from gutters and rills and rivers that overflowed with it. The soft green hills that surrounded the small city became softer and greener. Tiny white flowers appeared on the coffee plants. Avocado trees betrayed a slight yellowing. Other blooms opened their faces to receive the cool, heavenly bath. Hibiscus, frangipani, dahlias all in open competition to seduce the birds and the bees into tasting their nectars.

And what could be more romantic than a 500-year-old colonial city where puddled streets reflected the pleasing sightlines of the rooftops and the sturdy confidence of the sixteenth century cathedral? Horses not only clip-clopped, but they also splish-splashed.

The paving stones on the streets were washed clean and took on a promising new life. Children ran and jumped into muddy puddles. The rain was part and parcel of the natural beauty of the capital city.

La Capital was also a city that honored its past and eschewed modern entrapments. There were no shopping malls, nor office buildings, nor supermarkets, not even a tanning salon. And in the morning, traffic was light around the city before the rush hour which normally began at 9 or 9:30 (10 at the latest) before the universal gridlock set in.

Early on this particular morning a cobalt blue car resembling a small sea-going yacht, made its way through the pre-rush hour chaos. It was highly polished and highly praised by its owner, a former boxer and La Capital's leading taxi driver. William's slightly used Lincoln Town Car gave low growls around the corners, frightening lizards and stray dogs as he maneuvered the beast to avoid muddy puddles. All 365 horses under its very long hood, one for each day of the year, were just chomping at the bit to be let loose. William had dreamed of a machine like this when he was still driving the filthy death trap of a Buick.

It was going to be a busy morning. Dodging imaginary ring opponents, William jockeyed the car through the streets like he was competing in the Grand National Steeplechase. First to the Hotel Cinco Estrellas to pick up Steve Steele. Steele had sounded very tense on the phone. William couldn't help but chuckle, *I guess things did not work out for the CIA this time.* He checked his watch. *The pilot should be finishing breakfast right about now.*

He was wrong. Pulling his ship to its mooring post in front of the hotel he found a nervous sickly-looking CIA operative already at the curb, with his usual small "two-suiter" suitcase in his hand ready to board. "Let's go, ameegow. A La Chingada!"

"Good morning, Mr. Steele, right away. First a quick stop."

"A quick stop? Oh, no William. Not the overlook, please."

"No, *señor*, not the overlook although it is a fine overlook, yes. No, first I have another customer also going to the airport. It will just take a minute; he lives very close."

"Ok but make it fast! *Rápido-o.*"

"Yes," said the cabbie feinting to his left.

Steve slid into the back seat. "I like your new ride, William? Is this a Cadillac?"

"Lincoln Town Car!"

"Well done! Better'n that piece of shit you had before. No offense."

"None taken." They drove in silence for a while the pilot agonizingly reviewed the events of the past two days. "If I never return to Aguacate Province, it will be too soon," he said before forming himself into a ball in the corner and rolling over in a deep sleep.

William drummed his fingers on the steering wheel and hummed "The Girl from Ipanema."

⏳ ⏳ ⏳

"What is the purpose of your visit to the Presidential Palace?"

"I have come for the President, the Generalíssimo."

"Your papers, please. Who are you?" William passed his identity papers through the open window to the guard dressed as the head doorman at New York's Plaza Hotel. The officer bunched the papers in his fist and circumnavigated William's vehicle until he returned to the driver's window again and asked, "Is this a Cadillac?"

"No. As you can see by my papers, officer Gómez, I am William. And as you can see by my most fantastic vehicle, which is a Lincoln, I am the taxi driver. You know me, *pendejo*! I have come to take his excellency to the airport."

"And what is the nature of the Generalíssimo's trip to the airport?"

"I do not know and I am sure it is a state secret. Anyway he is waiting, I do not like to make him wait, so let me in."

"Wait! What is that?!"

"That, Officer Gómez, is Esteeve Steele, chief pilot."

"Why is he a ball? Rolled up like that?"

"He is sleeping as you can see. He had a very long day yesterday. I am taking him to the airport also."

"Of course, you may pass."

William entered the grounds of the palace and executed an elegant wide turn with the sleek Town Car and came to rest by the super-secret side door of the dictator's quarters. He saw a pair of matching green suitcases which he stowed in the Lincoln's ample storage, careful not to wake the pilot in the back seat.

Mandamás soon appeared from behind the false wall. He looked back wistfully at the immense French Baroque masterpiece, a proud piece of Republican patrimony. It was an historical moment with only one witness. Máximo walked to the vehicle and turned around for one last goodbye to his home for these past few years. "It is Izquierdo's prison now and he is welcome to it," he sighed before crawling silently into the front seat like a thief in the night. The pile of clothes in the rear seat prompted him to point a thumb at the back seat and ask William, "What is that? Your laundry?"

"Not what, who. That is your pilot to *La Yunae*," William answered. He engaged his cobalt blue machine and drove off with the deposed Dictator-for-Life, his luggage, and a CIA agent disguised as a pile of clothing to destiny.

Chapter 37
Return of Piojo

Corporate Chief Executive Officers are known to retreat to a special place in order to plan their next move. Special places like a family cabin in the woods, or company yacht, or private ranches to take down rare game animals, offered beleaguered CEOs shelter from the nagging press, the nagging board of directors, and the nagging first wife. In the rarified climate of the exclusive hunting lodge, a CEO could find comfort surrounded by his many trophies like the African Greater Kudo, a 300-lb. swordfish, or his new wife. Most importantly, it gave him time to reflect, self-assess, circle back, drill down, do a deep dive, retool, and pivot to the new paradigms so at the end of the day he could impact the bottom line.

Tirofijo was no different. He had his own special place, his Hideout, where he tasked himself for adjusting his business model. He had recently read with great interest, a college textbook mistakenly included in a shipment of goat entrails destined for a Santeria synod in South Florida. What drew his attention the most was a chapter called "Self-Assessment for the Self Starter," in particular the section dealing with something called "SWOT Analysis."

SWOT Analysis, the book's author famed Italian economist Clementus Sixtus, Ph.D. explained, was "Strengths, Weaknesses, Opportunities and Threats." Although poorly translated into English from the original Italian by editors at MidAmerica A&M Press, the lesson was still clear. Tirofijo read:

"You gotta have gooda analysis or you go *pazzo* (sic). Alla time, you look atta *forza* (sic) (strength) see what you makes you estrong. Be a go-a getter." There followed a handy "how-to" section suggesting "ideation" sessions, "spitballing" and advising there are "no bad ideas." Internally Tirofijo had laughed at the last concept, thinking the author had obviously never set foot in La República. Otherwise he took to the business exercise and had already started on the upper left quadrant, the one for Strengths. He was using his favorite pen, the one with the naked girl floating in a bubble of water and tapping it on his temples for thought stimulation. He had written:

Virility

Hung like a horse

Respected and feared

Under "Weaknesses," he felt it was too easy to write "none." Instead he listed:

Ron Aniversario

Romantic comedies

Paola (crossed out)

"Opportunities" stymied him. That *hijo de puta* Esteeve Steele disappeared on a fool's errand to Aguacate. That *pinche* Paola stole all his chicken money. And Piojo, who was like a son, melted into the jungle with his brigade of ragamuffins. With all that had been happening to him it was difficult to visualize any opportunities. And in the book Dottore Sixtus had written that the entrepreneur must always be ready to identify an opportunity. But where, *coño*?! His face brightened with an idea, and he wrote:

"Sell Macaw *guano* to the *gringos*."

At the front of the warehouse, at the door to Violeta's Sexx Shoppe, came a quick knock followed by the shop owner herself entering and bringing with her a sensuous smell wafting in like the force of a gale. "Are you decent?" She asked the room at large. Violeta was, as usual, well-adorned, -coifed, and -cured both mani and pedi. She walked in like she owned the place, advancing only a few steps not wanting to give her ex-lover any ideas of a dalliance in the making. "Hey," she raised her voice in a less than respectful manner.

"*Sí, mi amor,*" Tirofijo responded optimistically. Since she cut him off he was not the Tirofijo of old: virile and master of his domain. Still reeling a bit from the Paola situation, he was hoping for a thaw in Iceberg Violeta. He was glad to have doused himself with Hai Karate that morning. It was a manly smell. Highly irresistible. He stood, intending to approach Violeta.

"*No empieces, cabrón,*"[1] was her deflating retort; still keeping a wide distance from her ex's desk and holding the hand up, palm out, like the traffic policeman in front of the mercado. Violeta got down to business quickly and growled, "Tirofijo, there is someone in my shop to see you."

"From Hollywood?"

"Are you still on and about that stupid movie you made? No, *imbécil.* No Hollywood for you, just a poor and scared kid. Looking for you."

"For me? A kid? Look Violeta, I am in the middle of a very important business exercise from this very important textbook, *mira?*" He held up Clementus Sixtus' tome for her to see also hoping to impress her enough she might sleep with him. Trying to strike a serious note, he added, "I am self-evaluating, Violeta. Very critical in the world of business. There are new paradigms —"

"Whatever." She cut him off. "Piojo is in my shop probably feeling up the blow-up dolls or practicing worse perversions. He wants to see you, but I can tell he is scared you will yell at him and maybe hit him."

---

[1] Do not start *cabrón.*

"Violeta, you know I would never hit Piojo. Maybe a *ca-chetada*[2] now and again. But nothing hard, I love him. He is like a son."

"Whatever. I will send him in. Just be kind. He worships you."

"Of course he does, *mi amor*." Tirofijo admitted and sat back down behind his desk.

Piojo sheepishly entered the hideout. He had ridden all the way from Aguacate in the front seat of William's land yacht thinking how he would approach his mentor. He felt silly that such child's play, adventure comics, would have taken him away from the *Escondite* and Tirofijo's tutelage. Just returning made him feel he was back in the right place.

Still in the shadows of the vast warehouse space, Piojo hid behind a bird cage that was empty but for a smattering of scarlet macaw droppings on top of the front page of a week old El Día. He waited before walking toward the lamp shaped as a slutty woman's leg in fishnets, and into the circle of light it created. Behind the desk was his real-life idol, Tirofijo, pretending to be working out his "Opportunities."

"*Jefe?*" Said the boy shyly, remorsefully. Poor Piojo stood waiting to be cuffed. Tirofijo sat waiting to be hugged. The two were at an uncomfortable impasse. Neither, being men, wanted to show weakness to the other. There followed an uncomfortable silence that stretched out like a rubber band, tension building. Only the sound of a motorcycle speeding down the sidewalk could be heard. Piojo tried unsuccessfully to clear his dry throat. It was Tirofijo who finally broke the ice with a generous olive branch, "I need help Pi-ojo. Do you see Rafael Izquierdo as a 'Threat' or 'Opportunity?' I see it both ways, of course. As the Prime Minister (Interim) he can

---

[2] Cuffing.

make trouble for our, er, economic sector. On the other hand, he could be a new 'opportunity.' We may have to revise our budget *vis a vis* our bribe outlays, naturally, but I do not think that should be a problem. Our biggest weakness right now is revenue; we need adjust to the new paradigm Piojo. Do you agree?"

Piojo had no idea what Tirofijo was on about but agreed anyway. *"Sí, jefe."*

"Have you ever done a SWOT analysis?"

Capitán Freedom was big on SWAT as in "Captain Freedom Swats the Soviets" and not so much on SWOT analyses, leaving Piojo at a loss as to how to respond. It mattered little because Tirofijo was just deflecting away from the incidences of the last few days in order to mend fences with his protégé.

"So you are back?"

"Yes, and I am sorry, *jefe*. It is just that it all seemed so exciting. The *gringo capitán*, the *comunistas*, and you were busy with, you know, with the chicken money, I wanted to help, *jefe*, but I did not have a motorcycle and —"

There seemed to be some tears in the offing which would have made them both uncomfortable, so Tirofijo interrupted. "That is over, Piojo. You are back, which is important."

Piojo wanted to kiss the man's ring, but Tirofijo didn't wear much in the way of jewelry. Instead he looked upon the thug with shining, adoring eyes.

"We have new problems. Money is low, I may need you to help collect taxes, once we see which way the wind is blowing with the mayor, I mean Prime Minister. There's a shortage of parrots and pumas, people whining about loss of habitat, and nobody wants to deal in little mud men with massive dicks. Something about international laws against looting."

As Tirofijo poured out his woes and outlined the failing business, Piojo could not be any happier. He started to break into a smile, then remembered his place. Showing alertness, that he was paying attention and sympathetic to his boss's situation he asked, "What about the chicken money, *jefe*?"

"Stolen!"

"Stolen? By who?"

"Whom."

"By whom! Stolen by whom, boss?"

"By P —" Tirofijo stopped himself before admitting that he had been conned by his concubine. His EX-concubine, that *bitch*! "P-persons unknown. Never mind that, Piojo. We need some ideas. Let us spit some ball."

The concept of spitballing in a business context was new to Piojo who had not read Clementus Sixtus' textbook entry on the matter. His knowledge of spitballing was in another area entirely.

"I prefer *terrones*, dirt clods. They fly faster, more accurate. Like the time I hit that *basurero*?[3] It was when we first met. I made the garbage can ring! Remember *jefe*?"

"No, *idiota*!"

Piojo response to the verbal abuse was a feeling of elation, pure joy. Things were back to normal with his boss and the boy was ecstatic. "No?"

"Mira, *pendejo*, spitballing is a concept in big business." Tirofijo spoke with authority but his interpretation of spitballing was more literal than figurative. "This is how it works, Piojo. Pay attention. We come up with an idea, okay. We scribble it on a piece of paper. Then we put the paper in our mouth, get it good and wet, *con baba*,[4] then we throw it against the wall see if it sticks."

"Can we just write the ideas down and talk about them?"

---

[3] Garbage can.
[4] With spit.

"We can do that, I suppose. Anyway Piojo, we have got to get more money in the *Escondite*. ASAP!"

"¿Asap? *¿Que es* asap?"

"ASAP! It means *rápido* in English.

So the spitballing began, conceptually, without the saliva.

Chapter 38

Steve Steele Returns to Miami

Steve Steele slept during the entire trip to the airport and was unaware that he shared the ride with Máximo. Máximo had left the vehicle and carried his own bags to the terminal walking under the "Passenger Check-In" sign. Other passengers looked and pretended not to notice it was the iron-fisted dictator carrying his own bags without his wife barking in his ear. Afraid to be noticed staring at the Dictator-for-Life, there was a lot of close examination of luggage tags, checking of boarding passes, and interest in the terminal's ceiling. Max seemed melancholy, yet relaxed as he made his way past the onlookers to the Kiwi Airways counter.

The pilot, meanwhile, was still sleeping like an opium addict in the back of the Lincoln Town Car. William opened the rear door and reached in to nudge him. Steele shook himself awake and looked at his driver. "Thank you, William. I hope to be back soon." The cabbie gave a small twitch of his head and saluted Steve Steele as he walked away from the car. "I hope so, *Capitán.*"

The pilot entered the terminal and got into the queue for passport control. There seemed to be a lot more activity than usual, so Steele took advantage of the shorter lines reserved for diplomats and crew.

"Passport please. What was the porpose of jour visit, *se-ñor?*" The officer demanding documents and answers looked out of place wearing only a doorman's uniform. "I fly the airplane, you know that. Look, I need to board, can we speed this up?"

"Please cooperate, *señor.* I know jou believe the airplane cannot leave without jou —"

"That's right! It can't. So may I go?"

"Jour porpose in La República *señor*?!"

"I was here to put down a revolution." Steele replied without a trace of irony.

Whomp-whomp. "Proceed *señor.*"

The flight back to Miami from La Chingada was unusual. The plane was nearly full of passengers, many with quite a bit of luggage. Steve recognized many lower-tiered minions of the Mandamás administration representing various government divisions and ministries. The functionaries were recognizable by the waxy finish of their broad foreheads, the ink stains on their shirt cuffs, and their general demeanor of superiority. Apparently they had left their areas of dominant influence for a quick trip to Miami. *Shopping probably*, thought the pilot watching the line of passengers climb the shaky makeshift ladder up to the door of the airplane. "Who are they?" He asked the flight attendant checking tickets at the door. The girl followed his gaze down to the tarmac where a number of uniformed officers and their wives were queuing up to board the plane.

"Dey are leaving La Capital, *Capitán.* Exile in Miami."

Exile, what the hell?

"Exile?"

"Jes, *Capitán.* My seester tol' me. Máximo has left his wife and the palace; we have a new government soon." She reported the good news happily.

Not good, not good.

Next to board was an eerily familiar passenger that Steve Steele thought he recognized. He was on the short side, wearing a long heavy woolen coat totally out of keeping with local customs and lugging a very large valise, like a salesman's sample bag. Steele was drawn to his face, the familiar eyes, and *are those bug bites?* There were a number of razor knicks on the man's face with tiny bits of tissue to stop the bleeding. The man stowed his square black bag and slid into a window seat. Once settled, he reached into the right pocket of the overcoat and took out a magazine — a catalogue of fine jewelry — and proceeded to lose himself in the photographs of diamonds, sapphires, rubies, and the like. The other flight attendant offered him an avocado smoothie on a tray, which he accepted. "Thenx," the man whispered.

The pilot kept trying to recollect and continued to stare hard at the man in seat 1A. Soon the pilot was distracted by the only other first-class passenger who very quietly entered the cabin. Steve stared at the new arrival trying to place his face as he sat in the aisle seat next to the poorly shaven man.

Jesus Christ! Is that? It was. Máximo Mandamás! His nibs himself. The former generalíssimo a mere passenger on Kiwi Airways flight 2. "Darling, is that?" "*Sí, Capitán,* it is the former dictator."

"He's going into exile in Miami too?"

Checking the manifest, the stewardess nodded, "Jes Esteeve."

"Well, I can't chit chat all day, this bird won't fly herself." Chuckling he disappeared into the cockpit to join Indio, his co-pilot and chief mechanic. Indio wasn't really a co-pilot, per se, but the passengers seemed more at ease when there were two uniforms in the cockpit, instead of just the chief pilot.

The plane was loaded with passengers and Steve was ready to push off except there were problems loading the cargo. Too much luggage it seemed. Many bags of all descriptions, some tied with rope, some taped, some cinched with men's belts or extension cords. There were boxes upon boxes, and oddly shaped pieces: rocking chairs, paintings, sculptures, a few couches, and something shaped like a woman's leg. A brace of goats were turned back to the customs shed. The hold was finally full, and Flight 2 was ready to go.

La Chingada International Airport does not boast of a very long runway, and so the DC-4 museum piece needed every single foot of it to make its takeoff. "Shit on a stick, Indio, I thought we would end up in the ditch. We must be a flying flea market. I never saw such crap. Chairs, lamps, and all. That was something, huh, Indio?"

"Sí, *Capitán*." Indio was a man of few words and did not want to be distracted from his reading, the latest installment of comics, "Captain America Fights Jungle Rot."

⧗ ⧗ ⧗

The chief pilot executed a decent landing at Miami International (IATA Code: MIA), parked his aircraft, and quickly descended the stairs in front of his passengers. He was in a hurry and wanted to stay ahead of the mayhem created by a plane load of *republicanos* fleeing their country loaded down with possessions like depression-era Okies heading to California. He had CIA business and didn't want to be late.

After clearing customs and immigration, Steve found himself melting at the curb in the Floridian heat. He prayed for the rare, air-conditioned taxi to take him to his meeting in Little Havana. It was not to be, however. A dented, rusty cousin of William's old Buick painted green, with South Beach Yellow Taxi stenciled on the door screeched to a stop in front of him. The driver reached over and rolled down a scratchy and milky window causing a sweet cloud to waft around Steve. He choked a bit, but managed to stifle it, fearing that his coughing might be taken as racist.

"Where u go mon' ?"

"La Marseillaise. It's on —"

"Eight street. Ya mon, I know. Hop in. Ten dolla."

Because the cab was reminiscent of William's old Buick in nearly every detail, Steve Steele couldn't help but feel nostalgic for La Capital, Paola, the Cinco Estrellas Hotel Bar, Wulther. Would he ever see them again? Distracted by his thoughts he failed to anticipate the car's quick stop and slammed into the plexiglass divider face first, the ugly knot on his forehead leading the charge.

"We be here, mon. The Marsaylaise. Be ten dolla dude."

The captain rubbed his throbbing brow, paid the driver through the little door in the divider and stepped out on to the sidewalk in front of Miami's iconic Cuban/Latin American restaurant. Steve hoped the agents would let him eat something this time, maybe *lechon asado*. Mmmmm.

He pushed the heavy glass door inwards and immediately slammed into a tall skinny man in overalls who looked at Steve with his one good eye, the other swimming in its socket. "Gwach it meng."

"Sorry!" *Oh God it's the raft person again.*

"Estengle, he manayes." It was the password. Steele being an old pro by this time was quick with the countersign.

"Bucky Dent sucks."

"Turd boot on de right."

The CIA agent and recently failed operative in La República walked unsteadily to the third booth on the right and, as before, saw agents Blue and Orange sitting next to each other in the same seats, dressed in the same clothes, wearing the same stony expressions. The only difference was the order of *tostones* on the table they were sharing. Neither rose to greet him.

Steele decided to employ a friendly approach and nodded to each of the spies in turn.

"Blue, Orange."

"No names," they snapped in unison.

Steele sat.

"What the hell happened to you?"

Steele automatically reached up and touched his big ouchy. Grimacing, he responded. "Altercation with one of the Red rebels. I took care of it."

Blue, uncharacteristically spoke up with a hint of amusement. "We should see the other guy? Haha!"

"The book." Said Agent Orange looking over Steele's shoulder at who knew what.

Steele took out the slim yellow volume "Handy Phrases in Albanian" and laid it on the cheap Formica-topped table. The pamphlet quickly disappeared.

"The book." It was Agent Orange again. Steve looked at him, then at Agent Blue.

"He means the Oxford Edition of The Complete Works of William Shakespeare, Fully Annotated. You don't seem to have it."

Steve had not rehearsed an answer, and he sure didn't want to let them know he surrendered it to a bus driver in Aguacate. "Don't have it. Lost it in the … uh, the firefight. You have to admit it's a bit bulky to be —"

"You lost the book?"

"Y-y-yes."

"In a firefight?" Blue was positively garrulous.

"Do tell agent, we'd like to hear how one loses a book like that in a firefight. Wouldn't we, Agent Blue?"

Blue nodded ever so slightly, like he was bidding on a Monet at Sotheby's.

"Well, it went like this —" Steve Steele's mind was racing trying to invent a story that would satisfy his handlers. He was fortunate that the waitress came to the booth laden with piles of steaming pork, rice, garlic bread, beans, yuca, and other sundries. The pilot's eyes grew wide at seeing the repast.

"We eat," Agent Orange said pointing with the bent tines of his fork. "You talk."

While the Langley duo dug into the fabulous spread and made disgusting noises as they swallowed fistfuls of meat chased with rice, beans, and what not, Steve used the hiatus to concoct a tale worthy of a bestselling spy novel. He related a chilling account of the secret meeting in the Kiwi hangar, recruiting a small but determined cadre of battle-hardened men. "Very anti-communistic, gentlemen, and from the very best families." Then there was the planning, the meeting with Agent Weiss, Shakespeare codes and other skullduggery. Getting orders from the dago barber and his sneaky commie Korean friend. There was the story of the march on Aguacate, the suspicious border guard, and finding the sleeper cell engaged in receiving Marxist marching orders from El Corinto via coded messages in a television broadcast.

"Gentlemen, it was then that we were faced with treachery. There was a surprise ambush. Huts were burning in the firefight. We were soon surrounded, but my men held fast!" Agents Blue and Orange listened with fascination.

"Sadly, sirs, as brave as they were, we could not overcome the superior forces. Hundreds of tall dark warriors, very athletic, disguised as basketball players, with strange accents — they attacked from every direction. We retreated to fight another day."

"Venezuelans." It was Agent Blue again.

"Venezuelans?"

"Venezuelan mercenaries, Steele. We heard they were infiltrates in that area. Engaged by the sleeper cell to defend against your cadre. We couldn't commo the info."

"Commo the info?"

"Couldn't break radio silence to warn you."

"I didn't have a radio."

"There was one in the Jeep."

"I never turned it on."

"There you go."

"But if it was silent, then?'

Agents Blue and Orange looked at one another, their chins shiny with grease, their minds dulled by the pleasure of lunch at La Marseilles. Nodding in unison, they turned to a very hungry Steve Steele. Agent Orange, as usual, spoke:

"Excellent work, agent. You showed bravery under fire; that's a good thing. Greater forces were at play there. Venezuelans, Jesuits, Democrats, who knows what-all. Any way things have changed in La República, we are W.A.S. for now."

"W.A.S.?"

"Wait-and-see agent. It means we wait and we see. There seems to be some sort of coup in La Capital. We want you; the Company wants you somewhere else. You're being exfiltrated."

Confused, Steele avoided Blue's creepy stare and looked at Orange. "Wants me somewhere else? Exfiltrated? To Langley?"

"Georgetown."

Steele could not believe that after botching the sleeper cell situation in Aguacate they were sending him to Georgetown! In Washington, DC! That was right next door to Langley, CIA head-quarters. *Oh this is a great day!* He smiled broadly at Agent Orange and even snuck a look at Agent Blue. Neither reciprocated.

"What are you so happy about, Steele? You need to get to Georgetown right away. You're familiar with Georgetown? The capital of St. George in the Antilles? Here's what's happening, you are now assigned to the Island of St. George to usurp the commu-nistic government there. They are supported with dangerous *hombres* sent from Moscow fronting a vodka distillery and threatening American Interests. Capeesh?"

Steve Steele did not capeesh. Steve Steele had not heard anything after "… the capital of St. George" which he knew was a guano-covered rock in the Caribbean. Literally a pile of shit. And no soft hills, no good coffee, no *fritangas*, no Happy Fish. No Paola.

"Not the one in DC? No Washington Monument? No Lincoln Memorial?"

"No."

"Defend American Interests you say? What exactly are those?"

Agent Orange answered deadpan, "The C.C.C."

Steele, puzzled, "The *sí sí sí?* Like yes yes yes?"

"No no no. The C.C.C."

Steele, hopeful, "You mean C.C.C.?"

"Correct," Agent Blue volunteered. Then he added, "Medical School. CCC. Chiropractic College of the Caribbean at St. George, Steele"

The pilot's head was throbbing and in a spin. All he knew was he would not return to La Capital, much less visit Langley headquarters. Goodbye to that suite at the Watergate Hotel he had envisioned.

"It'll be a piece of cake. They speak our lingo, no need for a terp."

"Terp?"

"You know the drill," Orange ignored Steele's question and resumed driving the conversation. "Your cover is still Kiwi Airways, new route to Georgetown, St. George. We've requisitioned a DC-3 for that purpose. We will comm as per usual. Here's your book of cipher codes."

The new man in St. George looked down at a dog-eared copy of "101 Esperanto Verbs." *Here we go again.*

Orange continued, "Here's your book. You are to contact our agent on arrival; he's the head of customs in Georgetown." He dropped a large tome with a thud on the table, between the *yuca* and the *maduros*.

Steve reacted resignedly, "The History of the Decline and Fall of the Roman Empire (Abridged)," he read out loud.

"Abridged, we thought you would appreciate that. By Gibbon. It's good."

"But it's still so … never mind."

"Off you go, Agent Steele!"

Steve stood up, side-stepped the grouchy waitress, and trekked disconsolately across the restaurant with pounds of ancient history under his arm.

Orange called after him, "Don't be so disconsolate, Steele. Look on the bright side."

"There's a bright side, Agent Orange?"

"No names! Yes. There is. The Russian vodka. Made from yams. Smooth."

Chapter 39

The Trappings of Power

A new chapter in Ugueth Ugarte's History of La República was being written. Future generations would learn of the events that had unfolded. Not only had a book club mistaken for a communist sleeper cell been defended against a misguided CIA operative; but a dictator had been deposed. Generally speaking, it was always a good day when a dictator was deposed. These and other incidents were capped by the historical nomination and installation of an Interim Prime Minister under the legal constitution. The transition of power was signed and sealed as the last act of the Dictator-for-Life Máximo Mandamás who, presumably, was enroute to *La Yunae* to join the diaspora of deposed dictators. Dade County was rife with exiled despots.

Rafael Izquierdo, former mayor, former communist, former regular at the Hotel Cinco Estrellas Bar walked into the seat of power, the main office of the Presidential Palace, and looked around appreciatively. *This will do nicely.* He placed a moving carton full of his most personal effects on the corner of the desk and began unpacking. A rolodex with all his contacts, the pen and pencil set that had been a gift from Ché Guevara, a Mr. Met bobble head, some amulets, and other meaningful bric-à-brac. He looked out his picture window onto the grounds. "Mine," he said to his reflection. Looking down at the desk there was a handwritten note. Strangely, Mandamás had left a phone number, a long-distance phone number, that said "If you change your mind, call me."

"Not bloody likely," Izquierdo said to the note.

With everything in place, Izquierdo moved behind the desk and admired his interior surroundings. The trappings of power. He caught his reflection again and turned to look at his very authoritative pose. "Churchillian," he thought as he raised his strong chin and spoke in stentorian tones to test the sound of his voice in the chamber. As the words rolled off his tongue, Izquierdo greatly admired the timbre of his prime ministerial speechification. "I will have to renovate, these walls are so bare, and the floor needs polishing. What are those hideous grooves in the floor?" The man's observations echoed off the empty walls and floors.

"They were made by Mandamás, Mr. Mayor."

Rafael jumped straight up at the intrusion. It was Paola Labios there to welcome the new leader of La República! Izquierdo beamed. *Mine? The trappings of power?*

"Mandamás used to drag his spurs on the floor. What is funny is that the man was afraid of horses. Never got near one."

"What a nice thing, Paola, to welcome me personally." There were dirty thoughts in Izquierdo's mind. "But there is no need to refer to me as *Señor Alcalde*, dear Paola, you may address me as, Your Excellency, for I am now the Prime Minister."

"Interim."

"Merely a formality, Paola. Merely a formality. The Constitution says, I believe, that I can appoint myself full-time PM after the rains."

"That is very interesting, Mr. Mayor."

"*Primer Ministro.*"

"Whatever, perhaps you can show me where it says that, where it says that you can appoint yourself after the rains." Paola unrolled the Constitution of 1935 and spread it over the mostly empty desk like a picnic blanket at the city's overlook.

A stunned Izquierdo, not expecting this show of — whatever the show was, looked down at the document and did not see his name on the line which was dotted. He saw Mandamás' signature and initials here and there, but he did not see his own name.

"There must be some mistake, Paola. I was the clear choice of the plebiscite at the Cinco Estrellas Bar! Yet I do not see my name inked in as expected."

"No mistake, Mr. Mayor. There as you can clearly see are Mandamás' signatures and there are his initials and there is the name of the Interim Prime Minister. If you would, please read it."

He hesitated. "P-P-Paola Labioth."

"That's meeeee." She sung. "Now if you please, I need to begin prime ministering, Mr. Mayor."

Rafael Izquierdo's shoulders immediately sagged, he knew he had been hoodwinked and so glumly returned his rolodex, family photos, pen and pencil set, Mr. Met, and various bric-à-brac back to the box. He hefted the carton, took one look at the trappings, and walked to the far door and out the building. The mayor looked like Joe Btfsplk,[1] with his humiliation hovering like a dark cloud above his head.

Paola Labios, PTA president, former prostitute, one-time movie star, and recently appointed Prime Minister (Interim) of La República sat behind her desk and began enjoying the commandeered trappings of power. She looked bemusedly at the former dictator's note and phone number.

"Inga!"

---

[1] A character in the world of Al Capp.

Chapter 40

Paola's Constitutional Crisis

Paola was installed at the Presidential Palace and feeling quite lonely. It was a big place with many rooms occupying two wings of a masterpiece in the French Baroque style of architecture. Originally designed and built by an early 19th century French governor with grandiose plans for La República, or Le Republique as it was known in the days of occupation. By the French. American occupation(s) came later.

The governor, Federic Patek du Provence ("Little Freddie" to his intimate friends), did not get to enjoy the fruits of his labors. A small man and amateur architect, he spent months on the designs and took great pleasure in the overseeing the construction of his great work and all its concealed idiosyncrasies. Very hands-on.

What rankled most of those in his orbit, however, was the non-stop spewing of vulgar orders to servants, workers, and tradesmen. Anyone around him was subject to a poetic roux of polyglot profanity: crude English, French, Franco-Provençal, and Spanish expressions never before heard on this side of the Atlantic. The Frenchman yelled at his workers and supplicants accusing them of bizarre sexual practices with goats, sheep, swans, and other livestock.

A few weeks before the completion of the Governor's Palace, Patek contracted a particularly nasty strain of the Zika virus. Although many in his circle appeared to be grief-stricken, the news was taken rather well. Morale improved almost immediately on the palace grounds.

Little Freddie Patek was stricken by the virus while on an expedition to discover the sacred remains of La Virgen de Aguacate during La República's wet season. The governor was a known devotee of the Virgen and a fan of stuffed avocado salad, thus the foray into the far forest reaches of his governorship. His campaign included soldiers, two cooks, waiters, native bearers, his concubine, a priest, scouts, and his trusted equerry. They plunged deep into the forest of what later became known as Aguacate Province; a tropical fen infested with poisonous reptiles and airborne enemies of the crown; one of which landed on his excellency's neck. The assailant insect inserted his (or her) proboscis removing a small amount of blood and leaving behind many tiny friends.

Patek was ported back to the palace quite unceremoniously in his gilded, therefore heavy, sedan chair, the preferred mode of transit for governors and peers of the realm. Needless to say, it was a soggy slog back to La Capital, or La Capitale as it was known.

The Zika, an unknown strain at the time, wasn't even called Zika but the *"Qué Asco,"* or "How Disgusting," Virus manifesting itself in two ways: first breaking out into scarlet suppurating disks on his face. The unfortunate lesions were large, about the size of a U.S. twenty-five cent piece prompting the governor's servants to giggle and call him "Pizza Face Patek" behind his back. Second, the virus caused the rare "Reverse Tourette's" syndrome and to everyone's surprise the overly vulgar governor began speaking politely. When he heard the tittering behind his back, the governor wanted to scream accusing them of unspeakable acts with the palace dogs; instead all he could manage was "thank thee kindly" or "thou art most gracious," and "thank you for your attention in this matter."

Silver-tongued Governor Patek lasted but a few weeks before his tragic passing from the *Qué Asco* virus. He not only endured the humiliation of physical decomposition, but also the frustration of not being able to let loose his usual strings of multi-cultural obscenities. It was tragic.

Freddie managed to stay alive long enough to watch the final avocado trees brought back from his expedition and planted to grace the entrance of the magnificent palace he had built. However, as the groundskeeper tamped the soil around the last of the trees with his shovel, word came to the palace guards that the British had landed in the harbor and were at that very minute marching toward the palace with plans for the governor's gory execution.

It was then he uttered his final words, in response to the warnings of the guards who rushed into his chambers with the report of the English dogs marching toward La Capitale.

"The British are coming, the British are coming," they shouted.

"Fuck me!" Little Freddie Patek responded thereby signaling the joyous news that his "Reverse Tourette's" had been cured.

However, the governor died of unrelated symptoms and the French moved on to eat snails and other slimy things in France, Martinique, and Freddie's home province of Provence. As far as the monarchy's plans for La Republique, there were none — the Central American territory was abandoned by the French and soon after by the Dutch, then the Italians, then the Portuguese, then the English. Finally, abandoned by all the colonial powers, it returned to be called La República.

Fast forward two hundred years or so and …

… Prime Minister Paola Labios wondered if she was alone in the Prime Minister's palace. She was occupying Máximo's old apartments and office but couldn't help but feel a presence in the faraway opposite wing in the rooms where *La Bruja*, Máximo's ex-wife, had held forth with that monk Gregorio. *What happened to him, I wonder?* Ms. Labios was loathe to check into the noises mostly because they were very creepy but also because it would take forever for her to find the other wing in the veritable maze of the building and what if *La Bruja* was there? It was enough to send shivers up the spine.

It hadn't taken long for Paola to move in. One trip in William's newish Town Car, which he christened "Rocky," was sufficient to carry Paola's goods including the furnishings from the shared room that served as bedroom for Paola and her two sons, Axl and Slash. She looked around her office and told the floors and the walls, "This will do nicely."

Meanwhile the two kids were loving the adventure of moving from a two-room apartment into a 100-room house, which they explored endlessly when not corralled by their *au pair* who was preparing their breakfast before taking them to Colegio James Monroe (Manifest Destiny!).

"You must chew your toast twenty times, children. Then you will be strong."

"Inga, just get them dressed and off to school, they will be late."

Inga, former masseuse of the Dictator-for-Life was hired by the Prime Minister (Interim) to take care of her two boys while she (the Prime Minister) attended to the complicated task of running a third world nation without cracking heads or forced arrests. It was daunting.

Máximo had a personal secretary, his inept son-in-law Güicho, to handle mundane office tasks; so Paola was surprised that Inga said **she** was the Generalíssimo's personal secretary. Knowing the dictator's perverse proclivities, Paola quickly filled in the blanks without asking the lithe blond with the long legs exactly what her "personal secretary" duties were. Apparently, they were mostly horizontal.

During the course of their first private conversation, Inga unraveled the tale of her escape from her hometown of Malmö where she left her abusive husband Sven and a family that didn't understand her need to find a safe place for herself. "After all," they said, "Sven is rich! Sven hess a mansion und a yacht!" Sven was also a brute and treated Inga like chattel.

Inga answered a classified ad in her local newspaper, the Malmö Monitor that read: *Benevolent Dictator of tropical paradise seeks personal secretary. Immed. F/T Salary DOE. EOE. Benefits incl. med./dental.* So she fled her homeland, seeking something better, something away from the abuse of family and spouse, and landed in the spacious apartments of the dictator of a small republic in a part of the world unknown to her. She took pity on the man who battled his own demons with a wicked spouse and offered him what he wanted, which started with massages. He was kind to her, so she stayed on.

Máximo had left his post, so this new woman came in to replace him. This Paola who had come to call on the Generalíssimo from time to time, Inga knew she was a *prostituerad* as they said in Sweden. How she got to move in so quickly when the Generalíssimo moved out, she couldn't understand but Inga liked Paola, nonetheless. And her picaresque children made the Scandinavian smile remembering her own brothers Axl and Snedstreck back in Malmö.

"Yes, *Drottning* Paola."

"Just Paola, Inga."

"Yust Paola?"

"*Sí.*"

"Well, they are dressed; I take them now to the school *ja?*"

"*Ja.* I mean, *sí!* Go my babies, learn your maths, give your *mamita* a kiss."

"*Adios, mami,*" said Axl.

"*Farväl, mami,*" said Slash.

Paola exhaled deeply and watched her two boys leave with the *au pair.* She ached seeing them leave her sight; no mother likes to see her children go out any door. But it was time to run a country.

Paola Labios sat behind the large desk and examined her pitiful, non-Prime Minister type accessories. There were the photographs of her children, of course. And one of her best friends Yettsy who had found love with that nice *gringo* Dennis Martin and had left with him to the *Yunae*. And the small trophy Mrs. Mool had given her: a gold, plastic man holding a large sphere in his hand with a brass plaque that read, "MidAmerica Lanes, Indiana City." It was a gesture meant to congratulate her on playing Ilsa in that farce Tirofijo put together.

What an adventure that was, she remembered fondly. 'Casablanca' as imagined by the crime boss who thought he was a movie director. *Jajaja!* The scene was recorded on Chac Mool's camera and that *gringo* Dennis was supposed to take the tape back to Hollywood, in California, to the studio. But nothing happened. Paola, who thought she might become a star as a result, had begun to abandon such dreams a while ago.

Her attention returned to take in the offices, **her** offices. Something had to be done with the pictures Mandamás had left hanging. The collection was a who's who of tyrants: Máximo with Rafael Trujillo, Máximo with Fulgencio Batista, Máximo with Papa Doc, and his favorite, Máximo with *the* Generalíssimo himself, Francisco Franco. "These will have to go," Paola said. "I'll keep the mirror though."

There was a business-like knock on the door. "I wonder what —"

Paola set Mrs. Mool's trophy down and looked up to find Rafael Izquierdo's head poking inside the door. Presuming the rest of the former communist was attached to that head, Paola said "Come in, come in, Mr. Mayor."

She wasn't particularly wanting to see the man, but anything would be an improvement on the dullness of the day and perhaps he would help her get started on this business of governance.

"Good morning, Paola," he said cheerily as he walked across the sea of grooved wood.

"*Primera Ministra*, if you will. To what do I owe this pleasure, Don Rafael. Please sit."

"*Gracias*. It is so strange."

"What?"

Izquierdo turned serious and glowered, "Well that it was I, duly elected by his peers, the elites of our nation, I who was sitting in that very chair when you barged in to usurp my government."

"Ay, Rafael, I did not usurp anything. Duped perhaps. But usurped never. I simply took advantage and wrote my own name on the Constitution of 1935 naming me the Interim Prime Minister. It was an act of impulse."

"That is just it, Paola —"

"Prime Minister."

"Ok, Prime Minister then. But you, a woman, cannot be the Prime Minister! This whole charade provth it." Izquierdo, nervous and excited, was lispy.

"What proves what, Mr. Mayor." Paola was wavering. It was an internal battle between the forces of bemusement and armies of anger.

"Your act of impulse. We cannot have women lead the country. Women are ill-suited for the job. You are too impulthive, and your month —"

"Stop right there, *pendejo*!" The armies of anger had won.

"Well, look over the Constitution, Paola. I am sure the framers specifically said men and not women could be Prime Minister. You are, clearly, not a man!" The mayor's gaze had strayed a bit southward toward Paola's bona fides.

Paola was on shaky ground here. She wasn't sure of the exact wording in the constitution *vis a vis* male prime ministership. She thought that in 1935 it was entirely possible that whoever penned that legislation would specifically write in the word "man." Possible? No, it was probable, she thought.

"My eyes are up here, Izquierdo! Yes, you are indeed correct. Mr. Mayor." Paola was going to play a bluff. She heard Inga stifling a giggle in Güicho's old office where the Swede had made herself at home.

"I am?" Izquierdo was stunned by the quick capitulation. He began mentally rearranging the furniture to accommodate scholarly books, a globe, Mr. Met, and his bric-à-brac.

"Yes, I have reviewed the document very carefully. So as to stay within the limit of the law, of course."

"Of course."

"And it says the Prime Minister is a 'man' a 'he.' Not a 'she.' Just as you said, Mr. Mayor."

"You mean Mr. Prime Minister, *jajaja*." Izquierdo was giddy now that he knew he would be back in the saddle and continued to stare at Paola's breasts. They were heaving.

Paola ignored his breastward staring. "No, *señor*. I mean Mr. Mayor because as the Constitution of 1935 states that the Prime Minister is to be a man, it leaves the question of gender of the **Interim** Prime Minister up in the air. It is not defined."

Rafael Izquierdo's line of sight returned to look Paola in the eye. He gulped loudly and blubbered, "But I am Ithquierdo, I am more mathculine."

"So you see, *Señor Alcalde*, as Interim Prime Minister and a full-blooded woman, as I am sure you are aware, I am in control until a Prime Minister is so named in which case I wish you lots of luck."

Rafael Izquierdo was again a deflated man and who wouldn't be if they had attained the vaulted office of prime minister of their country twice, only to have had it wrested from their grasp twice by a scheming former lady of the evening. Rafael took inventory of the situation. He was somewhat relieved of the onerous task of running La República which was, not to put too fine a point on it, a miserable mess.

Izquierdo, known for his smart sophistication, rose from his seat and spoke a bit of Shakespeare that he saved for august occasions, "Let discretion be the better part of valor."

Paola Labios, not to be outdone, responded, "The quality of mercy is unstrain'd."

Thus, the Prime Minister (Interim) watched the mayor leave despondently for the second time in 24 hours.

Chapter 41

The Labios Cabinet

BANG! BANG! BANG!

Everyone jumped when they heard the gavel pounding; the sounds bounced off the empty walls of the palace. Paola, the Prime Minister (Interim) looked down the magnificent table at her seated cabinet, the leaders of the new La República, the gavel in her raised fist. The table, among the war reparations La República had exacted from El Corinto under the conditions of the Guacamole Act, was now to be part of history as the newly formed cabinet was convened ready to advance the glorious future of the republic.

The room, a large dining room meant for state banquets, had been forgotten during the Mandamás regime and unearthed by Axl and Slash on one of their explorations. It was large and, thus, useful for the gathering of such distinguished public servants. It was, however, quite dreary: a dank, dark space with no windows. Its only source of light was a dirty chandelier with six 50-watt bulbs jury-rigged by the Minister of Public Utilities, the palace handyman.

"Ministers, quiet please!" Paola was trying to establish some order as the cabinet was in full gossip and speculation mode. Ugarte and Izquierdo, Minister of Communication and Interior respectively, were arguing over the type of wood used in the grand table. "Izquierdo, I know through my research that this very table, which, as you know, was wrested from El Corinto as war reparations. I discuss this in Chap —"

"Enough with your book, Ugarte. But what forest woods were used? The table is elegant. Very palatial."

"You did not let me finish. In Chapter Six, I chronicle the Corinthian carpenter whose very labors produced the pride of the palace from the finest *ceiba* trunk in Aguacate province."

Meanwhile, further down the table toward the furthest end from the Prime Minister (Interim), Klaus Von Klaus, Minister of Health was making eyes at Inga. Tirso, the only one seemingly taking the proceedings seriously, had his head buried in a large tome, an English language encyclopedia.

"Ministers and advisors! Please report on your findings. First will the Minister of the Treasury *por favor*, please give us a state of La República's finances?" She looked past the other heads on either side of the table. All had cocked forward and turned in the direction of the Treasury Minister who sat far far away. It was a very large table, indeed.

Tirso Lee, perhaps La República's most successful merchant of legal goods, was beaming. Paola Labios, at the head of the table, took this to be good news from the third-generation Korean immigrant. She was silently patting herself on the back for her wise decision to appoint the country's only Asian to the important post of Minister of the Treasury. Tirso was known for his integrity and attention to detail after all.

The owner of Donde Tirso was glowing, ready to burst with the news.

"What do you have for me, Tirso?" Paola smiled with anticipation.

The man could not contain himself, using an index finger to punch the ledger he had been reading, loudly blurted out "326, 121, and 44!" He looked around at the blank visages of the other ministers, then at the hopeful Prime Minister whose glassy-eyed stare and smile were seemingly glued to her pretty face. It was so quiet you could have heard an assassin's spent shell casing drop. The quiet ricocheted off the blank walls.

"And?"

Tirso was ready to leap from his chair with the news that Carl Yastrzemski, his favorite player and famed Red Sox outfielder, had achieved the grand trifecta way up there in Boston. He won the American League triple crown.

"You can imagine madame, Prime Minister —"

"— Paola. Just Paola, Tirso."

"I beg forgiveness. I was just reciting some statistics. Base-ball statistics. From *La Yunae*."

"It is okay, Tirso." Her rolled eyes were lost on Tirso, too far away to see them. "Go on. You were going to say. About the treasury?"

"Oh, nothing."

"Not the *beisbol*, Minister. But the treasury. Please report."

"I was. Reporting, I mean. We have nothing. Nada. Only a handful of *tucanes*. Nothing really."

"That is impossible, the Mandamáses did not spend any money, that is why our infrastructure is in such a state. *¡By the Virgin!*, what is happening?" Paola in her exasperation had lowered her-self to invoking the patron saint of La República. *Not a good way to start a new era*, she chastised herself. "I am sorry friend. Did you find **anything** in the treasury?"

"I found," the Minister read from a yellow legal pad on the table in front of him, "Forty *tucanes* in small bills, a handful of jacks but no rubber ball, a can of tennis balls, uh Wilson Wimbledon Spe-cials, some kite string but no kite, and 100 boxes of these —." He held up a cheap, purple plastic tiara of the kind used in costume dress. "Each box has (looking down at his sheet) 144 tiaras."

A chair screeched sounding like fingernails on a chalkboard as Ugarte, the Minister of Communications, stood suddenly and de-clared, "That is gross, madame Prime Ministress," he said.

"I know Ugueth, it is a terrible situation, but you are not helping."

"But madame, *Primera Ministra*, I was just pointing out that the contents of the box are a gross. One hundred and forty-four. One gross."

The Prime Minister stared at the pompous pedant she had appointed to head up communications in La República. Paola Labios, in the first of many acts of self-control, resisted the urge to wedge one of her beautifully manicured thumbnails deep into the small space between Ugueth Ugarte's dull brown eyes.

"Whatever, Ugarte. Please refrain until asked. Now Tirso, if you please. Where does that leave us?"

"*Quebrados y jodidos*.[1] We have no money to pay our workers. Or the police, teachers, nurses, nada." She started to wonder if the appointment of Tirso was such a good idea. Fortunately, one of the cabinet ministers interrupted. Unfortunately, it was Ugarte.

"Madame, let the record show that the Minister of Interiorrrr has asked for the floor," he said pointing to Izquierdo who seemed to be in a daydream.

"*Que chingados*, Ugarte. No one is making a record. Perhaps you should be appointed secretary." Paola may have spent much of her professional life supine at the Happy Fish, but she did know her way around a boardroom.

The opportunity to knock down the journalist a peg or two was not lost.

Izquierdo woke up and declared, "I move Ugarte appointed secretary of the Cabinet!"

"Second."

"Third!"

"So moved. All in favor?"

---

[1] Broke and fucked.

"Aye."

"Aye."

"Aye."

"Ay-yay-yay!"

"Ugarte, you are now the secretary. Take notes. Tirso, give him your pad."

The Korean slid the pad halfway down the length of the table where it stopped in front of the frowning columnist.

"Ok, where were we? Mr. Secretary, please read back the minutes. Never mind. I believe Rafael Izquierdo, our mayor and new Minister of Interior (she bowed regally toward her erstwhile rival for the Republican throne) wanted the floor. Rafael …"

Rising to the occasion, Izquierdo stood up. "I wanted to ask the Minister of the Treasury to clarify our financial status. I do not believe I heard correctly."

"We are broke, *alcalde.*"

"Minister, please."

"We are broke MI-NI-STER."

Paola started chewing a nail.

"Surely you mean there is only enough to pay the cabinet, it behooves us to maintain —"

"No money, MINISTER. Not for you, not for the teach-ers."

"Not good."

"No not good at all. Where can we get funds, Tirso?"

"Well, Paola, I am at a loss," Tirso answered. "It appears that Mandamás and/or his wife took the money from the treasury, the *gringos* are furious because of the thing there in Aguacate, you know the CIA battle? The American Ambassador is not in residence, KFC says they cannot pay any sales taxes because someone stole their chicken money, other businesses are following suit. They do not trust the new government. Should I go on?"

Paola surprised her own atheist self and cried, *"Por la Virgen,* does anyone have good news?"

A chair scraped, and a minister rose. Izquierdo reluctantly ceded the floor and sat down, his own chair squealing. "Your excellency, if I may."

"What now Ugueth?"

"I wish to make a motion."

One of the heads, possibly the Minister of Parks and Wildlife, made the crack, "Then excuse yourself and go down the hall." Everyone exploded in laughter; it was good to clear the room of tension. Paola remained as serious as possible, "Yes, Ugarte what is your, uh, what did you want to add?"

"I move that we name the defeat of the CIA and the Brayan Buenaventura Brigade the 'Second Battle of Aguacate!' It will be a glorious thing, parades, pyrotechnics, pomp! And a wonderful addition to my History of La República which I am in the process of rewriting for the Second Edition —"

"—*Puta Madre*, Ugarte, stop! I need some real help here. Anyone?"

A knock on the door garnered everyone's attention. No one moved. Was it a coup? Was there a junta? Had *La Bruja* returned for her gross of gross tiaras? Paola optimistically turned her chair toward the door and bellowed "Come in!"

The door opened and a young man walked through it looking like an English gentleman of leisure down to his Harris tweed hunting jacket, pipe, and black felt bowler. Up and down the table, the ministers maintained a respectful quiet. Gravitas was coming out of the man's very pores. He greeted the Prime Minister with a courtly bow at the waist and saluted the gathering with the curved handle of a tightly wrapped Brigg & Co. umbrella. *"Buenas tardes,* Prime Minister, I am at your service." The man's diction was perfect and carried the musical notes of the *republicano* accent.

"Come in, come in. Ministers! I present to you La República's Minister of Foreign Affairs and Culture."

"*Hijo?*" Said the old mayor.

"*Papá!*" Said the new arrival.

"Yunior!" Said the cabinet.

Yunior, scion of the Izquierdo family, one of the heroes of the Second Battle of Aguacate, and former suspected communist was the newly appointed Minister of F.A. and C. Having an English public-school education, he was perfectly bilingual and the one to deal with, as Paola put it, "that ball sack in the embassy."

The meeting was paused as everyone welcomed the well-liked son of Izquierdo into their midst. There was some manly back-slapping and a polite curtsy from Inga before the chairwoman and PM (I) banged the gavel once again for attention. "*Ministros*, let us continue. We welcome Yunior Izquierdo to the cabinet. Yunior we welcome you! What do you have for us, something good?" *Please!*

"Madame Prime Minister, Ministers, Inga, Dad. We are in a very difficult situation. My sources at the British compound in El Corinto say the *gringos* are *encabronados*, or, as they say in the Queen's English, 'fucking cheesed off.' Mostly it is the CIA that is angry, but they are gone from our shores, left to fight another day for American Interests somewhere else. Anyway, there is talk of an embargo." He paused for effect.

The air went out of the room.

"An embargo of *republicano* goods until there is a democratic transfer of power," the Foreign Affairs and Culture minister clarified.

"What does that mean?"

"It means we can no longer sell, legally sell rum, coffee, cigars, etc., in *La Yunae*. The effects will be catastrophic to our tourism sector!"

"No, what does 'democratic transfer of power' mean?"

"It means we have to elect someone the *gringos* will approve."

"*Pinches gringos*, we have ensured due process as outlined in the Constitution of 1935. As I wrote in Chapt —"

"Shut the fuck up, Ugarte!" was the unanimous response.

I need a miracle, the Prime Minister (Interim) mused.

Chapter 42

Paola Calls For Help

Paola, feeling the loneliness of command, knew the cabinet meeting had not gone well. Nothing was accomplished. Her cabinet talked the talk but as far as walking the walk, they were more comfortable on a bar stool ordering another round of daiquiris from Wulther.

Paola did not have access to "SWOT Analysis" as delineated by Italian economist Clementus Sixtus, Ph.D. In it Sixtus reveals the benefits of introspection, particularly in the evaluation of one's weaknesses. Had she read the text she might have listed the following under "Weaknesses":

A depleted treasury

A constituency of businesses that claimed they couldn't pay their sales taxes

An ongoing chaos with traffic

Returning the schools back to a program of math, science, history, etc.

A rising petty crime rate

The American embargo on Republican exports

A million other things

Paola had a vision for the country's future: improved education, rights for women and gays, improved medical care in the provinces, an equitable relationship with El Corinto (those *jueputas*!), and other progressive concepts.

She had little confidence in the handful of maladroits she had assembled as her cabinet. Well-meaning idiots. But she had to start somewhere, she felt. Rome wasn't built in a day; a journey of a thousand miles begins with a single step. Choose your cliche. "They need a *cachetada*, a good kick in the ass," she thought.

"*Por la Virgen*, I do not have time for that, I need a strong second-in-command. Someone with leadership abilities and experience. That's what I need! This business of running a country, it takes someone to light fires under the assess of people like Ugarte and Izquierdo …"

"Café, Madam *statsminister?*" The blond assistant had come out of her cubby hole, the one occupied by the former first son-in-law, with a tray and a cup of steaming coffee.

"Bless you, Inga, set it right there."

The benefits of Central American coffee, specifically coffee with Republican provenance, are legion. Doctors in La República, many of whom owned coffee plantations themselves, advocated a couple of cups a day for physical and mental well-being. Some credited the *grano de oro*[1] with improved sexual potency. Coffee, as many have come to discover, stimulates the brain's synapses.

Installed in the highest seat of government, which was a classic ox-blood leather wingback chair with matching ottoman, Paola finished her delicious *tinto*.[2] She smiled at her secretary Inga who put the cup back on the tray and retreated into her closet space. A worried Inga sat at her desk and watched through the unclosed door as Paola paced, looked out the window, paced some more.

The pretty Prime Minister tired of her pacing and sat down with her head in her hands, elbows on the desk. Minutes passed, Inga worried until there was a snapping of fingers! Paola's fingers. It looked like Paola had experienced a brainstorm of some kind.

She, Paola, blurted out, "Yes! It's radical, but it might just work."

---

[1] Grain of gold. A soubriquet for coffee.
[2] Black coffee.

Inga was staring with her mouth open and wondering what was so radical, what was the Interim Prime Minister up to? The Interim Prime Minister hurriedly reached across her desk for the phone and dialed a number. After a pause Inga could make out an intermittent buzzing. The phone at the other end was ringing.

"C'mon, c'mon. Pick up, *idiota*." Paola was impatiently tapping her right foot.

Six or seven rings later, someone picked up the receiver.

Inga made out a man's voice. It was hard to make out his words. "Coca Cola?" He seemed to say.

"Hola, it is me. Listen. I need your help. There is so much to do, and I need a man like you, strong man, a leader, someone to be my second-in-command an underboss."

"Mmm quo," came the muffled response.

"It is Paola, *baboso!* Seriously, can you help? Are you willing to serve La República?"

"Mngun."

"I need a second-in-command."

"Nnguhn. Corleone. Stanito?"

"I guess. Sure, just like Sonny. You are James Caan, ok? But seriously, *pendejo,* will you be my underboss so that I can run this country?"

"Qeplu mixtolivia?"

"Simple. Just like a mafia family (Paola was inventing at this point). You be my underboss, my enforcer. But a nice one! No beatings. Threats maybe, but no blood. You would be it. The power behind the throne. Or in front of it, I cannot remember which. Anyway, I would be in the palace prime ministering to the country's needs. You would be, er persuading people to follow my policies, kick some *culos*, get the treasury replenished."

"Atdpula nvstergmmns!"

"I am sorry about that. It will be our secret no one has to know."

"Puffnta plu snetiv!"

"I know it is embarrassing. But I had no other option at the time."

"Pretta lxviun menu?"

"It is just me and Inga and my kids Axl and Slash, of course. I have the whole palace to myself. Even *La Bruja* and her monk are gone!"

"Cque folla sinq!!"

"Absolutely not! This is not an exchange of services! No conjugal visits, *cabrón*! Do it, you know, for old times' sake. This will earn you that respect you're always whining about."

"Whumma hopis hopis, ngumya?"

"What's in it for you? The honor of serving your Prime Minister. (Reluctant Pause) And 10% of any revenue you bring to the treasury."

"Znquit!"

"12%!"

"Znque!"

"Deal, you get 15% of the revenue. But I —." Paola paused, she thought she heard a gasp. She shook her head and went back to the conversation, "I need you to do other things. The ministers need, eh, stimulation. With the schools, the —"

In her tiny chamber, Inga's eyes were wide open. The secretary had figured out who was at the other end of the phone and couldn't believe that Paola was making a deal with her adversary.

"Mmano upanieme?"

"Good! Come to the next cabinet meeting. It is a week from today. Can you make it? I know it is a lot to ask, but I need you, the country needs you, and there is that 15%."

"Etoin shrdlu!"

"*Deacachimba!*[3] Remember one week from today, come to the palace. But wait outside with Inga until I announce you to the cabinet."

"Inga Cque folla sinq?"

"No, she's off limits. Put your dick away for once. See you at the meeting." Inga bit her fist to keep from laughing.

"Wagyu mropa?"

"What? I do not care. You can wear whatever. Come in tennis shorts if you want. What a question. See you at the meeting, *menso.*"[4]

Paola, dropping the receiver like a microphone after a great speech, it fell with a satisfactory clacking before settling into its cradle. She leaned back and said to the dusty ceiling, "It is a miracle."

---

[3] Really, really great!
[4] Stupid.

Chapter 43

The Underboss Takes Office

A week had passed and nothing had been resolved. Paola's inbox was empty. No resolutions, no laws to enact, no financial reports or reports of any kind. "What the fuck have those imbeciles been doing?"

She walked into the dining banquet-cum-cabinet meeting boardroom to a room full of actors auditioning for the role of Atticus Finch. Every one of her distinguished ministers was pacing, speechifying, making grandiose statesmen-like gestures, puffing chests, removing eyeglasses, putting on eyeglasses, banging fists into open palms, and carrying on with an air of self-importance.

She slammed the door behind her and as the discoursing ceased little by little, a paper airplane floated to a perfect landing in the middle of the oval table. "Kiwi" was written on its side in a childish hand. Paola approached her chair at the head of the table, looked around at her cabinet suppressing a gag reflex before sitting.

Chairs scraped annoyingly against the uncarpeted floor as the rest of the chamber took their respective seats one by one. Inga had nicely made paper tents with their cabinet posts written on them in an elegant hand. The ministers quickly realized their responsibilities did not match their paper tents, so there more scraping of chair against floor as they got up to switch seats, clumsily bumping into one another and with a lot of "excuse, no excuse ME, after you, no after YOU!" the men finally found their seats.

"You know you could have just switched the … never mind. I call the meeting to order, report to me whatever the hell you have to report to me." Paola was already feeling defeatist.

There was a pause. Ugarte took advantage and rose from his chair. The abrasive sound of his chair dragging against the floor only served to further irritate the Interim Prime Minister.

"Your excellency, if I may?"

"Yes, Ugarte, what is it? You have something to report?"

"Not specifically. More in the area of a recommendation."

"Recommendation?"

"*Sí*, madame Prime Minister. Our government is now ten days old or so, I think it is time we hold a press conference. Maybe open it to the general public. As the Minister of Communication —"

"And pray tell dear Ugueth, what would we say at this event?"

"Why, Paola, all the advances of the new government of course. It would be most propitious —"

"Advances you say, Ugarte?"

"Yes, Your Excellency. Advances." The journalist and historian stood holding a recently purchased authoritarian looking pair of glasses, referred to as a pince-nez, which he felt gave him an air of dignity appropriate in the proceedings. Instead he appeared to be more like a proud puppy after retrieving a soggy tennis ball. Had he a tail, he would have been wagging it happily.

Paola's famous temper oozed out of her every pore. "Advances, *pendejo*? Advances, you moron! There are no advances. Zero! You know what we have Mr. Minister?"

Ugarte began to sweat. He gulped. "No?"

"Whatever is the opposite of advances that's what we have. No advances. Who's next?"

No one wanted to be next of course so there was a lot of fidgeting, repositioning of name cards, and staring at the ballroom ceiling, which was badly in need of a coat of paint. Paola was face down, her head in her hands. She sighed and looked up toward Rafael Izquierdo the Minister of Interior and whose son, Yunior, was noticeably absent. He might have news from his son.

"What about the *gringos*, Izquierdo? Where's your son, Izquierdo? Has he met Two Dix? First order of business I should think. For the Minister. Of. Fucking. Foreign Affairs!! Where is he?"

"He'th back in Aguacate. Today is the weekly book club meeting. I think they are covering 'Valley of the Dollth.'" Rafael, sweating through his jacket, suddenly brightened. "They changed their name, Excellency. Now it is just the ABC."

"ABC?"

"Aguacate Book Club! No longer the Culture Commune. Sounds less communisty. That should make the *gringos* happy, yes?" Izquierdo was proud to be his son's proxy and bring this piece of information, this foreign relations coup, to the cabinet meeting. He looked around expectantly.

"Very, very good, Izquierdo. Oh, one question?"

"Ask away Paola."

Paola looked the grinning man right in the eye and, asked in a friendly voice saturated with sarcasm, "Did they lift the embargo?"

"Uh, no."

The head of government then gave a big sigh and heaving of her Latin breasts that diverted the assembly's attention in that direction. The only exception was Klaus Von Klaus, Minister of Health who was busy staring directly across the table at Inga's Nordic breasts. Klaus had been a natural for the post of Health Minister because of his experience in Germany during the war. He was a doctor and held the prestigious post of *Oberstabsveterinär*, he was the veterinarian responsible for the treatment of the German High Command's Rottweilers. Paola, thinking Klaus Von Klaus was an actual doctor, had him installed as the head of all things health in

La República. Paola had very high hopes for the former national socialist.

"Any news Klaus Von Klaus? What does the Minister of Health have for us today? Vaccination programs? Sex education classes? Distribution of condoms?"

Klaus Von Klaus slid-scraped his chair away from the table and stood at attention. "*Eure exzellenz!*" He loudly brought his heels together sending a CLICK that pinged off the bare walls. "*Achtung,* I have news."

Paola, in her despair, had disheveled her gorgeous mane and took on a look of desperation. She was coming apart at the seams but managed to look up at her reformed Nazi of a minister with optimism.

"You have news, Klaus? Wonderful! Attention ministers. Let us listen to the report of our Minister of Health!"

Klaus flashed a Germanic smile, white Teutonic teeth and icy blue eyes, threw back his broad shoulders and cleared his throat. He gave another CLICK of his heels, looked around the cabinet room and announced,

"*Jawohl,* here is another Zika outbreak on the Corinto border!"

"Klaus, my friend, how do you say 'sit your ass down' in your language?"

"*Sich Hinsetzen, mein ministerin.*"

"Well, *sich* whatever, you Teutonic twit and shut up!"

"*Jawohl,*" Klaus said and, cowed by Paola's sudden anger, sat.

She turned her eyes, pupils whirling like pinwheels, at Tirso. *Good old, reliable Tirso. What a wise choice I made putting Tirso atop the Treasury.*

"Treasury, what have you done about the state of our country's finances? Extended our loan payment schedules? Re-indexed the currency? Issued any bonds? Obtained new credits?"

The Korean shopkeeper seemed distracted by something. He stayed seated and replied, "Things are difficult, Paola."

"How difficult, Tirso?" Tirso represented her greatest hope for something, anything, just a scintilla of sanity in the chamber. His reputation as a businessman, educated at MIT, owner of many stores in La República was what had given Paola confidence.

"We just cannot get past Mr. Gibson."

"Is he with the World Bank?" she asked.

"Not exactly."

"The IMF?"

"Mmmm. No."

"The First Trans-Caribbean Bank of Broward." Paola had reached the limit of financial institutions known to her.

"No."

"WHAT then??"

"He is with St. Louis."

"Oh, I see, a bank in St. Louis. That's good. Branching out. So are you trying to make inroads with this Mr. Gibson?"

"Well not exactly. You see madame Prime Minister (Interim), he is just unhittable. Shut us down twice! It is the Curse of the Bambino. I can feel it hovering. And Gibson is taking the mound in game seven. Tomorrow!"

"*Qué fuckety fuck carajo* is my Finance Minister talking about?"

"The World Series of course. Oh, Paola, it has been tooth and nail. I have not been able to tear myself away from the radio, all the games are broadcast on Radio Martí. Plus the pre-game. And the post-game. Hasn't left me with much time for other things. A lot is riding on this for, for, for uh, for the Nation —"

"For the Nation of La República?"

"No, for the Red Sox Nation!"

She returned her gaze back to Izquierdo, Minister of Interior. *What does this schmuck have for me?*

"Izquierdo!"

Izquierdo jumped, banging his knee on the table apron, "S-S-Sí Paola?"

"What can you add to these proceedings? As Minister of Interior, I mean. What exciting things have you done? Voter registration? Plans to expand La Chingada? Fixing potholes? Addressing the green lights issue. What?!"

"Oh, well I have been very busy, ma'am. Very busy." Izquierdo responded, rubbing his knee. "I have ordered new curtainth for the officth. The old ones were just, well they had to go. Also I am getting rug thamples later today, I thought the Prime Minister's office should have thomething to cover up those unthightly grooves. Then there's the issue of —"

Paola shot him a glance stopping him mid-report. "*Imbecil!* I remind you, Izquierdo, you are the Minister of the Interior, not interiors. (*What a shit-for-brains.*) What do you have in the way of ministering to the COUNTRY'S interior, Señor Izquierdo?"

"I am not quite sure what that means exactly. But I have ordered new mattrethes for the Happy Fish? Gotta great deal."

Paola, for the first time in her life, was speechless. She heard a cough and looked up to see Inga "ahemming" into her fist. Inga nodded and gestured to the door by cocking her lovely Swedish head.

Finally!

Paola stood suddenly with a violent screech of her chair that sent a chill up the spines of all. The ministers believed it was proper protocol to stand so after a slight pause they decided to stand as well. The pulling out of the chairs creating shrill noises like the screaming in a bad opera where all the players sang a different tune. After the aria of the furniture was concluded the ministers were on their feet appearing alert.

"*Sich hinsetzen,* you idiots. Sit down!" Paola was feeling her new German vocabulary was very apt.

More scraping of chairs coupled with some mumbling between the ministers unsure if this was proper protocol. Ugarte had left his "Robert's Rules of Order" at home (it was bracing a table leg), so he was unsure.

"I have an announcement!" Paola banged the table.

There was respectful silence and a bit of excitement. Something was happening! The ministers exchanged glances with one another, Klaus managed another glance at Inga's magnificent Scandinavian embonpoint.

"There is to be a new appointment. Someone to lead you *huevones*.[1] A leader. A respected leader. Someone you all know very well."

The ministers immediately began to speculate who the new appointee was to be.

One of the ministers ventured, sotto voce, "She is bringing him back, I just know it."

"Presenting the Underboss of La República ..." Paola swept her arm toward the open door at the far end of the room.

Let the minutes show that there was a collective gasp in the room as the ministers beheld a man in jodhpurs, shiny English riding boots with small brass spurs, a tweed jacket and a dashing deerstalker. He paced toward the group, flourishing a riding crop, dragging spurs across the floor.

"Tirofijo?!"

"Tirofijo?"

---

[1] Good-for-nothings.

"T-T-Tirofijo!"

Yes, it was Tirofijo. local racketeer, trader of endangered species, and seller of the national patrimony. As he looked at her, the rakish gleam in Tirofijo's eye reminded Paola of those trysts at the Happy Fish; and now he was partnering with her to run the new government.

Which proves the adage:

Bedfellows make strange politics.

The end.

Extra

Ingredients for a perfect daiquiri
By Wulther

Two ounces of Ron Aniversario Blanco
One ounce fresh-squeezed lime juice
One-half ounce of simple syrup
Pour mixture with crushed ice into a cocktail shaker
Shake over the shoulder with great vigor 12-16 times
Strain mixture into a chilled stemmed glass
Garnish with lime wedge

If you enjoyed "Behind Every Tree," please take a minute to review the book on Amazon or any other reading sites.

Other Books from D M Flynn

La República Books
"The Kidnapping of Dennis Martin," Volume 1 of the La República Trilogy
"Behind Every Tree," Volume 2 of the La República Trilogy
"Stories From My Attic," A collection of unrelated stories and anecdotes

Marti Lay Art
"Take Me Home, Please," For Children 3-6. Illustrated by Marti Lay

Praise for "The Kidnapping of Dennis Martin"

Full of wit and energy … vivid, bold, very funny in a satirical, Borges-meets-Hiaasen world.
— ChatGPT

The Kidnapping of Dennis Martin is a tale that will have you laughing out loud. Author David Flynn has created a world populated by funny, charismatic, and very believable characters who come together in hilarious, cinematic scenes featuring sharp satiric portraits of corporate America and the fictional Latin-American country La República. Flynn has a strong insight into both worlds, having spent a lifetime in advertising and in traveling the globe.

… Every character in La República is memorable, flawed yet with redeeming qualities, and very real. Flynn has a gift for putting these people together with Dennis and each other in scenes that feature hilarious conversations, insights into the characters' thoughts, and descriptions of both exotic and mundane places that make you feel that you are there in the middle of it all. When all these characters come together despite all their selfishness, misunderstandings, defects and delusions, the unexpected results make for a satisfying conclusion. A great read! **— Amazon**

A hilarious story, written with wit and imagination. I loved all the quirky characters and their relationships. David Flynn has penned a well spun yarn and I'm looking forward to the next two installments! **— Amazon**

Flynn is a wordsmith like no other and combining his enormous world perspective with his talent for creating and spinning fabulous tales, readers will be left questioning if their values are as shallow as those of these characters are and if their life is just a hilarious mark in time. Flynn is part Hunter Thompson with some Vonnegut and a lot of Hiaasen, blended into an even saucier teller of enthralling and laugh out loud tales.**— Amazon**

A hilarious comedy, a satire in which none of the zany characters or quirky locations are safe from ridicule. I have not laughed out loud at a book like this one in years, as the author David Flynn has great insight into many cultures, having been a lifelong world traveler and a student of people from other worlds. Puritanical values in Mid-America as well as US businessmen's sole focus on profit margins at any cost are comically disparaged. How US Citizens have been made ignorant of world affairs and foreign cultures by our isolationist America first lifestyle are humorously brought to light and frizzled and seared. **— Amazon**

D M FLYNN was once a struggling journalist banging out sports stories and feature pieces in dusty New Mexico. Fortunately, he wasn't very good and switched careers saving him from death by reporting. His new vocation, advertising, kept him busy for some 35 years. So, now he turns to writing once more, drawing on a life of memories, experiences, and observations. Born in Chile and living in 10 Latin American countries made him a keen observer of every detail of local life in order to fit in. Now, alas, he struggles anew. With this second novel, David has once again crafted a story that could only happen in La República, a quiet nation of his own invention, in the past of his own imagination.

Based in Austin, Texas he is also a prize-winning photographer documenting the people and culture of the developing world.

David laughs out loud at his own jokes.

Author's website:
www.dmflynn.com
Photography:
www.theculturalphotographer.net

Coming Soon from the pen of D M Flynn

Hedgetrimmer
Frankie Pesto of Fantastical Films produces slasher movies in the Garden Tool Horror genre. He is in desperate need to find a cheap location to shoot his next blockbuster, "Hedgetrimmer."

Sipping a dry martini in his favorite Venice Beach fern bar, Frankie overhears some Hollywood suits talking about a place called La República. Apparently, some nut built a soundstage there and it's available.

Fantastical Films relocates production of "Hedgetrimmer" to Tirofijo's Hideout studios bringing with it their top star, Brock Brockton, to play the lead opposite part-time prostitute, PTA president, and Prime Minister (Interim) Paola Labios.

A new batch of characters mix with the old Hotel Cinco Estrellas regulars including the "electrical guy," the pretty and sharp Yoko Nono, who has an eye for local Tirso. There are also Brock, Frankie, and Billy DeMille the alcoholic director. Billy is a giant in the industry even though his feet don't touch the floor when he sits.

How will all this play out in La República?

Oh, one more thing. The country is in the grips of an election to determine the next Prime Minister as dictated by the Constitution of 1935.